Pu-239

and Other
Russian Fantasies

Pu-239

and Other
Russian Fantasies

Ken Kalfus

MILKWEED EDITIONS

"Pu-239" first appeared in *Harper's Magazine*
"Budyonnovsk" first appeared in *News from the Republic of Letters*
"Salt" first appeared in *Bomb*

© 1999, Text by Ken Kalfus

Distributed by Publishers Group West
Published 1999 by Milkweed Editions
Printed in the United States of America

Cover design by Patrick Nistler
Cover photo from the Moscow History Museum.
Interior design by Donna Burch
The text of this book is set in Legacy Serif

99 00 01 02 03 5 4 3 2 1
First Edition

The extract on p. 236 is from Vladimir Nabokov's translation of "Silentium," by Fyodor Tyutchev, in *Three Russian Poets: Selections from Pushkin, Lermontov and Tyutchev* (New Directions, 1944). Copyright © 1944 by Vladimir Nabokov. Reprinted by arrangement with the Estate of Vladimir Nabokov.

Milkweed Editions, a nonprofit publisher, gratefully acknowledges support from the Elmer L. and Eleanor J. Andersen Foundation; James Ford Bell Foundation; Bush Foundation; Dayton Hudson Foundation on behalf of Dayton's, Mervyn's California, and Target Stores; Doherty, Rumble and Butler Foundation; General Mills Foundation; Honeywell Foundation; Jerome Foundation; McKnight Foundation; Minnesota State Arts Board through an appropriation by the Minnesota State Legislature; Norwest Foundation on behalf of Norwest Bank Minnesota; Lawrence and Elizabeth Ann O'Shaughnessy Charitable Income Trust in honor of Lawrence M. O'Shaughnessy; Oswald Family Foundation; Ritz Foundation on behalf of Mr. and Mrs. E. J. Phelps Jr.; John and Beverly Rollwagen Fund of the Minneapolis Foundation; St. Paul Companies, Inc.; Star Tribune Foundation; U.S. Bancorp Piper Jaffray Foundation on behalf of U.S. Bancorp Piper Jaffray; and generous individuals.

Library of Congress Cataloging-in-Publication Data
Kalfus, Ken.
      Pu-239 and other Russian fantasies / Ken Kalfus. — 1st ed.
          p.   cm.
      ISBN 1-57131-029-0 (cloth)
        1. Russia—Social life and customs—Fiction.   I. Title.
PS3561.A416524P8   1999
813'.54—dc21   99-18183
                                                     CIP

This book is printed on acid-free paper.

For Sky

Because these stories are fiction, I should probably limit my acknowledgements of credit to the relevant Muse. But several friends have provided invaluable assistance in researching the material for these stories, and it's the author's prerogative to express his gratitude to them. These friends introduced me to the charms and peculiarities of Russian life, carefully read my work, and pointed out its solecisms—some of which, for my own perverse reasons, I have allowed to stand.

Alla Bourakovskaya read each of these stories with a sharp eye for its literary as well as factual qualities and gave me continued guidance on how things work, or don't, in Russia. Valentina Markusova, Natasha Perova, Masha Lipman, Viktoria Mkrtchan, and Aleksandra Sheremeyeva also provided significant comment.

In the Jewish Autonomous Republic, I enjoyed a productive interview with David Vaiserman, whose book *Kak Eto Bil* proved very helpful. My example of socialist klezmer is based on a song that appeared in Ruth Rubin's book *Voices of a People*.

In regards to "Anzhelika, 13," I wish to acknowledge the precedence of Ludmilla Ulitskaya's story "March 1953," which appeared in *Glas 6*.

The story about Sergei Korolev's journey from the gulag, recounted in "Orbit," is drawn from James Harford's masterful biography, *Korolev: How One Man Masterminded the Soviet Drive to Beat America to the Moon*.

My fable "Salt" is based on one collected in *Russian*

Fairy Tales, selected by Aleksandr Afanasev. The story's epigraph is taken from Robert Cottrell's article "Kremlin Capitalism," which appeared in the *New York Review of Books,* March 27, 1997.

No full accounting of my debts would be complete without mention of the *Philadelphia Inquirer* foreign desk, which named my wife, Inga Saffron, Moscow bureau chief in 1994, and thus sent our family on an extraordinary four-year adventure. The respect the *Inquirer* holds for the written endeavor extends beyond the perimeters of its staff, and I'm grateful for much incidental and vital support.

And I thank Inga, who was, as always, my stories' first reader.

Pu-239

and Other
Russian Fantasies

Stories

Novella

Pu-239

and Other
Russian Fantasies

STORIES

Pu-239

Someone committed a simple error that, according to the plant's blueprints, should have been impossible, and a valve was left open, a pipe ruptured, a technician was trapped in a crawlspace, and a small fire destroyed several workstations. At first the alarm was discounted: false alarms commonly rang and flashed through the plant like birds in a tropical rain forest. Once the seriousness of the accident was appreciated, the rescue crew discovered that a soft drink dispenser waiting to be sent out for repair blocked the room in which the radiation suits were kept. After moving it and entering the storage room, they learned that several of the oxygen tanks had been left uncharged. By the time they reached the lab the fire was nearly out, but smoke laced with elements from the actinide series filled the unit. Lying on his back above the ceiling, staring at the wormlike pattern of surface corrosion on the tin duct a few centimeters from his face, Timofey had inhaled the fumes for an hour and forty minutes. In that time he had tried to imagine that he was inhaling dollar bills and that once they lodged in his lungs and bone marrow they would bombard his body tissue with high-energy dimes, nickels, and quarters.

Timofey had worked in 16 nearly his entire adult life, entrusted with the bounteous, transfiguring secrets of the atom. For most of that life, he had been exhilarated by the reactor's song of nuclear fission, the hiss of particle capture and loss. Highly valued for his ingenuity, Timofey carried in his head not only a detailed knowledge of the plant's design, but also a precise recollection of its every repair and improvised alteration. He knew where the patches were and how well they had been executed. He knew which stated tolerances could be exceeded and by how much, which gauges ran hot, which ran slow, and which could be completely ignored. The plant managers and scientists were often forced to defer to his judgment. On these occasions a glitter of derision showed in his voice, as he tapped a finger significantly against a sheet of engineering designs and explained why there was only a single correct answer to the question.

After Timofey's death, his colleagues recalled a dressing down he had received a few years earlier at the hands of a visiting scientist. No one remembered the details, except that she had proposed slightly altering the reaction process in order to produce a somewhat greater quantity of a certain isotope that she employed in her own research. Hovering in his stained and wrinkled white coat behind the half dozen plant officials whom she had been addressing, Timofey objected to the proposal. He said that greater quantities of the isotope would not be produced in the way she suggested and, in fact, could not be produced at all, according to well established principles of nuclear physics. Blood rushed to the woman's square, fleshy, bulldog face. "Idiot!" she spat. "I'm Nuclear Section Secretary of the Academy of Sciences. I fucking *own* the established principles of nuclear physics. You're a *technician!*" Those who were there recalled that Timofey tried to stand his ground, but as he began to explain the flaw in her reasoning his voice lost its resonance and he began to mumble, straying away from the main point. She cut him off, asking her audience, "Are there any other questions, any educated questions?" As it turned out, neither Timofey nor the scientist was ever proved right. The Defense Ministry rejected the proposal for reasons of economy.

Timofey's relations with his coworkers were more comfortable, if distant, and he usually joined the others in his unit at lunch in the plant's low-ceilinged, windowless buffet. The room rustled with murmured complaint. Timofey could hardly be counted among the most embittered of the technical workers—a point sagely observed later. All joked with stale irony about the lapses in safety and the precipitous decline in their salaries caused by inflation; these comments had become almost entirely humorless three months earlier, when management followed a flurry of assuring memos, beseeching directives, and unambiguous promises with a failure to pay them at all. No one had been paid since.

Every afternoon at four Timofey fled the compromises and incompetence of his workplace in an old Zhiguli that he had purchased precisely so that he could arrive home a half hour earlier than if he had taken the tram. Against the odds set by personality and circumstance, he had married, late in his fourth decade, an electrical engineer assigned to another unit. Now, with the attentiveness he had once offered the reactor, Timofey often sat across the kitchen table from his wife with his head cocked, listening to their spindly, asthmatic eight-year-old son, Tolya, in the next room give ruinous commands to his toy soldiers. A

serious respiratory ailment similar to the boy's kept
Marina from working; disability leave had brought a
pretty bloom to her soft cheeks.

The family lived on the eighth floor of a weather-
stained concrete apartment tower with crumbling front
steps and unlit hallways. In this rotted box lay a jewel of a
two-bedroom apartment that smelled of fresh bread and
meat dumplings and overlooked a birch forest. Laced
with ski tracks in the winter and fragranced by grilled
shashlik in the summer, home to deer, rabbits, and even
gray wolves, the forest stretched well beyond their sight,
all the way to the city's double-fenced perimeter.

His colleagues thought of Marina and the boy as
Timofey was pulled from the crawlspace. He was conscious, but dazed, his eyes unfocused and his face slack.
Surrounded by phantoms in radiation suits, Timofey
saw the unit as if for the first time: the cracked walls, the
electrical cords snaking underfoot, the scratched and
fogged glass over the gauges, the mold-spattered valves
and pipes, the disabled equipment piled in an unused
workstation, and the frayed tubing that bypassed sections of missing pipe and was kept in place by electrical
tape. He staggered from the lab, took a shower, vomited
twice, disposed of his clothes, and was briefly examined
by a medic, who took his pulse and temperature. No one
looked him in the eye. Timofey was sent home. His colleagues were surprised when he returned the next day,
shrugging off the accident and saying that he had a few
things to take care of before going on the "rest leave" he
had been granted as a matter of course. But his smile was

as wan as the moon on a midsummer night, and his
hands trembled. In any case, his colleagues were too busy
to chat. The clean-up was chaotically underway and the
normal activities of the plant had been suspended.

Early one evening a week after the "event," as it was
known in the plant and within the appropriate ministries
(it was not known anywhere else), Timofey was sitting at a
café table in the bar off the lobby of a towering Brezhnev-
era hotel on one of the boulevards that radiated from
Moscow's nucleus. A domestically made double-breasted
sports jacket the color of milk chocolate hung from his
frame like wash left to dry. He was only fifty years old
but, lank and stooped, his face lined by a spiderwork of
dilated veins, he looked at least fifteen years older, almost a veteran of the war. His skin was as gray as wet
concrete, except for the radiation erythema inflaming
the skin around his eyes and nose. Coarse white hair
bristled from his skull. Set close beneath white caterpil-
lar eyebrows, his blue eyes blazed.

He was not by nature impressed by attempts to suggest
luxury and comfort, and the gypsies and touts milling
outside the entrance had in any case already mitigated the
hotel's grandeur. He recognized that the lounge area was
meant to approximate the soaring glass and marble atria
of the West, but the girders of the greenhouse roof impended two stories above his head, supported by walls of
chipped concrete blocks. A line of shuttered windows ran
the perimeter above the lounge, looking down upon it as
if it were a factory floor. The single appealing amenity was

the set of flourishing potted plants and ferns in the center of the room. As Timofey watched over a glass of un-
sipped vodka that had cost him a third of his remaining
rubles, a fat security guard in a maroon suit flicked a cigarette butt into the plant beds and stalked away.

Timofey strained to detect the aspirates and dental
fricatives of a foreign language, but the other patrons
were all either Russian or "black"—that is, Caucasian.
Overweight, unshaven men in lurid track suits and
cheap leather jackets huddled over the stained plastic
tables, blowing smoke into each other's faces. Occasionally they looked up from their drinks and eyed the people
around them. Then they fell back into negotiation. At
another table, a rectangular woman in a low-cut, short
black dress and black leggings scowled at a newspaper.

Directly behind Timofey, sitting alone, a young man
with dark, bony features decided that this hick would be
incapable of getting a girl on his own. Not that there
would be too many girls around this early. He wondered
if Timofey had any money and whether he could make
him part with it. Certainly the mark would have enough
for one of the kids in ski parkas waving down cars on the
boulevard. The young man, called Shiv by his Moscow
acquaintances (he had no friends), got up from his table,
leaving his drink.

"First time in Moscow, my friend?"

Timofey was not taken off guard. He slowly raised his
head and studied the young man standing before him.
Either the man's nose had once been broken, or his nose
had never been touched and the rest of his face had been
broken many times, leaving his cheeks and the arches

beneath his eyes jutted askew. The youth wore a foreign blazer and a black shirt, and what looked like foreign shoes as well, a pair of black loafers. His dark, curly hair was cut long, lapping neatly against the top of his collar. Jewelry glinted from his fingers and wrists. It was impossible to imagine the existence of such a creature in 16.

Shiv didn't care for the fearlessness in Timofey's eyes; it suggested a profound ignorance of the world. But he pulled a chair underneath him, sat down heavily, and said in a low voice, "It's lonely here. Would you like to meet someone?"

The mark didn't reply, nor make any sign that he had even heard him. His jaw was clenched shut, his face blank. Shiv wondered whether he spoke Russian. He himself spoke no foreign languages and detested the capriciousness with which foreigners chose to speak their own. He added, "You've come to the right place. I'd be pleased to make an introduction."

Timofey continued to stare at Shiv in a way that he should have known, if he had any sense at all, was extremely dangerous. A crazy, Shiv thought, a waste of time. But then the mark abruptly rasped, in educated, unaccented Russian, "I have something to sell."

Shiv grinned, showing large white canines. He congratulated him, "You're a businessman. Well, you've come to the right place for that too. I'm also a businessman. What is it you want to sell?"

"I can't discuss it here."

"All right."

Shiv stood and Timofey tentatively followed him to a little alcove stuffed with video poker machines. They whined and yelped, devouring gambling tokens. Incandescent images of kings, queens, and knaves flickered across the young man's face.

"No, this isn't private enough."

"Sure it is," Shiv said. "More business is done here than on the Moscow Stock Exchange."

"No."

Shiv shrugged and headed back to his table, which the girl, in a rare display of zeal, had already cleared. His drink was gone. Shiv frowned, but knew he could make her apologize and give him another drink on the house, which would taste much better for it. He had that kind of respect, he thought.

"You're making the biggest mistake of your life," Timofey whispered behind him. "I'll make you rich."

What changed Shiv's mind was not the promise, which these days was laden in nearly every commercial advertisement, political manifesto, and murmur of love. Rather, he discerned two vigorously competing elements within the mark's voice. One of them was desperation, in itself an augury of profit. Yet as desperate as he was, Timofey had spoken just barely within range of Shiv's hearing. Shiv was impressed by the guy's self-control. Perhaps he was serious after all.

He turned back toward Timofey, who continued to stare at him in appraisal. With a barely perceptible flick of his head, Shiv motioned him toward a row of elevators bedecked with posters for travel agencies and masseuses. Timofey remained in the alcove for a long moment, trying to decide whether to follow. Shiv looked away and punched the call button. After a minute or so the elevator arrived. Timofey stepped in just as the doors were closing.

Shiv said, "If you're jerking me around . . ."

The usually reliable fourth-floor *dezhurnaya,* the suppurating wart who watched the floor's rooms, decided to be difficult. Shiv slipped her a five dollar bill, and she said, "More." She returned the second fiver because it had a crease down the middle, dispelling its notional value. Shiv had been trying to pass it off for weeks and now conceded that he would be stuck with it until the day he died. The crone accepted the next bill, scowling, and even then gazed a long time into her drawer of keys, as if undecided about giving him one.

As they entered the room, Shiv pulled out a pack of Marlboros and a gold-plated lighter and leaned against a beige chipboard dresser. The room's ponderous velvet curtains smelled of insecticide; unperturbed, a bloated fly did lazy eights around the naked bulb on the ceiling. Shiv didn't offer the mark a cigarette. "All right," he said, flame billowing from the lighter before he brought it to his face. "This better be worth my while."

Timofey reached into his jacket, almost too abruptly: he didn't notice Shiv tense and go for the dirk in his back pocket. The mark pulled out a green cardboard folder and proffered it. "Look at this."

Shiv returned the blade. He carried four knives of varying sizes, grades, and means of employment.

"Why?"

"Just look at it."

Shiv opened the folder. Inside was Timofey's internal

passport, plus some other documents. Shiv was not accustomed to strangers shoving their papers in his face; indeed, he knew the family names of very few people in Moscow. This guy, then, had to be a nut case, and Shiv rued the ten bucks he had given the *dezhurnaya*. The mark stared up through the stamped black-and-white photograph as if from under water. "Timofey Fyodorovich, pleased to meet you. So what?"

"Look at where I live: Skotoprigonyevsk-16."

Shiv made no sign of being impressed, but for Timofey the words had the force of an incantation. The existence of the city, a scientific complex established by the military, had once been so secret that it was left undocumented on the Red Army's own field maps. Even its name, which was meant to indicate that it lay sixteen kilometers from the original Skotoprigonyevsk, was a deception: the two cities were nearly two hundred kilometers apart. Without permission from the KGB, it had been impossible to enter or leave 16. Until two years earlier, Timofey had never been outside, not once in twenty-three years. He now realized, as he would have realized if he hadn't been so distracted by the events of the past week, that it wasn't enough to find a criminal. He needed someone with brains, someone who had read a newspaper in the last five years.

"Now look at the other papers. See, this is my pass to the Strategic Production Facility."

"Comrade," Shiv said sarcastically, "if you think I'm buying some fancy documents—"

"Listen to me. My unit's principal task is the supply of the strategic weapons force. Our reactor produces Pu-239 as a fission by-product for manufacture into warheads. These operations have been curtailed, but the reactors must be kept functioning. Decommissioning them would be even more costly than maintaining them—and we can't even do that properly." Timofey's voice fell to an angry whisper. "There have been many lapses in the administration of safety procedure."

Timofey looked intently at Shiv, to see if he understood. But Shiv wasn't listening; he didn't like to be lectured and especially didn't like to be told to read things, even identity papers. The world was full of men who knew more than Shiv did, and he hated each one of them. A murderous black cloud rose from the stained orange carpeting at his feet and occulted his vision. The more Timofey talked, the more Shiv wanted to hurt him. But at the same time, starting from the moment he heard the name Skotoprigonyevsk-16, Shiv gradually became aware that he was onto something big, bigger than anything he had ever done before. He was nudged by an incipient awareness that perhaps it was even too big for him.

In flat, clipped sentences, Timofey spoke: "There was an accident. I was contaminated. I have a wife and child, and nothing to leave them. This is why I'm here."

"Don't tell me about your wife and child. You can fuck them both to hell. I'm a businessman."

For a moment, Timofey was shocked by the violence in the young man's voice. But then he reminded himself that, in coming to Moscow for the first time in twenty-five years, he had entered a country where violence was the most stable and valuable currency. Maybe this was the right guy for the deal after all. There was no room for sentimentality.

He braced himself. "All right then. Here's what you need to know. I have diverted a small quantity of fissile material. I'm here to sell it."

Shiv removed his handkerchief again and savagely wiped his nose. He had a cold, Timofey observed. Acute radiation exposure severely compromised the immune system, commonly leading to fatal bacterial infection. He wondered if the hoodlum's germs were the ones fated to kill him.

Timofey said, "Well, are you interested?"

To counteract any impression of weakness given by the handkerchief, Shiv tugged a mouthful of smoke from his cigarette.

"In what?"

"Are you listening to anything I'm saying? I have a little more than three hundred grams of weapons-grade plutonium. It can be used to make an atomic bomb. I want thirty thousand dollars for it."

As a matter of principle, Shiv laughed. He always laughed when a mark named a price. But a chill seeped through him as far down as his testicles.

"It will fetch many times that on the market. Iraq, Iran, Libya, North Korea all have nuclear weapons programs, but they don't have the technology to produce enriched fissile material. They're desperate for it; there's no price Saddam Hussein wouldn't pay for an atomic bomb."

"I don't know anything about selling this stuff . . ."

"Don't be a fool," Timofey rasped. "Neither do I. That's

why I've come here. But you say you're a businessman. You must have contacts, people with money, people who can get it out of the country."

Shiv grunted. He was just playing for time now, to assemble his thoughts and devise a strategy. The word fool remained lodged in his gut like a spoiled piece of meat.

"Maybe I do, maybe I don't."

"Make up your mind."

"Where's the stuff?"

"With me."

A predatory light flicked on in the hoodlum's eyes. But Timofey had expected that. He slowly unbuttoned his jacket. It fell away to reveal an invention of several hours' work that, he realized only when he assembled it in the kitchen the day after the accident, he had been planning for years. At that moment of realization, his entire body had been flooded with a searing wonder at the dark soul that inhabited it. Now, under his arm, a steel canister no bigger than a coffee tin was attached to his left side by an impenetrably complex arrangement of belts, straps, hooks, and buckles.

"Do you see how I rigged the container?" he said. "There's a right way of taking it off my body and many wrong ways. Take it off one of the wrong ways and the container opens and the material spills out. Are you aware of the radiological properties of plutonium and their effect on living organisms?"

Shiv almost laughed. He once knew a girl who wore something like this.

"Let me see it."

"It's *plutonium*. It has to be examined under controlled laboratory conditions. If even a microscopic amount of it lodges within your body, ionizing radiation will irreversibly damage body tissue and your cells' nucleic material. A thousandth of a gram is fatal . . . I'll put it to you more simply. Anything it touches dies. It's like in a fairy tale."

Shiv did indeed have business contacts, but he'd been burned about six months earlier, helping to move some Uzbek heroin that must have been worth more than a half million dollars. He had actually held the bags in his hands and pinched the powder through the plastic, marveling at the physics that transmuted such a trivial quantity of something into so much money. But once he made the arrangements and the businessmen had the stuff in *their* hands, they gave him only two thousand dollars for his trouble, little more than a tip. Across a table covered by a freshly stained tablecloth, the Don—his name was Voronenko, and he was from Tambov, but he insisted on being called the Don anyway, and being served spaghetti and meatballs for lunch—had grinned at the shattering disappointment on Shiv's face. Shiv had wanted to protest, but he was frightened. Afterwards he was so angry that he gambled and whored the two grand away in a single night.

He said, "So, there was an accident. How do I know the stuff's still good?"

"Do you know what a half-life is? The half-life of plutonium 239 is twenty-four thousand years."

"That's what you're telling me . . ."

"You can look it up."

"What am I, a fucking librarian? Listen, I know this game. It's mixed with something."

Timofey's whole body was burning; he could feel each of his vital organs being singed by alpha radiation. For a moment he wished he could lie on one of the narrow beds in the room and nap. When he woke, perhaps he would be home. But he dared not imagine that he would wake to find that the accident had never happened. He said, "Yes, of course. The sample contains significant amounts of uranium and other plutonium isotopes, plus trace quantities of americium and gallium. But the Pu-239 content is 94.7 percent."

"So you admit it's not the first-quality stuff."

"Anything greater than 93 percent is considered weapons-grade. Look, do you have somebody you can bring this to? Otherwise, we're wasting my time."

Shiv took out another cigarette from his jacket and tapped it against the back of his hand. Igniting the lighter, he kept his finger lingering on the gas feed. He passed the flame in front of his face so that it appeared to completely immolate the mark.

"Yeah, I do, but he's in Perkhuskovo. It's a forty-minute drive. I'll take you to him."

"I have a car. I'll follow you."

Shiv shook his head. "That won't work. His dacha's protected. You can't go through the gate alone."

"Forget it then. I'll take the material someplace else."

Shiv's shrug of indifference was nearly sincere. The guy was too weird, the stuff was too weird. His conscience told him he was better off pimping for schoolgirls. But he said, "If you like. But for a deal like this, you'll need to go to one godfather or another. On your own you're not going to find someone walking around with thirty thousand dollars in his pocket. This businessman knows me, his staff knows me. I'll go with you in your car. You can drive."

Timofey said, "No, we each drive separately."

The mark was unmovable. Shiv offered him a conciliatory smile.

"All right," he said. "Maybe. I'll call him from the lobby and try to set it up. I'm not even sure he can see us tonight."

"It has to be tonight or there's no deal."

"Don't be in such a hurry. You said the stuff lasts twenty-four thousand years, right?"

"Tell him I'm from Skotoprigonyevsk-16. Tell him it's weapons-grade. That's all he needs to know. Do you understand the very least bit of what I'm saying?"

The pale solar disc had dissolved in the horizonal haze long ago, but the autumn evening was still in its adolescent hours, alive to possibility. As the two cars lurched into the swirl of traffic on the Garden Ring road, Timofey could taste the unburned gasoline in the hoodlum's exhaust. He had never before driven in so much traffic or seen so many foreign cars, or guessed that they would ever be driven so recklessly. Their rear lights flitted and spun like fireflies. At his every hesitation or deceleration the cars behind him flashed their headlights. Their drivers navigated their vehicles as if from the edges of their seats, peering over their dashboards, white-knuckled and grim, and as if they all carried three hundred grams of weapons-grade plutonium strapped to their chests. Driving among Audis and Mercedeses would have thrilled Tolya, who cut pictures of them from magazines and cherished his small collection of mismatched models. The thought of his son, a sweet and cheerful boy with orthodontic braces, and utterly, utterly innocent, stabbed at him.

The road passed beneath what Timofey recognized as Mayakovsky Square from television broadcasts of holiday marches. He knew that the vengeful, lustrating revision of Moscow's street names in the last few years had renamed the square Triumfalnaya, though there was nothing triumphant about it, except for its big Philips billboard advertisement. Were all the advertisements on the Garden Ring posted in the Latin alphabet? Was Cyrillic no longer anything more than a folk custom? It was as if he had traveled to the capital of a country in which he had never lived.

Of course hardly any commercial advertising could be seen in 16. Since Gorbachev's fall a halfhearted attempt had been made to obscure most of the Soviet agitprop, but it was still a Soviet city untouched by foreign retailing and foreign advertising. The few foreign goods that found their way into the city's state-owned shops arrived dented and tattered, as if produced in Asian, European, and North American factories by demoralized Russian workers. Well, these days 16 was much less of a city. It was not uncommon to see chickens and other small livestock grazing in the gravel between the high-rises, where pensioners and unpaid workers had taken up subsistence farming.

Resentment of Moscow burned in Timofey's chest, alongside the Pu-239.

Plutonium. There was no exit for the stuff. It was as permanent and universal as original sin. Since its first synthesis in 1941 (what did Seaborg do with that magical, primeval stone of his own creation? put it in his vault? was it still there?) more than a thousand metric tons of the element had been produced. It was still being manufactured, not only in Russia, but in France and Britain as well, and it remained stockpiled in America. Nearly all of it was locked in steel containers, buried in mines, or sealed in glass—safe, safe, safe. But the very minimal fraction that wasn't secured, the few flakes that had escaped in nuclear tests, reactor accidents, transport mishaps, thefts, and leakages, veiled the entire planet. Sometime within the next three months Timofey would die with plutonium in his body, joined in the same year by thousands of other victims in Russia and around the world. His body would be brought directly to the city crematorium, abstractly designed in jaggedly cut, pale yellow concrete so as to be vaguely "life-affirming," where the chemistry of his skin and lungs, heart and head, would be transformed by fire and wind. In the rendering oven, the Pu-239 would oxidize and engage in wanton couplings with other substances, but it would always stay faithful to its radioactive, elemental properties. Some of it would remain in the ash plowed back to the earth; the rest would be borne aloft into the vast white skies arching above the frozen plain. Dust to dust.

Yet it would remain intangible, completely invisible, hovering elusively before us like a floater in our eyes'

vitreous humor. People get cancer all the time and almost never know why. A nucleic acid on a DNA site is
knocked out of place, a chromosome sequence is deleted,
an oncogene is activated. It would show up only in statis-
tics, where it remained divorced from the lives and deaths
of individuals. It was just as well, Timofey thought, that
we couldn't take in the enormity of the threat; if we did,
we would be paralyzed with fear—not for ourselves, but
for our children. We couldn't wrap our minds around it;
we could think of it only for a few moments and then
have to turn away from it. But the accident had liberated
Timofey. He could now contemplate plutonium without
any difficulty at all.

And it was not only plutonium. Timofey was now ex-
quisitely aware of the ethereal solution that washed over
him every day like a warm bath: the insidiously subatomic,
the swarmingly microscopic, and the multi-syllabically
chemical. His body was soaked in pesticides, the liquefied
remains of electrical batteries, leaded gasoline exhaust,
dioxin, nitrates, toxic waste metals, dyes, and deadly viral
organisms generated in untreated sewage—the entire car-
cinogenic and otherwise malevolent slough of the great
Soviet industrial empire. Like Homo Sovieticus himself,
Timofey was ending his life as a melange of damaged chro-
mosomes, metal-laden tissue, crumbling bone, frag-
mented membranes, and oxygen-deprived blood. Perhaps
his nation's casual regard for the biological consequences
of environmental degradation was the result of some
quasi-Hegelian conviction that man lived in history, not
nature. It was no wonder everyone smoked.

For a moment, as the hoodlum swung into the turning

lane at the Novy Arbat, Timofey considered passing the turnoff and driving on through the night and the following day back to 16's familiar embrace. But there was only one hundred and twenty dollars hidden in the bookcase in his apartment. It was the sum total of his family's savings.

Now Shiv saw Timofey's shudder of indecision in his rearview mirror; he had suspected that the mark might turn tail. If he had, Shiv would have broken from the turning lane with a shriek of tire (he savored the image) and chased him down.

In tandem the two cars crossed the bridge over the Moscow River, the brilliantly lit White House on their right nearly effervescing in the haze off the water. It was as white and polished as a tooth, having been capped recently by a squadron of Turkish workers after Yeltsin's troops had shelled and nearly gutted it. Shiv and Timofey passed the Pizza Hut and the arch commemorating the battle against Napoleon at Borodino. They were leaving the city. Now Timofey knew he was committed. The hoodlum wouldn't let him go. He knew this as surely as if he were sitting in the car beside him. If the world of the atom were controlled by random quantum events, then the macroscopic universe through which the two Zhigulis were piloted was purely deterministic. The canister was heavy and the straps that supported it were beginning to cut into Timofey's back.

He could have even more easily evaded Shiv at the exit off Kutuzovsky Prospekt; then on the next road there was another turnoff, then another and another. Timofey lost count of the turns. It was like driving down a rabbit hole: he'd never find his way back. Soon they were kicking up stones on a dark country road, the only traffic. Every once and a while the Moscow River or one of its tributaries showed itself through the naked, snowless birches. A pocked and torn slice of moon bobbed and weaved across his windshield. Shiv paused, looking for the way, and then abruptly pivoted his car into a lane hardly wider than the Zhiguli itself.

Timofey followed, taking care to stay on the path. He could hear himself breathing: the sound from his lungs was muffled and wet. Gravel crunched beneath his tires and bushes scraped their nails against the car's doors. The hood slowed even further, crossing a small bridge made of a few planks. They clattered like bones.

Timofey's rearview mirror incandesced. Annoyed, he pushed it from his line of sight. Shiv slowed to a stop, blinked a pair of white lights in reverse, and backed up just short of Timofey's front bumper. At the same time, Timofey felt a hard tap at his rear.

Shiv stepped from his car. Pinned against the night by the glare of headlights, the boy appeared vulnerable and very young, almost untouched by life. Timofey detected a measure of gentleness in his face, despite the lunar shadows cast across it. Shiv grimaced at the driver of the third automobile, signaling him to close his lights. He walked in front of his own car and squeezed alongside the brush to Timofey's passenger door.

"We have to talk," he said. "Open it."

Timofey hesitated for a moment, but the lengthy

drive had softened his resolve and confused his plan.
And there was a car pressed against his rear bumper. He
reached over and unlocked the door.

Shiv slid into the seat and stretched his legs. Even for
short people, the Zhigulis were too goddamned small.

"We're here?"

"Where else could we be?"

Timofey turned his head and peered into the dark,
looking for the businessman's dacha. There was nothing
to see at all.

"All right, now hand over the stuff."

"Look, let's do this right—" Timofey began, but then
comprehension darkened his face. He didn't need to consider an escape: he understood the whole setup. Perhaps
he had chosen the coward's way out. "I see. You're as foolish as a peasant in a fairy tale."

Shiv opened his coat and removed from a holster in
his sport jacket an oiled straight blade nearly twenty centimeters long. He turned it so that the moonlight ran its
length. He looked into the mark's face for fear. Instead
he found ridicule.

Timofey said, "You're threatening me with a knife? I
have enough plutonium in my lungs to power a small
city for a year, and you're threatening me with a *knife?*"

Shiv placed the shaft against Timofey's side, hard
enough to leave a mark even if it were removed. Timofey
acted as if he didn't feel it. Again something dark passed
before Shiv's eyes.

"Look, this is a high-carbon steel Premium Gessl
manufactured by Imperial Gessl in Frankfurt, Germany.

I paid eighty bucks for it. It passes through flesh like water. Just give me the goddamned stuff."

"No. I won't do that," Timofey said primly. "I want thirty thousand dollars. It's a fair price, I think, and I won't settle for anything less. I drove here in good faith."

Timofey was the first man Shiv had ever killed, though he had cut a dozen others, plus two women. He wondered if it got easier each time; that's what he had heard. In any case, this was easy enough. There wasn't even much blood, though he was glad the mark had driven his own car after all.

Now Shiv sat alone, aware of the hiss of his lungs, and also that his armpits were wet. Well, it wasn't every day you killed a man. But Timofey hadn't resisted, it hadn't been like killing a man. The knife had passed through him not as if he were water, but as if he were a ghost. Shiv sensed that he had been cheated again.

He opened and pushed away Timofey's brown sports jacket, which even in the soundless dark nearly screamed Era of Stagnation. The canister was there, still strapped to his chest. The configuration of straps, hooks, and buckles that kept it in place taunted Shiv with its intricacy. He couldn't follow where each strap went, or what was being buckled or snapped. To Shiv it was a labyrinth, a rat's nest, a knot. To Timofey it had been a topographical equation, clockworks, a flowchart. "Fuck it," Shiv said aloud. He took the Gessl and cut the thin strap above the cylinder with two quick strokes.

Already the mark's body was cool; perhaps time was

passing more quickly than Shiv realized. Or maybe it was passing much more slowly: in a single dilated instant he discerned the two cut pieces of the strap hovering at each other's torn edge, longing to be one again. But then they flew away with a robust *snap!* and the entire assembly lost the tension that had kept it wrapped around Timofey's body. The effect was so dramatic he fancied that Timofey had come alive and that he would have the opportunity to kill him again. The canister popped open—he now apprehended which two hooks and which three straps had kept it closed—and fell against the gearshift.

Powder spilled out, but not much. Shiv grabbed the canister and shoveled back some of what was on the seat, at least a few thousand dollars' worth. He couldn't really see the stuff, but it was warm and gritty between his fingers. He scooped in as much as he could, screwed the cylinder shut, and then dusted off his hands against his trousers. He cut away the rest of the straps, leaving them draped on Timofey's body. He climbed from the car.

"Good work, lads."

The two brothers, Andrei and Yegor, each stood nearly two meters tall on either side of their car, which was still parked flush against Timofey's bumper. They were not twins, though it was often difficult to recall which was which, they were so empty of personality. Shiv, who had called them from the hotel lobby, thought of them as pure muscle. By most standards of measurement, they were of equally deficient intelligence. They spoke slowly, reasoned even more slowly, and became steadily more unreliable the further they traveled from their last glass of vodka. Nevertheless, they were useful, and they could do what they were told, or a satisfactory approximation of it.

"What do you got there?" said Yegor.

"You wouldn't understand, believe me."

It was then that he saw that Andrei was holding a gun at his hip, leveling it directly at him. It was some kind of pistol, and it looked ridiculously small in Andrei's hands. Still, it was a gun. In the old days, no one had a gun, everyone fought it out with knives and brass knuckles and solid, honest fists, and pieces of lead pipe. You couldn't get firearms. They never reached the market, and the mere possession of one made the cops dangerously angry. But this was democracy: now every moron had a gun.

"Put it away. What did you think, I was going to cut you out?"

Yegor stepped toward him, his arm outstretched. "Hand it over."

Shiv nodded his head, as if in agreement, but he kept the canister clutched to his stomach. "All right, you've got the drop on me. I admit it. I'll put it in writing if you like. They'll be talking about this for years. But you're not going to be able to move it on your own."

"Why not?" said Andrei. He raised the gun with both hands. The hands trembled. For a moment, Shiv thought he could see straight down the barrel. "You think we're stupid."

"If you want to show me how smart you are, you'll put down the fucking gun."

"I don't have to show you anything."

"Listen, this is plutonium. Do you know what it is?"

"Yeah, I know."

"Do you know what's it's used for?"

"I don't got to know. All I got to know is that people will buy it. That's the free market."

"Idiot! Who are you going to sell it to?"

"Private enterprise. They'll buy it from us just like they'd buy it from you. And did you call me an idiot?"

"Listen, I'm just trying to explain to you"—Shiv thought for a moment—"the material's radiological properties."

Shiv was too close to be surprised, it happened too quickly. In one moment he was trying to reason with Andrei, intimidate him, and was only beginning to appreciate the seriousness of the problem, and had just observed, in a casual way, that the entire time of his life up to the moment he had stepped out of Timofey's car seemed equal in length to the time since then, and in the next moment he was unconscious, bleeding from a large wound in his head.

"Well, fuck you," said Andrei, or, more literally, "go to a fucked mother." He had never shot a man before, and he was surprised and frightened by the blood, which had splattered all over Shiv's clothes, and even on himself. He had expected that the impact of the shot would have propelled Shiv off the bridge, but it hadn't. Shiv lay there at his feet, bleeding against the rear tire. The sound of the little gun was tremendous; it continued roaring through the woods long after Andrei had brought the weapon to his side.

Neither brother said anything for a while. In fact, they weren't brothers, as everyone believed, but were stepbrothers, as well as in-laws, in some kind of complicated way that neither had ever figured out. From Yegor's silence, Andrei guessed that he was angry with him for shooting Shiv. They hadn't agreed to shoot him beforehand. But Yegor had allowed him to carry the gun, which meant Andrei had the right to make the decision. Yegor couldn't second-guess him, Andrei resolved, his nostrils flaring.

But Yegor broke the long silence with a gasped guffaw. In the bark of his surprise lay a tremor of anxiety. "Look at this mess," he said. "You fucking near tore off his head."

Andrei could tell his brother was proud of him, at least a bit. He felt a surge of love.

"Well, fuck," said Yegor, shaking his head in wonder. "It's really a mess. How are we going to clean it up? It's all over the car. Shit, it's on my pants."

"Let's just take the stuff and leave."

Yegor said, "Go through his pockets. He always carries a roll. I'll check the other guy."

"No, it's too much blood. I'll go through the other guy's pockets."

"Look, it's like I've been telling you, that's what's wrong with this country. People don't accept the consequences of their actions. Now, *you* put a hole in the guy's head, *you* go through his pockets."

Andrei scowled but quickly ran his hands through Shiv's trousers, jacket, and coat anyway. The body stirred and something like a groan bubbled from Shiv's blood-filled mouth. Some of the blood trickled onto Andrei's hand. It was disgustingly warm and viscid. He snatched his hand away and wiped it on Shiv's jacket. Taking more care now, he reached into the inside jacket pocket and pulled out a gold-colored money clip with some rubles, about ten twenty dollar bills, a few tens, and a creased five. He slipped the clip and four or five of the twenties into his pocket and, stacking the rest on the car's trunk, announced, "Not much, just some cash."

Yegor emerged from the car. "There's nothing at all on this guy, only rubles."

Andrei doubted that. He should have pocketed all of Shiv's money.

"I wonder what the stuff's like," said Yegor, taking the closed canister from Shiv's lap.

He placed it next to the money and pulled off the top, revealing inside a coarse, silvery gray powder. Yegor grimaced. It was nothing like he had ever seen. He wet his finger, poked it into the container, and removed a fingerprint's worth. The stuff tasted chalky.

"What did he call it?" he asked.

"Plutonium. From Bolivia, he said."

Andrei reached in, took a pinch of the powder, and placed it on the back of his left hand. He then closed his right nostril with a finger and brought the stuff up to his face. He loved doing this. From the moment he had pulled the gun on Shiv he had felt as if he were in Chicago or Miami. He sniffed up the powder.

It burned, but not in the right way. It was as if someone—Yegor—had grabbed his nostril with a pair of hot pliers. The pain shot through his head like a nail, and he saw stars. Then he saw atoms, their nuclei surrounded by hairy penumbrae of indeterminately placed electrons. The nuclei themselves pulsed with indeterminacy, their

masses slightly less than the sum of their parts. Bom-
barded by neutrons, the nuclei were drastically deformed.
Some burst. The repulsion of two highly charged nuclear
fragments released Promethean, adamantine energy,
as well as excess neutrons that bounced among the other
nuclei, a cascade of excitation and transformation.

"It's crap. It's complete crap. Crap, crap, *crap!*"

Enraged, Andrei hoisted the open container, brought
it behind his head, and, with a grunt and a cry, hurled it
far into the night sky. The canister sailed. For a moment,
as it reached the top of its ascent beyond the bridge, it
caught a piece of moonlight along its sides. It looked like
a little crescent moon itself, in an eternal orbit above the
earth, the stuff forever pluming behind it. And then it
very swiftly vanished. Everything was quiet for a moment, and then there was a distant, voluptuous sound as
the container plunged into the river. As the two brothers
turned toward each other, one of them with a gun, everything was quiet again.

Anzhelika, 13

Анжелика, 13

Thickened by a myopia left undiagnosed, a mist gauzed the small town, rounding the forms of the low, pale concrete buildings and the naked trees. The trees' branches were brown, smelling of color in a shadowed, variously grayed landscape. Patches of mud rose from the depths of the snow and ice. The horizon loomed, a wall only a few paces ahead. A truck drifted down the street, powered by a breeze. Otherwise, the town's capacity for motion was lost. The smoke from a chimney froze, curled like a beckoning finger.

The girl, Anzhelika (the stress rested on the penultimate syllable), was entirely enveloped in warmth, more warmth than could have been latent within her ragged coat. The heat dampened her hair and the hollows under her arms. This odd, close nimbus, which had swelled around her in the course of the day, was composed of two envelopes, the innermost a soundless vacuum. The outer envelope had been fed on the squeal of desks swinging open on their hinges, the dull, brute clatter of shoe leather in a hallway, and the brassy din of a schoolyard. She heard the clamor only at a distance. Her own shoes, loosely wrapped in oversized galoshes, pressed silently into the tender late-winter road, leaving a precise record of the weight she brought to this world.

Little Kolya was playing with some boys in the gaping

alleyway between two houses, poking a stick at something in an oily puddle. He was ten years old, the son of Aunt Olya and Uncle Fedya, who lived in the front room. Anzhelika occasionally watched over him when Aunt Olya was out, and even helped him once with his mathematics homework, though she was not good at sums at all. He had paid close, devoted attention, contemplating every question at length. Anzhelika had liked being in that room, working at Uncle Fedya's rolltop desk alongside the dark mahogany wardrobe that had been constructed in Vilna in 1879, according to an inscription inside the mirrored door. Kolya had showed the inscription to her; it was the year of Comrade Stalin's birth. The room smelled sweetly of the polish with which Uncle Fedya cleaned his boots.

That was last year. Yesterday she had passed Kolya playing in this same alleyway, a favorite place for the neighborhood boys, and when he saw her he had smiled, but not at her. A meteor had whistled by her right ear twenty seconds later. It landed on the ice ahead and skidded to an impact against a smaller stone, propelling it forward against some pebbles, propelling them in turn, a cascade of insults. She had walked on, hunched in her coat.

Today she expected the same rock to whistle by at exactly the same distance and velocity, and with the same melody. As she waited for it, she understood that the warmth that surrounded her had the character of an expectation, an intimate connection to something that was about to happen, born at the moment of the First Bulletin. Incomprehensible and unexplained, the bulletin had set off the ticking of a clock. The entire world heard it.

Even though the missile was never launched and she reached the door to the house unmolested, the sense of imminence never left her, it remained a warm, abiding presence through the rest of the day. She sought to capture and interrogate it, but after a hurried mental chase it eluded her around a rock and under a floorboard. The clock kept ticking.

Afternoon glided into evening, the haze imperceptibly passing into dusk and then night. Anzhelika sat on the bed in her family's room, with her books open around a notebook in which, so close to the page her breath moistened it, she drew pencil sketches of gowned women. The sketches were minute, so as not to waste paper, but each had a label: "Nadia," "Aleksandra Semyonovna," "The Countess of Wallachia," "Lyubov Orlova." Distracted by the laden clouds gathering around her, she hardly thought of the drawings as she composed them. Anzhelika's mother arrived from the dairy. Just before she entered the room, the girl turned the page of the notebook.

Her mother took some *kolbasa* and potatoes from the windowsill, prepared dinner in the kitchen, and brought it back to the room. Their table had once belonged to Anzhelika's mother's mother and still deserved a room a trifle larger. An inlaid stitched pattern of interlocking diamonds and rectangles ran the table's perimeter. Anzhelika traced the clean end of her fork along the pattern, a road on which she was driving a red automobile, through open country at the edge of a high plateau.

After supper she went to the privy, an unpainted shed shrouded in fumes and resting on cinderblocks a few meters from the back of the house. There was some long-running dispute about the arrangements for cleaning it. Anzhelika hurriedly did her business in a half crouch over the hole, counting each shallow inhalation. Yet tonight she was not repelled by the odor; its extravagance nearly attracted her; there was something meaty and real about it. She wiped herself with some newspaper.

At that moment, a series of massive, earth-devouring steps came up the back path to the house. They belonged to Father. She waited until he passed and then—she thought it was important to do this tonight—she took one more half breath, trying to taste the essence of what appealed to her. She gagged on it.

Every evening when Father arrived home, after her supper, it was as if for the first time. Anzhelika had been in the privy then, four years before, a misty winter night like this one. The pounding of his boots had been immediately recognizable as a stranger's, and was even more frightening than the privy, in whose hole, when she was nine, resided elves and bottom-grabbing demons. She had waited, shivering. Time passed and she wondered if the boots had either left through the front of the house or had never come at all. She returned to the house and stopped at the open door to the back room.

That evening her mother had been in tears. Never would Anzhelika consider the possibility that these had been tears of either relief or joy. A man had loomed in the shadows, the crevices and gnarls of his face starkly lit by the outside light. His eyes possessed a cold yellow illuminant of their own. A heavy bag, a grotesquely misshapen gray soldier's satchel many times torn and patched, lay at her mother's feet. Neither the man nor her mother turned in her direction.

Before that night, Anzhelika had shared the room with her mother and Aunt Lyuda. Afterwards, she slept in the kitchen. The other residents had bitterly objected to her usurpation of their common area. Threats were made. Father had replied with few words. He stood with his clenched, meaty hands on his hips, staring into the face of every opponent as if his glare could mark it. Now Anzhelika could not recall the final time she had seen Aunt Lyuda. She had simply left, a cousin had come for her. Those had been confused days and nights of agony. Sharp and sour odors had coagulated in the dark kitchen, taking fearful shapes. Anzhelika had imagined a great hand forming out of the murk.

No one ever spoke of Aunt Lyuda again. Anzhelika could hardly remember her. People were easily forgotten: like dreams their faces and the sounds of their voices were lost in the rush of daylight. Anzhelika herself would dissolve from memory no less quickly than Aunt Lyuda had.

Tonight her parents dined in silence, while Anzhelika sat among her schoolbooks on their bed. Father ate with enormous energy, tearing at his food. He was always hungry, never satiated. When he lay down his cutlery among the ruins of his meal, it was with a sour grimace, an expression of defeat. Anzhelika stared at the pages of notes that she had taken from the day's lesson about the war. The words and fragments of phrases were only what had drifted into the range of her hearing: "national-patriotic forces," "resolution," "communiqué from the front," "Voronezh," "Hitlerite," "by decision of the Central

Committee." She hadn't been able to read the black-board's corresponding chalkmarks. The precise meanings of these words eluded her, except that she recognized them as the building blocks of a construction that, if it could ever be completed (it couldn't be), would constitute an all-inclusive description of Comrade Stalin.

Uncle Fedya and Aunt Olya were having cutlets and soup. The aroma of their dinner entered the room as a rebuke. They ate better than Anzhelika's family did. Her parents didn't speak, they didn't even look at each other as their nostril hairs twitched around the vapors emitted by Aunt Olya's cutlets. Their anger intensified and their silence deepened. They too were listening to the somber, implacable unwinding of the gears inside the clock set off by the First Bulletin.

What made Father so frightful a figure to his family and to the other residents of the house was neither his great strength nor his angry aspect, but rather the four shrouded, silent years that had lapsed between the end of the war and his return from it. There had been no letters, and no one had notified her mother of his whereabouts nor of his imminent arrival. He never spoke about what he had done in the eight years of his absence. He hadn't said whether he had been in prison or in a camp and if so, whose, or whether he had been free and simply reluctant to take up the reins of his previous life. Whatever the reason, when he returned it was as if he had come back from the land of the dead.

After Uncle Adik had prepared his dinner, Anzhelika swept the kitchen floor and made her pallet under the table used for cutting food. No one begrudged her the space anymore, the table was her own house, thatched-roofed and built from logs somewhere on the wind-scoured steppe, where she waited for Yevgeny Samoilov to come home. Sorrel soup simmered on the stove. She had used candle wax to stick onto the wall under the table small newspaper pictures of Samoilov and other actors, Vladimir Druzhnikov, Mikhail Kuznetsov, Lyubov Orlova, Deanna Durbin, and Tamara Makarova. Last summer Aunt Nina had taken her to the cinema to see Samoilov in *The Boy from the Country*.

But another picture luminesced within the constellation of actors arrayed on the wall, a red-tinted charcoal sketch that she had won at school as an award for good penmanship: Comrade Stalin in his marshal's uniform. He gazed directly ahead, a few strands of gray in the dense growth of his moustache, a kind smile hidden beneath it. His eyebrows were slightly arched, an expression of punishing sternness that lay in contradiction to the warmth around his eyes.

Anzhelika went to the privy one last time that evening, carrying under her nightdress her notebook and the small sewing scissor she had stolen from her mother months before. The glow of a distant lamp seeped through the nearly parallel cracks in the privy door, illuminating an hieroglyphic that for years had refused exegesis.

She took great care, her hands sure, as she cut the page of drawings from the notebook and pulled away from the stitching the sheet that had been attached on the other side of it. Then she cut the pages into pieces, balled them up, placed them into the privy's hole—her hand detached itself, weightless over the pit—and let them drop. Never before had this subterfuge, this paper wastage, been so thrilling; never before had she felt so shamed by it.

As she returned to the house, the heat of her body cut a luminous swathe through the night. Under the table, she examined each of the photographs, looking for evidence of wear, or for signs that either Druzhnikov or Kuznetsov had become tiresome. They hadn't; she was newly charmed by the small rebellious sneer in the turn of Kuznetsov's mouth. Now the feeling that had accompanied her the entire day intensified. She recognized it as warmth, as expectation, as the creepy stink of the privy, and now as something else as well, a familiar, beckoning, taunting, and sickening itch. She kissed the picture of Samoilov, felt the starch of the paper on her lips. Then she lay on her back, the underside of the table eclipsed in shadow but as visible as the unlit side of the crescent moon after dusk, the photograph above her, her right hand beginning the long rustling arc through her bedclothes.

But Comrade Stalin watched too. He drew her eyes to his. It was said that if you were in the same room with him, or even with him and tens of thousands of others in the cobblestoned vastness of Red Square, you could not resist looking into his eyes, he had that power over men and women. Scientists couldn't explain it, the only man who could have explained it would have been Stalin himself. It was also said that those eyes could see the future.

Anzhelika's teachers had deeply immersed her in the history of the *Revolution*—the roar of marching crowds, a blur of red flags, a storm of dates—but the word *revolution,* whispered at night in her solitude, made an entirely different impression upon her. An incandescent globe had somehow been lowered from the sky. It hovered above Russia. It *revolved.* She gazed directly into the ball, a solid sphere of goodness, her face warming to its radiance. The miracle was augmented by mystery: Stalin had either summoned the sphere or had stepped from it, Lenin at his side.

Stalin was as handsome as any actor, men all over the world brushed back their hair and let their mustaches grow out like his. Anzhelika dreamed of marrying him. There had been girls worthy of Stalin: the young partisan spy tortured and hung by the Nazis, Zoya Kosmodemyanskaya; the Krasnodon Young Guard who had organized acts of sabotage against the Germans, Ulya Gromova; the little orphan in the song who had sent him her teddy bear. Fate had refused Anzhelika the possibility of similar acts of heroism, she was just some drab little girl living in a drab little town. Her eyes stung at the thought.

Yet at the same time, and this was the miserable secret rattling around the chambers of her heart, she was afraid of him. The fear had sprouted from something evil inside her, and she was not sure exactly what it was, but it was there and Stalin could name it. One line was never erased from Aleksandra Semyonovna's blackboard: *Although you do not know him, he knows you and is thinking of you.*

Stalin knew the evil was something worse than wasting notebook paper. The real evil was something deeper, indelible and pervasive, something that lay in the under water provinces of her body. Anzhelika knew the itch was wrong, or rather, that the pleasure she derived from touching it was wrong. The itch (it wasn't exactly an itch: it was a kind of incipience, something on the verge, a craving to be touched, a pulsing infection) would be all right if she left it alone. To silence it one night she had bit her hand. In class the next day she gazed at the mark, proof, if not of her goodness, then at least of her desire to be good.

Tonight she mumbled the bedtime words repeated by millions—*Thank you, Comrade Stalin, for a happy childhood*—and passed unevenly into sleep, her lips parching, her eyes fluttering open to the pictures on the wall. She woke to arrest her hand in its drifting fall. Don't touch it, it'll stop. But it spread through her body like water pouring into an empty vessel. Although no dreams lit the dark, her sleeping mind entered into a dialogue with the itch, which whispered entreaties and made demands, asked seemingly innocent questions and gave malicious answers. And then at last, hours deep into the night, she touched it and it was as if the liquid had turned to ice, and then as if the ice had caught fire.

She woke again, wet between her legs. Urgently she searched the bedclothes and closed her eyes in gratitude when she discovered that they weren't damp, that she hadn't peed. Her relief was so profound that she almost returned to sleep and would have if not for the thought that she might still wet the pallet and face terrible consequences. The warmth seized Anzhelika in an embrace under the blankets, insisting against the cold, middle-of-the-night journey to the privy. A different entity now,

more distinct but still enigmatic, the warmth suggested
that there was no pressure on her bladder and no need to
urinate. But Anzhelika climbed from beneath the table
anyway.

The night was as cold as promised, the wetness
clammy, almost reptilian, against her skin. The privy's
stink carried no attraction now. Her urine flowed in
hardly a dribble, but when she wiped she sensed that
she wasn't coming clean. She returned to the house, removed her coat, shoes, and galoshes, closed the door to
the kitchen, and turned on the electric light.

A little brown fish swam across the white front of her
nightdress. Anzhelika nearly swooned as she made the
identification: blood.

She extinguished the light at once. The realization
that the stain was blood cut through the fog of her childhood. She would need to dispose of the nightdress in the
privy (but it was too big, the scissor wouldn't cut the
cloth) or bury it in the rubbish tip at the end of the yard
(physically possible, but her mother would miss the
dress immediately).

Anzhelika returned to the pallet and lay awake, nau-
seated, wondering how long it would take for the wound
to heal. It was freshly wet when she touched it. From the
pallet, she could make out only a black oblong of sky
in the window over the wash basin, most of the sky occulted by a wall alongside the next house. She watched
the sky for hours, imagining stars and comets and the
ticking of a clock, until the moment she perceived the
first thin gray spill of daylight.

She crawled from beneath the table and washed at the

basin. When her mother and the other women arrived to prepare breakfast, no one noticed that Anzhelika had already rolled her pallet and dressed. With her father in the privy and her mother in the kitchen, Anzhelika hid the stained nightdress under the linen in their dresser, putting off a decision about it until nightfall. Then she stole a large scrap of yellow cloth from her mother's sewing kit. When it was her turn to use the privy again, she stuffed the cloth into her underwear to stanch the flow.

The cloth had belonged to a favorite, long-outgrown and long-outworn dress. As she returned through the early morning chill to the house, Anzhelika tried to smooth out the suspicious bulge in the lap of her uniform. It resisted elimination. Uncle Fedya, still unshaven, passed her in the hallway and halted. He pushed his eyeglasses up the long bridge of his nose, contemplating what was different about her. His breath that morning ascended from somewhere unspeakably deep within his body.

She turned, threw her coat over her shoulders, and rushed from the house before she would have to speak with him or anyone else.

Outside, past the front gate, she was alone again. She stood for a moment with a single foot in the street, as if caught between one place and another entirely different. Then she ventured onto the blackened ice and the fossilized imprint of a truck tire. The neighbors were already picking their way across the road that led to the dairy. They passed before her like shadows, weightless and speechless. The town's small homes and buildings were composed of the same wan, chipped concrete as the sky.

Anzhelika arrived well before the first bell and opened her coat, checking for stains on her uniform. She entered the classroom and carefully took her place, intent on maintaining the position of the cloth between her legs, which was bunched not quite flush against her. She shifted and it squirmed slightly, like a small animal. The regard of the other girls, her enemies, as they came into the room was neither casual nor blind, but direct and knowing. Blood again: Anzhelika heard it coursing through her cheeks and ears.

The torrent deafened her. She was unaware of Aleksandra Semyonovna's entrance until her bench-mate Masha swung open her desk and rose with the class. Anzhelika stood abruptly and the cloth slipped a little. It was horrible, the blood had wadded it.

The teacher carried a pointer and immediately began poking it at a large map of the world. With long auburn hair, a bright complexion, and slim, long legs, she was the prettiest woman Anzhelika had ever known. She liked Anzhelika. Once, when the girl had volunteered the correct answer to a difficult geography question—she almost never spoke in class, unless directly called upon—Aleksandra Semyonovna had stepped behind her bench and squeezed her by the shoulders. The answer was Paris. According to Masha, Aleksandra Semyonovna had been jilted by a cavalry officer from Ufa, a lieutenant with a clipped blond moustache. Anzhelika had once thought of growing her hair long like her teacher's, but her mother objected. She said it would get dirty and tangled.

The memory of her teacher's caress suggested to Anzhelika that she could be an ally, but the form and even the purpose of the alliance eluded her. Gazing ahead as the lesson began, Anzhelika recalled the steppe and the house she shared with Samoilov. Aleksandra Semyonovna also lived on the steppe, in another house across the way, still pining for her cavalry officer. Anzhelika and Aleksandra would borrow eggs and cheese from each other, and sometimes each other's dresses, and comb each other's hair, and in summer they'd sit on the porch waiting for their lovers to ride up on horseback.

But Boris Sergeyevich arrived instead, at the door to the classroom, his youthful, unlined face bleached, his expression grim. Aleksandra Semyonovna fell silent and the class, which had been listening attentively, found a level of stillness that approached the absolute. The principal beckoned the teacher. She took a lingering look at her students before she stumbled from the room.

The children were alone. An excited murmur rose from the seats and benches, like the humming of an engine. Its heat fell upon Anzhelika's back and the exhaust singed the hairs on her neck. The girls behind her snickered. She stared into her desk, focusing on a single scratch in the wood dashed across the grain, an imperfection less than a millimeter wide, and forced all her being into it. Drifting down the crevice, she bumped against its ragged walls and settled onto a ledge. Rapidly moving water rushed below her and foamed crimson against the rocks.

She luxuriated there in the heat fed by the springs below. Her feet dangled over the ledge. The light descending from above the desk was softened by its fall, and sound could not reach her at all. She dozed, making up for the previous night's sleeplessness, until a shiver, Masha's, was telegraphed through the bench.

Aleksandra Semyonovna had returned to the classroom, soaked in tears. The humming ceased abruptly. The teacher's face appeared to have been broken in two, skewing the bones of her nose and jaw. Her pale blue eyes, framed in fear, rested for a moment on Anzhelika. She looked as if she were about to speak, but surrendered instead to a fresh, disfiguring storm of tears. The students were paralyzed by the spectacle.

Something emerged from her trembling lips that Anzhelika could not hear. A wind swept through the room, cold and fetid, carrying the gasps and moans of the children and then the children themselves. As notebooks and papers gusted against the windows and walls, Anzhelika and her classmates were lifted from their benches and borne to the general purpose room.

The boys in their year were crying as they poured into the hall alongside Anzhelika's class, as were many of the older children. Boris Sergeyevich stood before them, tears streaming from his eyes. Anzhelika had never before seen a man cry, hardly knew it was possible. Something warm tickled the inside of her thighs. *Please stop please,* she prayed against the flow of his tears and her blood.

The day passed without any sense of movement. A few teachers attempted to make speeches, but most of what they said made no sense, as if the speeches were about why the sun had risen in the west, bearded, or why a cow drove the trolleybus on the left side of the street, rather than the right. Most of that day the children were not

spoken to, they remained in their places, sniffling. Else-
where grown men and women took their own lives.
Others mutilated themselves to show penance. Candles
were lit in churches and prayers were said in mosques
and synagogues. In the Far East, political prisoners wept.
Two days later, panic would seize a grieving crowd in
Moscow's Trubnaya Square and more than five hundred
people would either be trampled to death or suffocated.

The schoolchildren didn't stir in their seats, but they
never expected to be dismissed. They bathed in the liq-
uids of eternal purgatory. No bells ended the schoolday.
At some undefined, unclocked moment, several children
rose and filed out. Others followed, Anzhelika with them.
Aleksandra Semyonovna was no longer present, but other
teachers were at the door, embracing their favorite, most
affected students. Outside the school, adults waited in
the yard, and they too were embracing each other, talking
in low tones. Not a single one was without a cigarette. As
Anzhelika passed them, every chafing stride announced
that the insides of her thighs were wet.

Little Kolya was with his friends again. This time the
boys didn't have a stick, but they were standing around
the same oily puddle between the two houses. Anzhelika
went by and they turned with her. Their faces were as
dead as walls, but their little bird eyes stayed alert and
predatory.

She didn't enter the house but went right to the privy
and closed the door. Reaching over her head, she fastened the hook into the bolt, forcing it deep into the eye.
She opened her coat. In the gray light admitted over the
top of the door, she could not determine whether the

uniform was stained. She removed her coat and hung it on a nail. After hitching up her dress and dropping her underwear, she pulled on the rag. She shuddered as it slithered out of her. Thoroughly soaked, it dropped into the privy hole without returning a sound. Anzhelika tried to make out the lower portion of her body, but couldn't. She let go of the hem of her uniform and stood there, her underpants around her ankles.

A kind of noise surrounded her now, a ringing sheath that insulated her and deadened her senses to the privy's odors and the stickiness. She heard music, from "The Fall of Berlin":

> Through the terrible fire
> He fearlessly led the Soviet people.
> We passed through the storm as if it were a
> springtime gust. . . .

The song was punctuated by footsteps, recognizable by their echoing tread. They stopped and the door to the privy creaked and heaved. The little hook tugged on the screw and even in the gloom she could see the screw give. The plank to which the screw was fastened yawned away from the doorframe.

Too frightened to move, she didn't lift her underpants. The door hook was pulled hard to the horizontal, spanning a chasm of daylight, before it fell back into place. After a moment of silence, a fist thumped twice against the door. The privy's timbers rattled like the bones of a skeleton. She made a choked, wordless sound, signaling herself. Father left.

She would need another piece of cloth. This morning

she had seen in her mother's sewing basket a second
scrap alongside the yellow cloth, a piece of her old nightdress. Why hadn't she taken both of them? She wished
she could travel back in time and steal the second piece
of cloth, or better yet . . . further back, to prevent everything that had happened. Using what was left of the
newspapers (there would be complaints), she wiped herself. Tossed off its cinderblocks, the privy was spinning
now, she was sure her father would return any minute.
Why was he home so early? What time was it anyway?
Was her mother home? If she could get past him, she
could steal what was left of the old nightdress.

She quickly pulled up her underwear and, forgetting
her coat, hurried from the privy. Father wasn't waiting on
the steps. She went around to the front of the house. She
stepped through the door, removed her galoshes, and
shuffled through the hallway, unaware of the swelling
music. Her progress carried her to the door of the front
room. Uncle Fedya and Aunt Olya's big glass doors, usually shut and curtained, had been swung open. Anzhelika
stopped. Surprise carried her hands to her face.

All the adults who lived in the house were there, sitting around a circle in the failing light, listening to Uncle
Fedya's radio. They had never done that before, they dis-
liked each other too much. Still wearing her dark blue
smock from the dairy, her mother cradled her head in
her hands as if it were a cabbage. In the dusk, her person
seemed no more substantial than an image in an old photograph, and that is how Anzhelika would remember her.
Uncle Fedya sat alongside her mother, and on the other

side were arrayed Aunt Olya, Aunt Vera, Uncle Adik, and then Father, occupying the place closest to the door.

In sacred devotion to their grief, they were all perfectly still, except Father, who was clenching and unclenching his fists. The tendons rose in his arms and neck. The choir continued, *Forever he is true to that vow, which he gave Lenin.* Only gradually did the adults' eyes register the child's presence, at first with indifference. And then a few eyes widened and held their gaze. Father turned in his chair. He was red in the face, which was greasy with sweat. His eyes were raw. He too had been crying.

It was only then that Anzhelika realized that her fingertips had been wet and that now her cheeks were wet as well. She glanced to the right. Across the room, the full-length mirror of the 1879 wardrobe neatly framed her. She was betrayed in it, what was left of the day coalescing around her like a spotlight. The blood was all over, streaked brown across her face, up and down her legs, and across her bare left arm. The uniform was stained too, finally, in her lap and in a big swipe across her chest. There were even dried bits of blood caught in her hair. Her body lifted from the floor, buoyed away on a rush of sorrow. New tears flooded her face: she could taste the blood with them. She gasped for breath. The adults didn't move.

"It was me," she sobbed. "It's my fault!"

Father's blow, when it came, was like a bolt of divine lightning.

Birobidzhan

Биробиджан

One

Israel's prayers were answered.

A young woman stood in the shadows, hugging herself as if she were cold, though body heat and the fire of political dispute had steamed the flat's windows. Against the imagined chill she wore a shapeless brown cardigan that ended high above the waist of a long, incongruously flouncy blue dress. She was tall and almost swaybacked, with slender, bony limbs. Clearly a city girl, probably a student, possibly a Party worker. A casual glance might not have discovered her prettiness in the angular thrust of her jaw or in the firm, unsmiling set of her mouth, but he appraised her with the care of a jeweler. What summoned his attention was the penumbra of loneliness that extended from her person and merged into the room's dim places. In its indeterminate contours, he perceived the precise impress of his own need.

He had stepped from the kitchen only to stretch his legs (and to register his disgust with the course of the conversation). The flat's former dining room had been turned, or requisitioned, into the living space for a family of five. This evening it had been requisitioned yet again. Its fine parquet, shadowed by Chinese lanterns, now served as a dance floor. A gramophone recording unwound a length of insistently jazzy music, not quite current. In the center of the room a young red-haired student was trying to show her partner and another couple a new dance step, but she was unsure of it herself. Now she laughed at her own ineptitude.

"Back left foot, Israel? Side right foot and then the glide?"

He smiled distractedly, his gaze on the woman in the corner. She was staring into the room as if watching an entirely different scene, something unpleasant. Israel now noticed the menorah behind her, the *shammes* candle askew and a single light burning beneath it. The menorah was the only religious artifact in the room, even though Hanukkah was the Cultural Traditions Committee's ostensible reason for the party.

"Yes, but you must lift your arms. The gentleman steps, and then follows. No, no, *up*. Back left, side right, chassé, *up*. Here, let me show you."

In three quick strides he had reached the woman in the brown cardigan. "Please," he said, offering his arms. "I would like to demonstrate the Paterson Hop."

She shrank back from him, startled. She kept her arms around her chest.

"Ir ret Yiddish?" He asked if she spoke Yiddish. She shook her head.

"Please," he said in Russian. "I would be most honored."

"I don't know how to dance."

"You will, within three minutes."

The two couples on the dance floor giggled. The needle was brought to the perimeter of the disk. He lightly held the woman and fixed his eyes on her face, but she looked away. As the song began, Israel ascertained that the woman had lied: the ability to dance was not easily concealed. She took some shuffling, flailing steps, exactly the steps that a good dancer thought were the trade of the clumsy. He was pleased with this lie; his smile burst upon his face like a sun shower. She tossed boyish hips in time with the composition's complicated rhythm, unable to resist it. But she didn't know the Paterson Hop. He said, "It's a one-two, one-two, and then glide, with your arms, so"—he gently guided her—"so that the lady can pass under, and then, like this, that's the hop part. My name is Shtern. Israel Davidovich. Are you involved with Komzet?"

"No, my friend Rachel Labanova invited me."

"Lydia," he said to the red-haired girl. "Try it with Maxim. One step back, two steps forward. It's a dance for Nepmen. Now, glide. Almost. Again." Turning to his own partner, he added: "You have some potential as a dancer, but you'll need to practice. At least four times a day. Is Rachel Labanova involved with Komzet?"

"She heard only that there would be a party. We've just completed our exams." The woman frowned, sorry to have given him an explanation.

"I see. Glide, glide! And with whom do I have the pleasure of performing the Paterson Hop on behalf of the striving proletarian masses?"

"Larissa," she said dully.

"Larissa," he repeated, contemplating the fact.

Israel had a thick, pugilist's nose, as well as a pugilist's muscular, hairy arms. He was a compact, balding man

with bushy eyebrows, and in repose his expression was
fiercely birdlike. Yet he moved gracefully, his touch light.
His instructions to the other couples were clear and direct. Soon the small dance floor was filled. Larissa gave
up her pretense of inability and unsmilingly matched
him step for step. At twenty-nine, Israel was the youngest
man on the Komzet presidium, but he was older than
most of the men and women attending the party.

The needle slid into the disk's gutter. Israel stopped
and bowed to his partner. She didn't return the bow.

"Excuse me, Larissa, but I must leave you for a moment," Israel said. "The fools in the kitchen are giving
away my birthright. I'll be back."

"Thank you for the dance, but I'm leaving now—"

"Stay," he commanded.

At the kitchen table a half dozen men were sitting
around a large, crude map that had been heavily marked
and annotated. The map was sketched in heavy black
ink; the regions it denoted were labeled in handwritten
block letters. The irregular but inconspicuous shape of
the depicted area represented an idea only to the men at
this table, and perhaps to two or three others. At the
edge of the map, in the outland territories, lay a sheaf of
smudged, typed pages. Mikhail Beinfest had picked up
one of the sheets and was reading from it in an urgent
whine.

Israel interrupted, "We're still talking about soil
acidity?"

A few men grimaced, a few others shook their heads
to express their annoyance. Israel glared. This informal
meeting of the Komzet presidium was intended to be

decisive. But not everyone on the executive committee was present; there was not even a quorum. It looked less like a deliberative body than a game of pinochle. They were speaking in Yiddish.

"Israel, it's important," Leo Feirman said wearily.

"No, it's not."

The agronomist Bruk explained again. "We must quantify the arable land. There's a direct correlation between the soil's acidity—and it's very acidic—and how much livestock the land can support. And, Israel, it's not only a matter of soil quality. There's a single bridge across the Bira in the vicinity of Tikhonka, and it won't carry a truck or a tractor. The roads, such as they exist, haven't been tended in years. How will we supply the settlements? We also have to recognize the high, persistent activity of midges from April through August—"

"Midges? Midges? This is the most important moment in the history of the Jewish people in two thousand years, and you're worried about *midges?* Of course there's going to be midges. There's going to be locusts and hailstorms too. And you're lucky there's *any* bridges! You're lucky it's not the damned tundra, for God's sake. You have to *build* a homeland, just as you have to build communism. What did you think, they were going to give you Cornwall?"

One of the men said, "They promised us part of the Ukraine, or the Crimea."

"Forget the Ukraine! Forget the Crimea! Not in a million years are they going to give you the Crimea. The Crimea! They'll give the Crimea to the Zulus before they give it to you, you stupid, ungrateful kikes!"

Felder growled, "Don't raise your voice. This fucking kitchen's hot enough."

"Midges. Let me tell you something. You blow this, and you blow it for all time. The Jewish people are just about at the end of their history. Count the Jews who have been forced off the land in the last ten years. Count the Jewish shopkeepers who have lost their businesses— more than a million, according to Leshchinsky! Count the Jews who have fled to Moscow and Leningrad since the Revolution! How long do you think the Russians will tolerate it? Soviet power won't be enough to stop another round of pogroms. And then do you think we'll ever have another opportunity like this again? Or are we supposed to wait for the Messiah?"

"Israel," said Feirman, and sighed. "The midges bother the cattle. The Cossacks report very low milk yields. The Koreans don't even eat dairy."

"Good, we'll live like the Koreans."

"Israel."

A swirl of brown caught his eye. The cardigan was being passed across a doorway framed by three intervening thresholds. The sweater had been borrowed, he surmised, and now it was being returned.

"Wait a minute," he said. "I'll be right back."

"Israel, we can't wait—"

"Comrades, this issue must be decided by a quorum of the full presidium." He stopped and look back at the six gray, revolution-worn men. All had once carried guns and banners, faced bayonets and declaimed to thousands. Now their moment had passed or was passing. Israel had been the one to insist on this ad hoc meeting, under the cover of a holiday party, hoping to hand the presidium an accomplished fact. Now he shrugged at the need to change tactics. "This is a pointless argument in any event. Comrade Stalin has offered you something. Tell me how you would quantify the possibility of refusing it."

Israel found Larissa in the foyer on the edge of a chair, struggling with a pair of high, fashionable brown boots. They were probably borrowed too.

"We've hardly talked."

"About what? Look, it's been a long day. I made a mistake coming to this party."

"It may have been the best mistake of your life. Allow me please to walk you home."

She shook her head. "I live close by, in a student dormitory. Anyway, my friend Rachel is leaving with me."

Israel hadn't noticed the other woman, for whom I'm named, standing beside her, already dressed for the street in a luminous red coat and shawl. She smiled pleasantly, amused at Israel's persistence.

"I'll accompany you both . . ."

Larissa said dryly, "This matter of walking a woman home: it's a rather bourgeois manifestation."

Israel stared at her for a moment. Only the slightest suggestion of playfulness, nearly a mirage, shimmered around her eyes. He grinned at it.

"So they'll shoot me for walking you home. Let me find my coat."

In fact, the dormitory was only two blocks away and Israel had just begun to explain the work of the Committee for the Rural Placement of Jewish Toilers by the time they arrived. Thick snowflakes tumbled from the black sky. Larissa did not invite her companions into the lobby. She politely shook Israel's hand, kissed Rachel, and then fled beyond the building's single heavy wooden door. Rachel lived on the other side of the city. She told Israel he should accompany her only to the tram stop.

"No, I'll see you to your place," he insisted, and did, paying her fare and walking her up four flights to her communal flat, all the time talking, talking, talking. It was all politics, about which Rachel maintained a resolute indifference, but she basked in the heat of his attention. He lectured, he orated, he parodied, he cited, he argued (with absent interlocutors), and he asked rhetorical questions that, so that she would not miss the point, he answered himself.

And then he rushed back to Larissa's dormitory. It was a barrackslike affair, converted from a shoe factory and named for Lenin. He pushed open the door into a dim, gaslit corridor guarded by an armed young woman in an ill-fitting Red Army uniform. His smile was not returned. At the head of the corridor another woman, stout and middle-aged, sat behind a heavy desk. She glowered as he approached.

There was no possibility of being allowed upstairs; as he made the request, he perceived that the soldier tightened her grasp on her rifle. The woman at the desk would not even accept a letter for Larissa, grimly shaking her head.

"How about flowers? Would you give her my flowers?"

The matron laughed abruptly, a short, unpleasant

bark, but a laugh nevertheless. After all, this was
Moscow, in December of 1927.

"So you *would* deliver flowers? You would make sure
she received them?"

"Young man, the day you bring her flowers, I will
make sure she receives them."

"Thank you. Comrade-soldier, you are my witness."
Israel reached into his briefcase and removed from it
copies of *Pravda, Izvestia,* and the Yiddish newspaper he
worked for, *Der Emmes.* "Madame Comrade, do you have
a pair of scissors I may borrow? Well, never mind."

In Belorussia he had bunked with a young Polish
communist who had performed magic tricks to entertain
the troops. The Pole believed that magic belonged to the
people and that it was a hegemonic misappropriation
of universal cultural property to keep the secrets of the
trade from them. Every fifteen-minute performance was
followed by at least an hour of instruction. He was a good
teacher: after the company was routed, the surviving
troops drifted back to their villages, their sleeves lined
with playing cards and their pockets rattling with loaded
dice and trick handcuffs (the Chekist grinned when he
snapped his more reliable manacles around the Pole's
wrists). From this legacy—and from speeches by Comrade
Stalin to a visiting Italian delegation, a photograph of a
power plant built into the walls of a former monastery,
news of the flyer Comrade Shestakov's triumphant arrival
in Tokyo, a first-person account of the 1905 revolution
in the Presnya district, greetings from the Komsomol
to young French workers, denunciations of the Left
Oppositionists by Lipetsk peasants, compliments from

Indochinese anti-colonialists on the successful completion of the Fifteenth Party Congress, an enthusiastic report on the Dnepr dam project, warnings that the British were plotting an economic blockade, a Central Committee resolution on revolutionary vigilance, and congratulations tended to the state security apparatus on its tenth anniversary—Israel tore and folded and coaxed into bloom a bouquet of black-and-white flowers. With a copy of *Trud*, he made smaller arrangements for the receptionist and the soldier. The soldier smiled primly at the gift but refused it. The dormitory matron promised to bring the bouquet to Larissa at her tea break.

Two

Rachel in her bedclothes stepped softly through the room. Her roommates snored undisturbed by the pale, diffuse light thrown off by her smile. Despite a tragic adolescence (both her parents had been killed in pogroms during the civil war), Rachel smiled easily and made emotional attachments fearlessly. I believe that, by the end of the evening, she had fallen a little in love with Israel. Perhaps more than a little—supposing, as Israel did (though he wouldn't own up to it, in precisely those terms), that it was possible to fall in love with another person after a single encounter. Rachel descended into her bed as if into an embrace. But it was her romanticism and fearlessness that persuaded her that Larissa was the proper target of Israel's affections, and it would make her Israel's critical ally in the coming campaign. The newsprint flowers were soon followed by invitations to rallies, plays, political lectures, and gallery openings. Rachel congratulated Larissa on the arrival of each and encouraged their acceptance.

At first Larissa was flattered by the attention and, despite herself, pleased by the approval conferred by her dormitory girlfriends. They insisted upon putting the origami in a vase. One of them, a Russian country girl from beyond the Urals, asked if flowers made from newspapers were something Jewish. For her part, Larissa voiced the hope that this gesture would be the last and, as the invitations and humorous notes continued to arrive in the post during the next several weeks, she told Rachel, "What does he think? That I sit around all day attending to suitors?"

"You should write back. *Tell* him what you do."

"I'll send him a report on my last dissection. I'll send him the dissection."

But then the invitations ceased. No letter warned that he was surrendering to her resistance. She was surprised to find herself annoyed. Where was his determination? Men characteristically failed to persevere; it was proof of their insincerity. But what had she expected? That the invitations would continue indefinitely? She didn't mention her disappointment to Rachel. Nor did Rachel mention her own. And then late one afternoon at the precise minute of the day when Larissa had begun to wonder at her closed-mindedness and timidity, another student arrived to say that Israel had presented himself downstairs at the dormitory reception and had demanded to see her.

She didn't hurry, but neither did she primp before the mirror. She was wearing the same plain olive dress

that she had worn to her lectures that day. At the foot of
the stairs, at the place where the shoe boxes had been assembled, Israel now kept vigil, fashionably dressed in a
pressed shirt and vest beneath his open wool coat, a fedora
in his hands. He bowed at her arrival. The guard who had
been there the first night monitored their exchange.

"I received your invitations," Larissa said, by way of a
greeting.

"And the flowers?"

"The flowers too. They've become something of a fire
hazard. You seem surprised to see me," she observed.
"You did call on me, didn't you?"

"Yes, many times. This is only the first I've been able
to persuade someone to give you a message. You'd think
this was a convent."

She replied stiffly, "The working people of this country
have paid with their blood so that I may attend university. I didn't come to Moscow to dance in nightclubs."

This time she was fully sincere. She added, "I'm the
first in my family to receive a higher education."

"Who said anything about nightclubs?" Israel shook
his head, frowning. "I'm a former commissar in the Red
Army. My unit fought in Belorussia and Bashkiria. I
never received a higher education, but, you're correct,
among the things we fought for was for the right of peasants, workers, and Jews to attend university."

She bit her lip. "Sorry."

"And we also fought for the right of the people of this
country to produce the world's first example of proletarian high culture, free of bourgeois cant and chauvinism.

Look, I have two tickets to a concert tonight. Will you join me?"

"I need to study."

"Then why aren't you at the library?"

"What kind of concert is it?" she asked suspiciously.

"If I give the wrong answer, you won't come? It's music. What can be bad?"

She frowned, exposing a dimpled chin. He loved it. "Where?"

"At the Jewish State Theater," he conceded. "It's klezmer. Jewish music."

She betrayed not the slightest inclination to agree, but he had her trapped. It was the klezmer. She paused before she answered, as if to consider the proposal. At the mention of the Jewish State Theater, the soldier had screwed up her eyes. Larissa raised three fingers.

"Get another ticket. Rachel will come too."

"Can we ring her?"

"She doesn't have a telephone."

"A ticket's not a problem. But the concert begins at eight," he said, gesturing helplessly at his wristwatch. "If you want to fetch her, we'll never get to the theater in time."

But Larissa insisted, unsure of the source of her obstinacy. Did she think she needed a chaperone? Or a witness? Forty-five minutes later, Rachel was startled to discover the two of them in her foyer and in each other's company. She tried to hide her smile of wonderment. Embarrassed, Larissa studied her muddied, unborrowed boots.

A wet snow was falling when they returned to the street. After a quarter of an hour, Israel gave up the hope of a taxi. A densely peopled tramcar lumbered by, and he rushed the two young women onto the back of it. The car bolted forward. In the swaying, steaming throng, Israel, Larissa, and Rachel lost sight of each other—except for Israel's outstretched arm, which gripped an overhead strap, severed from his body. His wristwatch bobbed before Larissa's eyes, showing the time well past eight. As the second hand clicked through its stations, the heat and the sour, familiar odors of garlic and un-washed bodies made her drowsy.

Outside the tramcar, a sliver of electricity flew from the conducting wire and froze in white ice the gallery of pedestrians to be found along Myasnitskaya that winter: gesticulating sidewalk vendors, grimacing prostitutes, gypsies, rag-sellers, comb-sellers, and old women holding like icons other small household goods for purchase. They seemed no less distant than Tokyo.

Just when the tram made its turn onto Sadovaya, the humming of its electrical motor died. For several min-utes none of the passengers spoke nor took any notice of the thickening coagulum on the highway. The car was stalled precisely so that it obstructed not only the traffic exiting onto the ring road, but also the flow of vehicles already on the inner, clockwise lanes. Time passed. Perhaps all the passengers were lost in reverie, except Israel, who somehow managed to bully his way to the driver's box at the front of the car. There was a distantly heard argument before the doors sighed and the passen-gers, at first lingeringly and regretfully, clattered out.

Israel ran his two companions to the other side of the boulevard and at last succeeded in forcing a taxi to a halt.

"This is going to be some great article," Israel moaned.

"You're supposed to write about the performance?" Rachel asked, wincing. "Oh dear, I'm sorry."

"That's all right, it's already half written."

The concert had just completed by the time they arrived at the theater, which was down a flight of stairs in a courtyard off the Arbat. They swam against the rising surge of the departing audience, variously outfitted: semiformal evening dress, khaki military-style "French" jackets, threadbare overcoats. Since the proletariatization of culture and the distribution of free tickets by the unions, overalls and flowered peasant kerchiefs had come to dominate the theater halls. This audience was no less proletarian, but by its physiognomy, speech, and bearing it was also indisputably marked as Jewish. Israel led Rachel and Larissa to a large room behind the stage, where several men and women milled around a samovar and a plate of pastries. Their eyes lit when Israel strode through the doorway.

"Don't ask," he said, his hand raised and his face contorted in a parody of epic suffering. "I'm sure it was a wonderful concert. Please, allow me to introduce my friends."

Israel seemed to be known by everyone at the theater, even the visiting musicians, young men from the Ukraine no older than Larissa or Rachel. They had performed in conspicuously unfrayed work clothes. Now they brought some folding chairs together, again raised their instruments, and offered Israel a brief, remedial recital.

"It's not for me," Israel said agreeably. "It's for my readers. But I'll take a little vodka, if you have."

There were four men with instruments: a violin, a set of drums, a standard tenor clarinet, and a wide bass clarinet of ebony and chrome. An accordion and a trumpet lay on the chairs. A fifth musician, a thin man with a sparse red beard, was the vocalist. They all looked to the bass clarinetist for their lead. He kissed the reed and embarked on a growling, slithering crawl through the scale's nether regions. The clarinet and the violin came in, not timidly, but with great care. At first the music was something alien, hardly music at all, and then it was established as klezmer by the arrival of the giddy, fiddling violin. The vocalist stepped before his colleagues and began to sing in Yiddish, looking directly at Israel.

> *Af di fonen, af di fonen,*
> *Zaynen royte farbn.* . . .
>
> On the banners, on the flags,
> There are red colors.
> It's so good to be alive now,
> No one wants to die. . . .

When it was over, Rachel whispered to Israel, her face stretched into a gesture of incredulity: "What was that?"

"Socialist klezmer. No kvetching, no schmaltz, just good honest folk songs for the Jewish working man. Comrades, please, one more piece."

The second song was also political, something,

Rachel murmured to Larissa in explanation, about a young boy who gives up *cheder* for the Komsomol. But Larissa took little notice of the explanation. She was completely absorbed in the music, which was not about the Komsomol at all, but about something and someplace intimately familiar. Her lips were dry and slightly parted, her head cocked, her eyes blind, like those of an animal that had just caught a scent.

"All right, friends," Israel said when the musicians had finished. "That was wonderful. You've exceeded your norms. Come on, let's have a drink."

The vocalist thanked him on behalf of the band, self-consciously bobbing his head, and retired to a cup of tea. Officials from the theater approached Israel to be congratulated. He said some encouraging words to a few lingering stagehands.

But the bass clarinetist wasn't finished, even after the other musicians had laid down their tools. At first it appeared that he was blowing and fingering his instrument without musical intent. Then Larissa detected the familiar, submerged melody, and the low notes tongued her entrails. The song, "At the Casting Away of Sins," was something that had belonged to her grandmother, a hymn at bedtime. No one, she was sure, had ever before heard it played this way: fast, syncopated, loose, and ironic. The musician's eyes were closed behind a pair of heavy black-framed glasses. Sweating, he rocked as if in prayer. The violinist slid back to his chair and in a moment had stealthily joined him. The other musicians, minus the singer, came in too, each either playing for himself or in competition. The four brought the piece to an unexpectedly raucous conclusion.

Israel smiled. "The old sentimental tunes. They were the best, of course. But these are new times—"

He was interrupted by the bleat of the bass clarinet. Another song. The tall, dusky musician burrowed into the music like a feral animal, and his colleagues followed. The vocalist remained seated, for political reasons. The song was immediately recognizable: A mother braids her young daughter's hair while describing the man she is destined to marry. The man is strong and kind and the lyrics promise a happy future—but the melody reveals the mother's sorrow, for the passing of time, as well as for the ruins of her own marriage. Larissa's hair had once been braided; this melody was as familiar as the swollen, unjeweled hands that had braided them. But now when she closed her eyes, it was not as if she had returned home; it was as if she had never left the tramcar. She was enveloped again by garlic and body odor, hateful and seductive.

No one took notice precisely when Larissa began to sing. She herself first thought she was only humming, but in fact she was silently mouthing the words and then whispering them. The musicians adjusted, leaving just enough room for her voice to edge in between them. By the time she opened her eyes, she was singing fully, her diction distinct and knowing. Her face displayed intense concentration and something like disapproval, the same expression that she had assumed during the Komzet party. The mother's personal sorrow expressed a race's, and it became thoroughly Larissa's own.

In deference to the newcomer, the musicians at first reverted to the traditional arrangement, but the bass clarinetist forced the music across the measure and brought the others with him. Larissa didn't need to struggle to keep up: jazz seemed to be the way she had sung it her entire life.

No applause or comment followed their performance. The musicians put away their instruments almost furtively, as if caught in a shameful act—and in fact, they had been. The girl's husband was destined because the marriage was contracted by a broker, a disgusting practice outlawed by the Soviets. Such nostalgia would never have been approved for the evening's official program. The bass clarinetist gave Larissa a long, appraising look before dismantling his instrument, and then a nearly imperceptible, conspiratorial smile.

Larissa had never sung for Rachel, nor for anyone else in Moscow. Despite their years of friendship, Rachel hadn't known Larissa even *liked* music. This surprise did not amuse her; very quickly, like the last frames of a torn cinema film, the confidences she had offered Larissa flickered by in recollection. This time her smile obscured a wince.

Grinning, Israel said to Larissa, "I thought you didn't know Yiddish."

"I do. A little."

Larissa reddened. Her parents and grandparents had spoken Yiddish at home only when they didn't want her to understand, but there had been so much they didn't want her to understand that she had become fluent.

At the same time, she had developed another facility. Her father and grandfather played violins and her mother the clarinet, and in the small, overfurnished drawing room cluttered with photographs of forgotten and never-known ancestors and relatives, plus her own cot, she sang to their instruments. She carried the memory of this intermittent family harmony like armor.

"Comrades, I thank you," Israel said, placing his emptied glass next to his chair. "Take a look on page three tomorrow. You'll like what you'll see."

"You work for Komzet on the side, don't you? That's what they said. Am I right?"

These words were spoken by the vocalist, who had reapproached Israel with tentative steps.

A wide, welcoming smile stretched across Israel's face. "Damn right."

"Well, Comrade Shtern. Sign me up. I'll go."

"Of course you will. You're a Jew."

"And the Russians won't let me forget it."

"In Birobidzhan, you won't want to forget it. And you won't have to perform in some *kockenshteindit* basement underneath a bakery either. We're going to build you a theater with five hundred seats, cloakrooms, dressing rooms, recital rooms, lobbies walled by mirrors and lit by chandeliers, everything. It will be entirely for the preservation—and celebration—of Jewish culture. There'll be Yiddish music, drama, cinema, and wireless broadcasts. Our cultural works will be all around us, as plentiful and natural as the air we breathe. And why shouldn't they be? I want all you boys to come. Will you make me that promise?"

The drummer chuckled and turned his head away, avoiding the question. The other musicians didn't reply.

Israel went on: "It's remarkable how many times in the course of a day I'm approached by young, brave, healthy, hard-working Jews who ask me about colonization. It's taken hold of our national imagination. There's no denying it: we are about to write a new chapter in the history of the Jewish people. My friend, leave me your name and address. We'll be in touch."

In the past hour the evening had turned clement. Israel and the two women stepped out onto sidewalks wet but free of ice and largely empty of pedestrians. Through some aural illusion, the sound of the bass clarinet continued to snake through the moist night air, moaning pastiches of other familiar compositions, Larissa's own voice in accompaniment, richer and lustier than she had ever known it. She wished to preserve this illusion, and to that end she closed her senses to the Arbat's rough cobblestones pressing through her thin-soled boots, the twinkling streetlamps and the presence of her friends. She imagined that in the basement theater she had somehow exposed herself, yet she felt no remorse for it.

And then she thought to ask: "Birobidzhan?"

"The Jewish national homeland."

"Is it in Palestine?"

Israel laughed derisively. "Palestine is a lost cause. A strip of desert enshrined in myth. The Arabs will never let it exist and neither will the British. Any so-called Jewish national state in Palestine will always be an instrument of British imperialism."

"So what is it then?"

He stopped and reached inside his coat pocket. From it he withdrew a small square of folded paper. He maneuvered Larissa and Rachel within a street lamp's spotlight and executed another feat of prestidigitation. The square began to unfurl, apparently without end, its folds inexhaustible. Passersby turned their heads, first in wonder and then in fear, before scurrying away: was this a political demonstration? As solicitous as any stage performer, Israel asked the two women to open the last fold. Larissa took one end, Rachel the other.

"Voila!" Israel cried. "The Jewish national homeland. Created by Jewish workers and peasants, supported and protected by Soviet power, respected by the international proletariat. It's near Khabarovsk. On the Chinese border."

They had opened a standard wall map. The Union of Soviet Socialist Republics sprawled dizzyingly across the sheet. Its southern rim ran jagged against ancient empires. Its north petered out among uninhabited islands, archipelagoes, and deserts of ice. Three time zones east of Vladivostok, the country stretched nearly off the upper right-hand corner, trying to escape its own borders. Larissa held the familiar section of the map, the upper left corner, which tucked central Europe, Moscow, and Berlin in the same creased square. "Look here," Israel said—and she couldn't: he was pointing to a Russian dip into China several feet away. Leaning awkwardly, but still trying to keep the map open, Larissa teetered above the peach-colored steppes. Israel touched her arm, to steady her. His touch was warm, high up her arm. Then he let go and pointed to the place again. The light was too dim for the small print to be intelligible. A breeze stirred the map, tugging it between her fingers like a fish on a line.

"Forty thousand square kilometers," he said. "Virgin land rich in mineral deposits, lumber, and fertile soil. Bigger than Belgium, bigger than the British Mandate area of Palestine—and no Arabs. Just a few indigenous people and Russian and Cossack settlers, all enthusiastic about Jewish colonization. And it has just been given the full support of the Central Committee."

Rachel squinted into the map, and then at Israel. "You're building a theater there?"

"In time. And also Jewish schools, a Jewish cultural center, a Jewish publishing house, a Jewish newspaper, a Jewish party secretariat—"

Larissa abruptly asked, "How about Jewish places of worship?"

Israel shrugged with studied disregard. "Freedom of religious belief is guaranteed by Article 65 of the Soviet Constitution."

Three

Another woman may reflect on the story of her life and marvel at the chance encounters, odd remarks, freak accidents, slight misunderstandings, and trivial decisions—*if only I hadn't gone back for my hat!*—that have located her in this place at this time in this life. Perhaps respect for the personally serendipitous is a "Western" concept, a tenet of the cult of the individual. I myself live east of Istanbul, Delhi, and Beijing, where we prefer to give credit to fate or, in latter times, to history. My mother, Larissa, had gone to the Komzet party on a whim, which she regretted as soon as she arrived, but in the end she considered her life the product of unflagging historical determination.

In these late days I'm in a reflective mood, and I often look at the large local map I keep in the bureau drawer. On the map, the oblast's form is so irregular that it is still not immediately recognizable nor memorable. I know that countries often parody their own shapes. The Italians, for example, tirelessly exploit their cartographical image to promote their football teams and footwear industry. I once saw the Irish island figured as a small bear behind the wheel of a car. I have yet to see such a caricature of our autonomous region, not even by our most imaginative local cartoonist. Beyond our borders, the map attenuates toward tundra and desert, hills of naked rock, the great unknown Bureinsky Range, unpronounceable Manchurian place names, all of it virtually uninhabited.

And here I am, an insignificant spot on this improbable map, shlepping my groceries in a badly worn plastic shopping bag along a wind-carved boulevard that is as wide as a ravine and is neither the Arbat, nor Delancey Street, nor the Rue des Rosiers, nor the Allenby Road, but is in compensation named after Shalom Aleichem. The shopping bag is emblazoned with the scratched and faded photograph of an ample young woman posing shirtless on a similarly ample motorcycle, the American flag behind her. Well, so here I am: after sixty-five years of terrestrial existence, the thought continues to amaze me. Like Larissa, I insist against all reasonable argument that my presence on this map is too unlikely to have occurred by chance. It requires resolute design.

And what of Larissa? Is any of this history her design, or was hers a chance contribution? Standing in the shadows at the Komzet Hanukkah party, was she waiting to be made part of history? Was she really the lonely, unconnected girl that Israel took her to be?

Not quite. First, her future lay before her as readable as a book, her patients awaiting her, anesthetized, on an unbroken line of white-sheeted trolleys. And there was a boyfriend, an engineering student active in the Party and also a Jew—though a lanky, tennis-playing one with sandy hair and a Ukrainian's blue eyes. Ilya and Larissa had known each other for more than a year and had begun to make the small, necessary adjustments in their habits of living and dreaming. And they had made love once, imperfectly, a few weeks earlier, shortly before the Festival of Lights.

She didn't tell Ilya right off about Israel—what was there to tell?—but she mentioned the Jewish homeland.

He scowled.

"That's for what we fought a revolution? To create another Pale of Settlement? In China?"

"It's a theoretical question, a philosophical one," she said. "How should the Party break the cycle of repression and pogroms?"

"Through the *international* revolution of workers and peasants. There are significant numbers of Jews in nearly every Soviet republic and in nearly every European country. Jews will survive only if class solidarity overcomes national differences—that is where their salvation lies, as internationalists. Jews are the *original* internationalists."

"But isn't that the end of Jewish identity? Doesn't that mean the Jews will eventually assimilate into non-existence?"

"Neither Marx nor Lenin ever wrote anything contrary to assimilation; they foresaw it as a historical consequence of industrialization. And it's already happening. Do I really live any differently than a Russian student? I speak and write Russian, I obey no dietary laws, my holidays are the Soviet ones, it's no difference to me whether the girl I marry is Jewish or Gentile. So what?"

That was a misstep—she thought they had agreed he *would* marry a Jewish girl, herself—but Ilya was pleased with himself, even as he felt the wind shift. By the time he finished his speech the probability that they would make love again that night had declined to something less than even. Yet he didn't regret his stand. In the forceful assertion of doctrine lay a satisfaction that could not be found in lovemaking.

"Ilya, self-determination has been promised to more than a hundred nationalities. The Kalmyks, the Tatars—they all have homelands. Why shouldn't the Jews?"

"Because Jews are not Kalmyks or Tatars. Lenin was very explicit about this: the Jews have no scientific claim to nationhood because they have no territorial ties. It's living in Kalmykia and Tatarstan that *defines* what it means to be a Kalmyk or a Tatar. What do the Jews have to do with Birobidzhan? Why would they want to live there? Do *you* want to live there?"

It was a rhetorical question, but it startled Larissa. She realized it was not the first time since the evening on the Arbat that she had imagined living in Birobidzhan.

She didn't repeat Ilya's objections to Israel. But the next time he came to call on her, she declared that she already had a beau. Standing in the corridor under the righteous gaze of the dormitory guard, she said she was willing to continue her comradely friendship with Israel, but would understand if he did not. Her statement emerged flat and metallic, without conviction—though she meant every rehearsed word. By the time she had finished, she was annoyed at Israel for forcing her to deliver the speech. A more considerate man would have promptly interrupted her, said a few words in polite acknowledgment and saved her the discomfort.

Israel waited for her to finish but didn't appear to hear her. He proposed that they attend a film. He had already invited Rachel. Larissa didn't want to go, she needed to study, but she agreed anyway, weighted by the obligation to cement the friendship she had just proposed.

The film was something forgettably Bolshevik. Coming from the cinema, they walked along Hertsen Street and Israel performed feats of clairvoyance, anticipating his rival's objections.

"We *had* no territory, so we couldn't develop as a normal people, but now we *have* a territory. Everything that has plagued the Jewish people for two thousand years—their divorce from the land, their insularity, the ghettos and the shtetls, the blood libels, the pogroms, the dependency on exploitative capital—will be finished. We will

witness—in our lifetime!—the evolution of an entire
race. The Jews will develop a relationship with the land,
work it with their own muscle and intelligence, and in
the process develop a proletarian culture. And this
will happen outside the historical conditions that developed anti-Semitism in Europe, specifically, capitalism.
Birobidzhan has already won support from the Soviet
government, and it will also draw assistance from the
international proletariat and progressive world Jewry.
Even the American Jewish capitalists have promised us
money! This is a country where we can raise our children
as Jews, teach them Jewish culture, speak Yiddish—and at
the same time serve the Soviet state!"

And so on, into the night and the following days
and weeks. Israel talked about almost nothing but
Birobidzhan, neither about his family nor his past,
nor did he ask Larissa or Rachel about themselves. The
words *our children* hung in the air like smoke from a small
explosion.

Was this the first time that Israel had fallen in love?

No. His best friend on the Komzet presidium, Leo
Feirman, counted at least two previous courtships in the
last year or so. Each time, Israel had believed that he had
found his future wife, and his disabusement eventually
brought him paralyzing, unutterable grief. Leo also
knew that Israel had done the bouquet trick before—
which didn't make it a less sincere or less gallant gesture,
only less of a sudden inspiration. He thought that Israel
was foolish in thinking that love was something to be decided in a moment and then won by argument and siege.
But as the weeks passed and he witnessed Israel's resolve

and intimations of success (Larissa was reading his annotated copy of Lenin's book on nationalism), he reconsid-
ered his disapproval. He himself was not married. An old
Bundist, a portly, hard-boiled veteran of tsarist prisons,
the seizure of the Winter Palace, and the forced collectivization of agriculture, Leo was willing to concede that
his theories about romantic love were not fully developed.

He more easily comprehended the solid pragmatism
that drove the urgency with which Israel pursued ro-
mance. Israel desperately wished to be among the first
settlers in the new land. Hundreds had already left in
the weeks since the Central Committee had given its
approval, and Leo himself was about to depart. Israel
would not, however, emigrate unmarried. He expected
a poor choice of single women among the pioneers.

I once asked Larissa about Ilya, about why she didn't
marry him. We were in the kitchen on the rare occasion
that we were alone (we shared the flat on Kalinina with
another family). Glasses of tea cooled on the unpainted
wooden table. According to some privately held principle,
Larissa took hers without sugar.

She didn't immediately reply. I sensed that I had wandered onto dangerous terrain, but I was fourteen or fifteen
at the time and was thrilled by the danger and also by the
possibility that the question would cause her anguish. My
mother and I were separated by an entire continent of
dangerous terrain, much of it pimpled by watchtowers. I
was about to ask again, when she said, "I loved him."

Her eyes downcast, Larissa revealed neither pleasure
nor regret in this statement. She pronounced it with the

flatness of a diagnosis. I was stunned. She had never before spoken to me of anything so personal. Emboldened, I pressed her.

"Did you love Israel?"

"No, probably not, not at that moment."

"Why did you marry him?" I asked, with the direct fearlessness of a fourteen year old.

"It has something to do with this place. He had never been here of course, but how he described it . . . He spoke of trout running in clear rivers . . ."

I laughed unkindly. "It charmed you."

She considered this. I looked beyond her through the iced kitchen window, where loomed the gray shadows of trees and nearby buildings.

"No. But he made the place real. Ilya never succeeded in making the future real, our future together, no matter how often he spoke of it. I did love your father, only everything happened too quickly for me to realize it."

My godmother was more explicit about the way Israel pursued Larissa: single-mindedly, persistently, ruthlessly. There were picnics in the Park of Culture supplied by sausage, wine, and sweets from Yeliseyev's; presents of books chosen with nearly as much care as with which they had been written; an ardent patter to accompany illusions and sleight of hand; a deft, unsentimental poem; and a clumsy, sentimental confession. According to Rachel (we were on the divan, cuddling for warmth, and she stroked my hair as she unwound a skein of memory, while my mother read a newspaper at the table), Israel had convinced himself that Larissa was his last chance to find love. He had also reasoned that success with Larissa would make all the romantic failures of the past several years historically necessary.

Larissa knew this, and resented that Israel's supposed love for her had so little to do with who she actually was, that she was no more than a last chance. Also, he was a bit short. One preternaturally warm spring Sunday Rachel accompanied them on a picnic. They shared a blanket near the river edge, Israel between them. Both women lay on their backs, basking, the backs of their heads cradled in their hands. Israel was speaking, but his words were as tangible as the bars of martial music that occasionally drifted over from the attractions. Larissa looked over to her friend, gilded by the sun, her muscular arms bare, her chest broad, her cheeks aglow, and she realized that Israel had committed a signal error: it wasn't herself that he should be courting. Rachel's robust constitution was suited to pioneer the virgin lands. She cared about the preservation of Jewish culture. Israel had merely seen Larissa first—at the moment when the woman whose destiny was truly intertwined with his was standing right alongside her. It was Israel's absurd doggedness that kept him after Larissa. He didn't notice the stellar luminosity in Rachel's eyes when she gazed at him; nor did he remark his own pleasure in her company.

This realization should have freed Larissa, but it didn't. She contemplated both Israel and Rachel and couldn't imagine how she would summon the frankness to tell them of Israel's mistake. For weeks she was oppressed by her knowledge. And then one morning after the late return of the frost, she met Rachel as they filed into an unheated lecture hall. Rachel squeezed her by the arm, almost shaking loose her notebook.

"Guess what?" she said. "I've made a decision. I'm going to Birobidzhan too."

The words passed through Larissa like a sharp wind. She was instantly vouchsafed an image of Rachel in the Far East: astride a tractor, buxom and erect, her face to the sun. And there was something additional to this image: Israel standing next to the tractor, his arm lightly about her hip. Larissa knew now what it meant to be bankrupt, it didn't apply only to capitalists.

"That's wonderful," she croaked.

"Isn't it?" Rachel whispered. The other students were settling down in anticipation of their lecturer. "What's wrong?"

"You're so brave. I admire you. And Israel too, of course. I couldn't do it."

Larissa was astonished at her own bitterness. After all, the world had been set right. But she now looked at Rachel with fresh eyes. The girl was attractive and smart all right, but her easy enthusiasm often verged on the silly; this life-wrecking decision proved it. Larissa wondered how she had become so attached to her, and whether this attachment was the last manifestation of her own childishness.

And she also wondered now how she had gotten her life so mixed up with Jews. She had never expected to. In the cosmopolitan, revolutionary Petrograd of her adolescence, where she did not know the location of a single synagogue, her supposed Jewishness had rarely laid claim to her attention. In Moscow her attachments to Rachel and

Ilya had preceded her realization that they were Jewish. It had been only a coincidence of birth. In the future, she resolved, she would avoid such coincidences.

"But you *can* do it!" Rachel insisted. "You will! I'm counting on it!"

"You shouldn't. I have a career ahead of me here. A whole life."

"Israel's counting on it! He told me so!"

Larissa flinched. This was like one of Israel's displays of magic. A trivial object gains in value the moment it's put out of sight under a hat or in the pink blur of a quick hand movement. How gladdened we are by its return!

The lecturer arrived and the students briefly rose from their seats. Throughout the lecture, cartoon bubbles of frosted breath puffed from his mouth, but neither Larissa nor Rachel could read what were in them. There would always be a certain lacuna in their knowledge of the neural function of the microglia. But something had been settled.

When the lecture ended, Rachel turned to Larissa, her eyes moist. "I'm going to the Far East as soon as I finish my exams. I don't know Israel's plans. He's waiting for you. I wouldn't be so sure that I was going if I weren't so sure that you'd be going too."

Four

They were married that spring. By then Israel had left *Der Emmes* in order to devote his days and nights entirely to Komzet work. Intending to produce an agitprop cinema film, he campaigned for funding from various state

and Party organizations and even the American Joint
Distribution Committee, which had promised the
colonists material assistance and duly shipped Israel a
newsreel camera. Israel appeared on stage before nearly
every performance of the Jewish State Theater, as well
as at the other Jewish theater, the Habima, on Malaya
Bronnaya. He pitched the colonization plan to the
Russian papers, which devoted whole pages to speeches
by members of the Komzet presidium, as well as one in
which Soviet President Mikhail Kalinin promised the
creation of a Soviet Jewish republic: "national in form,
socialist in content!" Telegrams of encouragement
reached the Komzet offices from all over the USSR and
the world, from Uzbekistan, Arkhangel'sk, New York,
and London. The camera, however, was requisitioned by
the Commissariat for Enlightenment.

And suddenly the date of their departure impended.
Larissa made the journey to Petrograd—now Leningrad—
to explain her intentions. Her parents were too shocked
to object. They stood motionless in the foyer of their flat,
blinking their eyes as if against a very bright light. Larissa
herself had lost the power of speech. She couldn't explain
anything to her friends. All the farewells were muted. No
one expected to see her again. They laid their bloodless
lips against the cheeks of a memory.

A military band came to the Yaroslavl station to
salute the latest carload of departing settlers: the
"Internationale," followed by "Tsu a Yiddish Land," "Af di
Fonen," other martialized Yiddish songs, and, for good
measure, the overture from *Carmen*. A representative of
the People's Commissariat for Land Issues read a speech

that cited Lenin castigating the Left Oppositionists from the grave. Two dozen Komzet activists precipitated from the clouds of early-morning commuters with presents of flowers and sweets, carrying the same red flags wielded by Israel and Larissa at Rachel's departure a few weeks earlier.

Komzet had provided them with a clean and comfortable car, hitched to the rear of a long, Siberia-bound train. The car's interior was open, without private compartments, but each passenger had his own bunk, either above or below, and families and couples staked out adjoining places. Laying out her linen, Larissa missed the precise moment when the train broke from its moorings and the world she knew slipped from the edge of the window. She looked up. The departure committee had already foreshortened into the invisible. The band was now playing to an empty track. Steadfast against sentimentality, she returned to her unpacking.

Afterwards, as the travelers became accustomed to their surroundings, the first day of their journey would be recalled as one of wonder and novelty. In fact it was only marginally more eventful than those to come. The trip would occupy more than a month of their lives, an expanse comprised of forward lurches, hypnotic rocking, and stops of long, unexplained durations.

An incantation of place-names: Ryazantsevo, Yaroslavl, Sharya, Shabalino, Yuma, Buy, Neya, Vyatka, Yar, Kez, Perm. The train had not yet reached the Urals. Israel proposed that their car be renamed Settlement No. 1 and exhorted the passengers to keep it habitable: "How can we conquer the taiga if we can't even make our beds!" Every day the travelers washed the car's floors, windows, and toilet and even arranged several times a week to fill a large tub with hot water for laundry. Meanwhile they read, argued, gossiped, and planned. A map of their destination covered one window of the train; arguments were brought to it for adjudication. The settlers made pencil marks to illustrate where certain crops could be cultivated and roads should be built; names for new settlements were invented and written in. From afar, the transformations of the map seemed almost geological.

Shortly before they left, they had received reports and letters from the first settlers. In total, these reports didn't amount to much, but in the weeks of their journey they were repeatedly scrutinized for every piece of intelligence, their nuances interpreted, their omissions debated, their casually written details extrapolated, their many complaints reevaluated in light of the hardships that had befallen all settlers to new lands: the American Pilgrims, the Boers. Leo had arrived among the first echelons and had sent Israel a hastily scrawled note demanding a seeder. Israel hadn't even been sure what a seeder was, much less where to get it in Moscow.

As for Larissa, she had kept her textbooks unpacked so that she could review the chapters on primary care. They lay open on her lap, exposing the settlers to disease and trauma, while she gazed through the window at the slowly passing trees and small buildings along the rail line. Israel suggested that she change her first name to something more Jewish. "Naomi? Do you like Naomi? I like it. It means Delight." At first she thinly smiled and said no, she thought Larissa suited her. "Have you considered it? I just now suggested the name. How can you reject it so quickly?" He called her Naomi for several hours, just to see if it would catch on. But it didn't and she told him, with some annoyance, that Larissa derived from the Jewish name her parents had given her at birth: Leah. But she didn't care for that name either. In the end, the name she would be called in Birobidzhan would be Shtern.

Although they crossed seven time zones on the journey, the travelers did not set their watches ahead until the day of their arrival. The clocks on the railway platforms at which they stopped also remained in lockstep with Moscow. As the summer sun rolled and dipped along the edge of the horizon, the periods of dark seemed to come at random, like passages through long tunnels. Keeping faith with their loved ones back home, the settlers slept and rose according to Moscow time. Almost every day after 6 P.M., they took turns giving political lectures, performing skits, or reading aloud from the works of their favorite authors, like Maksim Gorky, Isaac Babel, Charles Dickens, and Shalom Aleichem. Nearly all of it was in Yiddish. Israel gave dance lessons and performed card tricks: the Hindu Shuffle, the Novel Reverse Discovery, the Invisible Transit, the Snake in the Garden, Two-by-Two, Wrestling with Angels, Crossing the Desert.

There were enough instruments and musicians aboard the train for concerts, sometimes classical and jazz—but usually the performances melted into folk music and klezmer. All but Larissa would take part in the sing-alongs; and then at some undetermined, unprompted point, they would desist and she would begin. Israel rested his head against the train window and listened as the upward spiral of her song seemed to fill the steppe.

At many of the stations, particularly early in the journey, the pioneers were met by delegations from the local Party, as well as from the local Jewish community. It always surprised them. As the train slowed, the first notes of the "Internationale" rose among the whistles and hydraulic gasps of the locomotive. Municipal officials and party secretaries were on hand, even when the arrival was at an inconvenient hour. In some of these towns food was scarce or expensive, but at least a basket of fruit or fresh pastries would be waiting for them. The Red Army bands were joined by folk singers and dancers in peasant dress, often Cossacks. The travelers muttered, giggled, and shook their heads in wonder at this latest manifestation of Soviet internationalism. Cossacks dancing for Jews!

In Sverdlovsk, a city with a sizable Jewish population, the train was stopped and the settlers marched off to a banquet, where one speaker after another thunderously praised them. In turn, Israel took the podium, wine glass in hand, and exhorted his hosts to join them in their adventure.

"There's room for you! There's room for your *children*. There's room for your *grand*children. A lot of room: forests untouched by man and vast fields of grain brushing the horizon. Forget these cramped ghettos, these stinking, narrow streets, poisoned by centuries of bigotry. I give you a land that we will be proud to call Jewish *and* Soviet." Vigorous applause. "It will be only there, free of bourgeois nationalism, free of capitalism, free to live off the land, fully employing our brawn and intellect under the guidance of the proletariat, that we will succeed in developing the true qualities of our race." Cheers, more applause. "This land, someday a full Union republic, shall become the repository of world Jewish culture and genius, with world-class universities, libraries, and theaters. It is our guarantee against assimilation. Our children shall *speak* in Yiddish, *write* in Yiddish, and *invent* in Yiddish." Rhythmic clapping. Israel acknowledged the audience's appreciation, then raised his finger to show that he wasn't done yet. "So, in conclusion, I say to you, comrades . . ."

He stared down at his audience. One wouldn't call it a congregation, even though the large wooden building in which he was speaking had been a synagogue just a few years earlier. Now he looked *over* the audience's heads, at the walls and the women's gallery on the second floor. All the religious objects had been removed, but there were still sectarian architectural details here and there: a six-pointed star inlaid in the parquet, menorahs in the plaster molding. He smiled benevolently at these symbols and then, nodding toward a rectangular shadow on a wall where a plaque had once been fixed, at the ghosts of the dead.

"So, I say to you, comrades! *Next year in Birobidzhan!*"

This was followed by applause—explosive and emphatic, accompanied by cheers and amens, and sustained for several minutes—but not immediately. Immediately there was a silence as complete as the silence between the earth and the heavens. Feeling a chill, Larissa tugged at her sweater. And then the vice-chairman of the local soviet, a Jew, raised his hands to his chest and drew them apart. Before he could bring them together, scores of other hands were slapping at one another.

Most of their stops were less eventful. The train often came to rest on a track distant from the platform. Surrounded by walls of freight trains, laid into this strip of track as if into an uncovered grave, the settlers never saw the station nor anything of the town in which they had arrived. Just a slice of white sky was visible above the roof of the next train. A jolt and then stillness: they had been detached from the locomotive and the other cars. They lost entire days on these sidings, apparently forgotten by the railway authorities. Larissa once stepped from their car for some air, onto the sparse, muddy grass alongside the track, casually intending to walk around the neighboring trains to the station. But the train alongside their track stretched a kilometer in either direction and there was no way of telling how many tracks away, or in what direction, the platform was located.

Motion! Motion! Idled in Ingashskaya, Larissa would have preferred to move anywhere, even if the train had been shuttled onto a circular track around the station. Under way, the train tauntingly, maddeningly, dawdled across Asia, at no faster than a horse's trot for hours at a time. Some days the image of the steppe outside her window never changed, as if the settlers were parked inside a natural history museum. Face to face with the terrestrial, Larissa came to understand by extravagant extension the distances and the emptiness embraced by the word interstellar. The nearest star was five billion times further from Moscow than was Birobidzhan. She opened Israel's map of the Soviet Union and located their minute progress across it. The scale was one to eight million. If single copies of the map fell evenly upon the surface of the Union of Soviet Socialist Republics, at the rate of one per second, the entire country would be covered sometime in the afternoon of the second day of the fourteenth week. She did these calculations in the time it took to complete three of the 8,358 kilometers to Birobidzhan, occupying thirty-six hundred thousandths of the journey. The maps would fall with their illustrated sides down, presenting a comforting vista of white paper stretching from the Baltic to the Pacific.

The deeper they crawled into Asia, the less likely they were to come to towns and villages whose people knew anything about Birobidzhan, or knew anything about Jews except to hate them. Militiamen would come on board and study their travel warrants as if studying for a test. The railway was a key strategic link and officials were wary of organized groups traveling along it. At some stops the settlers were not even allowed to disembark to stretch their legs. Although annoyed, Israel defended the precaution. Then at Kisly Klyuch, less than a week from reaching their destination, he overheard one militiaman on the platform call to another, jokingly, that the prisoners all looked like Yids.

Israel, who had been standing at the car's open door, was out onto the platform in a flash. Three rifles were raised in unison.

"What did you say?" he demanded.

Israel's face had flushed to his ears and his eyes bulged like eggs.

The soldier, a beardless young Russian giant, snapped, "Immediately return to your place."

"Who told you we were prisoners?"

"Go back to your place!"

Israel was already waving his passport and travel warrant, as well as other papers provided by Komzet. He appeared ready to beat the soldier with them. "Look at these! We're a colonization detachment under the auspices of the All-Union Committee for Settlement and the People's Commissariat for Land Issues. Can you read?"

The militiamen said sullenly, "I can read."

"Do you see anything here that says we're prisoners?"

The Russian wouldn't look at the papers. He said, thin-lipped: "Get into the car right now, or you'll be *my* prisoner. We've got a cell just for kikes."

"No."

The militiaman, his rifle above his waist, winced in disbelief. *"What?"* The two other militiamen, Asiatics, closed in on Israel.

From her seat, a textbook warm as a kitten on her lap, Larissa watched this scene performed in pantomime. Israel appeared to ignore the two Asiatics. He was lecturing the Russian, a stubby index finger laid against the soldier's chest. Larissa's mouth went dry as Israel began poking him with it. The Russian reddened and shouted back at Israel. Larissa couldn't tell what was being said, only that Israel was doing most of the talking. Kisly Klyuch: they called this place *Sour Spring.* The men were joined by four more soldiers, including a gray-haired officer. For a moment Israel was lost among them, as if under an ocean wave. Then she saw him whirl at them, brandishing his papers, pointing at the train and then down the track, back at Moscow. The officer, another Russian, his impassiveness nearly royal, rested a hand on his holster.

The settlers filled the seats by the windows, poised with their knees digging into the upholstery, their hands wrapped around the bunk supports. "Oy vey," someone said without emotion. Another whispered, "What happened? What is he *doing?*" By their gestures, Israel and the militiamen seemed to be speaking loudly, but the car was engulfed in a subterranean silence. Nearly every passenger received a new sense of the remote, lonely continent to which they had journeyed in the last month. As communists, they had believed they had mastered history; now, as Jews, they knew that history still possessed a stick, a pitchfork, or a gun, hidden in a cellar or a corncrib.

The officer abruptly turned, his back to Israel. The other men fell silent. Israel set his jaw and looked up the platform. Several moments later a square, thick-necked man entered the picture framed by the car window. He wore a black leather jacket, tightly belted. Now the settlers returned to their seats, fearful of demonstrating undue interest in Israel's fate. Not a man or woman made a sound, not even to clear a throat.

On the platform, Israel and the soldiers looked sullenly at their feet, like schoolboys found truant. The officer, his imperial bearing now diminished, addressed the newcomer. Then Israel spoke. Larissa recognized by his expression that he was arguing with restraint, avoiding fervor and importunity. And then he stopped.

The man in the black leather jacket spoke very briefly. His words received an immediate response. Israel and the soldiers filed down the platform and out of sight. None of the passengers dared look at Larissa. When the officer and two of the soldiers appeared inside at the head of the car, it was as unexpected as if they had stepped from a cinema screen.

The Jews (that's how they thought of themselves now) sat rigidly at attention. The ones who sat with their backs to the soldiers didn't move, paralyzed by indecision about the most appropriate gesture of respect. They were all aware, suddenly, that the train car smelled of dirty laundry and the hard-boiled eggs that had become their most reliable diet. Several other soldiers came aboard, followed by Israel and the black jacket, both of them stone faced.

"Comrades," someone said.

The passengers with their backs turned thought at first that it was the jacket who had spoken, because it was his judgment they awaited. But the words were barely articulated, rising just above a murmur. Facing ahead, Larissa stared cold eyed at the Russian soldier. He removed his cap, revealing an unkempt stalk of straw-colored hair. Without the cap, he looked to be no more than sixteen. "Comrades," he repeated. "Respected comrades. I beg your forgiveness."

He turned, but the gray-haired officer blocked his way and whispered something. The soldier glumly faced the settlers, again.

"I beg your forgiveness for what I said."

A flash of impatience lit across the officer's face. He

spoke at length to the soldier. The soldier nodded, his face pale.

"I beg your forgiveness for a statement made while performing my duties as a member of the Kisly Klyuch People's Security Detachment. I was talking with my"— he paused here, unable to locate the appropriate word— "my *fellow*, and I referred to you esteemed travelers as 'prisoners.'" Blinking furiously, he looked over to the officer, who whispered something. "This was an error of thinking, the result of a faulty political education. I thank your representative,"—he stopped again, and received more coaching—"I thank Comrade Israel Davidovich for kindly pointing out this error. I beg your forgiveness and promise to reflect on this incident further."

The settlers didn't respond. There was nothing in their experience that would have suggested what their response should be. Two red rims appeared around the soldier's eyes. The officer gripped the militiaman's neck and spoke to him again. The soldier listened carefully. He announced, his voice nearly breaking:

"We of the Kisly Klyuch People's Security Detachment, on behalf of the workers and peasants' state, wish you success in your important work!"

For another moment the settlers remained impassive. Then from the car's last bunk, Morris Kugel cried out, "Bravo! Well said, comrade-soldier! Bravo!" More cheers immediately flooded the car, in both Russian and Yiddish.

The soldier was momentarily bewildered. He blinked. What began as a polite, wary smile slipped from his control and ended as the full exposure of a mouth crookedly crammed with white teeth. The settlers started up a round of rhythmic clapping and produced a set of drinking glasses and a bottle of schnapps. With the approval of the officer, the soldiers each took a taste, accompanied by more applause. Israel was beaming now, his arms around the "lads."

Only the man in the black leather jacket didn't take part. He hung back by the entrance, closely watching the proceedings. His gaze appeared to rest on each settler's face long enough to commit it to memory. When his scrutiny reached Larissa, she looked away, but she found his image shimmering in the window glass. The ghost's eyes held hers.

The settlers were long under way, their visitors gone, before the embers of their merriment were extinguished. Israel's comic retelling of the confrontation in Kisly Klyuch, embellished by his commentary, comprised that evening's entertainment. The bottle of schnapps was emptied. As he concluded his presentation, Israel promised that the militiaman's simple words would stand as their welcome to the Far East. The settlers had told the soldier—his name was Kolya—that if he were to come to Birobidzhan, they would find him a beautiful Jewish wife.

Larissa's relief left her skin cold and salty, and the remnants of her anxiety left her fatigued for the remainder of the journey. Israel's jokes about the encounter mocked her fear. She suspected that she was not alone in her unease.

The travelers' knowledge that they were almost there

now disrupted the routine of their days and heightened
their appetites. Their impatience was transforming and
consuming. They could no longer bear to read or play
cards. They scrubbed the bathroom, the windows, and
the floor until their knuckles bled. The desire to have the
trip ended was like a lust. In these public quarters, the
sexual wants of vigorous young men and women had
been stifled for a month. As the train crossed the map
crease into the square that contained Birobidzhan, the
settlers' jests and comments became more risqué, the at-
tire of the women less modest, the looks of the men more
direct. Now Larissa would wake in the middle of the
night and hear the furtive rustlings of bedclothes, a sup-
pressed gasp or giggle. In the morning, she would search
the faces of her traveling companions. Once she imagined
that the entire passenger car had been engaged in sex, an
orgy that had begun in Belogorsk and ended in Zavitaya.
But it was not sex the travelers most hungered for. They
stared through the windows, seeking there the image that
would present itself when they arrived. Closing her eyes
against the sun beating through the tops of the passing
trees, Larissa thought she could smell the Pacific.

From the day they had left Moscow the travelers had
been beset by arguments, none of them petty. The cor-
rect approach to bourgeois nationalism. The success of
the New Economic Policy. Its failure. The Five-Year Plan.
Collectivization. The Left Oppositionists. The Right
Oppositionists. The Trotskyites' false charges of anti-
Semitism in order to defend counterrevolution. The
Shakhty wreckers' trial. What Marx and Lenin did or

didn't say. What Comrade Stalin says. What Comrade Stalin *means.*

Now the debates picked up their fervor. Men and women would shout. Fingers would fly through the air to snare a point. Polemics. Leading questions. Rhetorical questions. Hyperbole. Sarcasm. Irony.

At first Larissa believed the settlers were being incautious. It was only this past December that the Fifteenth Party Congress had expelled Trotsky and warned against deviation from the general Party line. Statements made in the heat of argument were bound to swerve from it. But now, as they neared a land as distant from the Kremlin as the Congo, she came to consider these arguments as expressions of liberty, the promise of their new lives. This was evident in the way the settlers argued: taking every charge and countercharge personally, claiming every issue a matter of principle, seeking alliances among those they secretly admired, turning on those they secretly loathed—all without spoiling their good humor or unity of purpose. And political positions that were taken in the evening were forgotten by the following morning.

Five

But someone did remember, and that memory persisted through a decade of days and nights, and it lurked in puddles and the glint off farm machinery, hissed in blizzards and flushed summer sunsets that took up half the sky, until it surfaced again on a gray metal desk in a dim, panelled office in the city of Khabarovsk.

It was not as if a mere ten years had passed; the fire

with which Stalin cleansed our country consumed entire lifetimes. It had left one of the men in the office with but two teeth in his head and no hair upon it. A gray, weedy beard hugged the hollows of his cheeks. His left eye was closed from a beating and would never admit light again.

He summoned nearly all his physical strength to remain upright on the wooden chair in which he had been placed. The odor of his soiled clothes revolted him. So did the cologne off the man across the desk, a tall, thin, dark man in a tailored, blue double-breasted suit. He had expected to recognize this man, but didn't. The official had only briefly looked up when he was brought in and had then occupied the next quarter of an hour studying papers in a file on the desk.

And then the official, glaring, said, "Shtern."

The prisoner made no acknowledgment.

"The Lenin Toilets," the official declared. "The Stalin Clap Ward."

Even in his condition, Israel could not feign forgetfulness. His voice hardly more than a whisper, he replied, "It loses something in the translation."

The man then read the remark flawlessly in the original language.

Israel tried to smile but something seemed to be broken in his face. *"Ir ret Yiddish?"*

"I was born in Kherson and attended *cheder* there until I was fifteen years old."

"My mother was from Kherson."

"Grinspan. Elena Samvilovna. Her family operated a laundry that employed six workers. Now, can you explain this remark?"

"You have to place it in context."

"All right," the man said, and read the following:

D. B. LIPSHIN: Spinoza? Why Spinoza?

M. I. KUGEL: He was only one of the world's greatest philosophers.

LIPSHIN: Yes, and a Jewish philosopher.

KUGEL: What's wrong with that? So was Marx.

S. V. BESSERMAN: Marx was a historian.

KUGEL: If you're going to build a great university in a Jewish republic, you should name it after a Jew.

LIPSHIN: That's chauvinistic! Shall we name the concert hall after Mendelssohn?

M. B. VEYNSTOK: We could!

LIPSHIN: And the sports stadium after some great Jewish athlete? And must the Chuvash university be named after some great Chuvash philosopher? Good luck. The revolution was founded on internationalism, and if we're going to succeed in Birobidzhan, we'll have to overcome these petty national chauvinisms.

KUGEL: But what's the point of Birobidzhan, if not to secure our national identity?

LIPSHIN: In an internationalist context! Our first allegiance is to the world proletariat. Before we start naming our heroes, let's examine their class credentials.

I. D. SHTERN: All right, I go along with Lipshin. I say we name everything after Lenin and Stalin and get it over with. Lenin University. Stalin Stadium. The Lenin Concert Hall. The Stalin Library. The Lenin Toilets. The Stalin Clap Ward.

The official returned to the papers in his file folder. His brow creased, he riffled through the papers until he found the sheet he wanted, and then began to write. He suddenly stopped, put the tip of the pencil in his mouth, thought for a moment and then resumed writing. The office had several windows, but they had all been white-washed and admitted only a wan light. Israel guessed it was daytime, but even though no more than two weeks had passed since his arrest, he couldn't recall the season.

He said:

"I was being ironic."

The man finished his composition before he looked up.

"Ironic? You were being ironic about the two leaders of the world revolution? The two greatest minds Europe has ever produced? Did it ever occur to you, Shtern, that there are some subjects, some ideals, too important to be mutilated by satire and ridicule? Or that this characteristic rhetorical effect, this racial stance, could be a curse upon the Jewish people? That it is their inbred sense of irony that prevents their social progress and threatens their physical survival?"

"Well, that's irony for you."

"Are you being ironic now?"

Israel's open eye was glassy and unfocused, his expression vacant.

"No," he said.

This is an invention. Somewhere in Moscow there is located the true record of Israel's interrogation, shut in a file in an overstuffed drawer in a locked, unattended room, a probable fire hazard. The file can be presumed to contain trivial data about Israel's origins, secondary school education and work history, the name of his accuser, the pretext for his arrest, the charges against him, the date of his conviction, his sentence, and his fate, the story of his life that Larissa never knew. But it's not really information; just markings on sheets of paper, unexposed to human sight for six decades. I suppose I could travel to Moscow (no, I couldn't, I'd prefer to go to the Congo) and apply (to whom?) to see the file. But invention is easier. And there are still a few facts loose upon the earth.

One afternoon in the early 1960s, Larissa boarded a train in Khabarovsk, by then no more than a five-hour journey from home. Her purchases (a washboard, a *kolbasa,* a dress, etc.) were tied in squirming, odd-sized bundles. With her single free finger, she pried apart the lips of the door to a second-class compartment and slid it open. She carefully lifted her packages onto the overhead rack and took a place on the upholstered bench facing the direction of travel. Only then did she glance at the man who would be her traveling companion. Again their eyes locked.

"I never forget a face," he said. "That's my sorrow."

Her gut turned to ice. She considered whether she should leave the compartment. But that would prove she was guilty. Of what? She didn't know, but she was sure that she *was* guilty. She pursed her lips and stared through the window at a long grassy field browning in the late summer heat.

"You have a daughter, Rachel Israelevna."

He said it gently, a slight interrogative perched at the end of the sentence. But to Larissa's ears, the pronouncement was as sinister as a malediction. She made no sign as she reviewed her choices: flight, denial, confession, supplication.

"She should be in her thirties now. Is she married?"

The motion she made in the affirmative was barely detectable.

"Any children?"

The twitch of a flea: no.

"She lives in Birobidzhan?"

It was a while, measured in kilometers, before she spoke. Larissa was aware that the man was studying her face the whole time, peeling back the wrinkles, creases, and folds, interrogating her skin for its secrets. Her first thought was to ignore the question, play dumb. She studied the passing fields and stands of trees as if it were the newfound land. Yet her companion's patient gaze kept the question alive, like a rat scuttling under the seats. It was a trick you learned at the Lubyanka.

Phlegm in her throat, she flailed at the question with a muttered reply: "She's a schoolteacher."

The train slowed and then lurched to a halt. The couplings between the cars relaxed, something electrical ceased to hum. The train was between stations, on another area of flat grassland, hay brushing against the window. This was a typical pastoral, a vista suitable for lowing cattle—but on the other side of the glass, the midges were murder. There were no cattle. Bitterness spasmed along her nerves. Why did the train stop? How many hours of her life had been lost on stopped trains? She turned toward the other passenger, venom pooling in her eyes. In the time it had taken for this breakdown, he had become an old man. Age had carved tracks in his face and burned his skin. His jaw quivered.

Terrified of her own anger, she blurted, "Why was my husband arrested?"

His laugh was abrupt and mirthless and seemed to cost him something. When his mouth opened, it revealed gray stumps of teeth.

"Sections eight and eleven. Terrorism. Same as me." He paused to see what effect this admission had on her. None was visible. He went on: "I went in three months before he did. We met in Magadan, winter of '39. He was very ill. Consumption, I believe, though he said, no, no, don't worry, it's only a touch of pneumonia."

"Did he die there? I was never notified."

The former policeman shrugged. "I suppose so. People were dying less ill than he was. I passed this way last week. They're doing track work. A Chinaman and a shovel."

We were never notified about anything, neither about his trial nor his conviction. During the winter and spring of 1939, the two of us—I was eight years old—traveled to Khabarovsk nearly every Sunday morning and hugged ourselves in the frigid shadows of the prison, hoping that Israel would see us from his cell. By then not even the most assiduous appraiser of women would have discovered feminine beauty in Larissa's hard, rilled face, but she tried to flirt with the guards and policemen anyway. She gave them gifts and feebly winked. Now she knew that he hadn't even been there.

"He tried to get word to you, but he had nothing with which to bribe anyone. Pathetic, the ruses he tried . . . I didn't know him very well, we were in different work brigades. But we talked in the barracks. He thanked me for my intervention in Kisly Klyuch. He told me about you and your daughter, and about the colonization—in the most optimistic language. I didn't correct him. Also, he talked about his arrest. The politicals always talked about their arrests, it was our favorite subject. We always compared who was sent for, who was invited to come in on their own, who was beaten, what kind of a trial we got, that sort of thing. We were looking for some kind of pattern, a moral order that would give our punishment meaning. You'd think the state security men would have had the answers, but we didn't; all we knew was that *our* arrests had been a mistake. The pattern was never quite established, at least not in Magadan. Perhaps other camps succeeded where we failed. I understand that at Okhotsk, where they had some first-rate German intellectuals, they developed some very provocative theories."

"What did Israel say about his arrest?"

"The usual. He protested his innocence. He said he had made a remark that was taken out of context. We laughed at him. They all said that. We told him that it was his duty as a citizen of the Union of the Soviet Socialist

Republics not to make a remark that could be taken out of context by the enemies of the workers' revolution."

"It had nothing to do with any remark. They arrested everybody. Nearly the whole Komzet presidium."

"Yeah, a bunch of bourgeois nationalists. Really, no better than Zionists."

"On the contrary," Larissa said evenly. "They were all ideologically sound."

The man was not accustomed to being contradicted, not even now. His eyes turned cold and as hard as two marbles. He spoke now deliberately, his voice resonant with indignation:

"And they were saboteurs. Wreckers. There was no doubt about it."

"Was sabotage one of the charges against Israel?"

He waved his hand dismissively at the middle-aged woman. "They couldn't have messed up as badly as they did without intent. The first year, they did virtually no planting and no building and lost nearly their entire herd of cattle. They misused and broke equipment. They ruined horses. None of those Yids could plow a god-damned straight line. Two thirds of them took one look at real work and got back on the train."

"We had floods," she protested. "It was the rainiest summer of the century, roads and bridges were washed away. We had a plague of Siberian tick."

"Excuses. History accepts no excuses."

Larissa turned away. She again recalled those lost Sundays, how we returned in the evenings along these same tracks, unable to speak.

"I always assumed you had something to do with Israel's arrest."

"No, at the time of his arrest I was felling timber in Kolyma."

"But before that you were state security," Larissa insisted. "They were watching us all along. You must have prepared a report on the incident in Kisly Klyuch."

He smiled as if he had been congratulated. Now his mirth was genuine.

"I noted that he was a troublemaker," he said cheerfully.

The train bolted forward. One of the packages on the overhead rack teetered, but remained in place. As if the train had been momentarily halted in a foreign country, its motion now carried Larissa to a place of familiar fear. She peered along the line, studying the buckle and weave of the rails for signs of an approaching station.

The former policeman didn't speak for another hour. Then he said, "One more thing. In the hospital, Shtern showed me a card trick. He was very odd about it. First he performed the trick, and then he showed me how he had done it. I was grateful afterwards: it's passed time over the years."

In a monotone, Larissa asked, "Do you have a pack of cards?"

He nodded and removed them from inside his coat. He handed the pack to Larissa. She shuffled and returned the cards. He said, "This is called the Paterson Hop, I don't know why. Please, take a card, any card. Now hold it for a moment while I place the king of hearts and the queen of hearts at the top and bottom of the pack, like so. You've seen this trick before?"

"Yes. Go on, please."

He performed the trick, perhaps not as smoothly as Israel would have, but every time after great complication and travail the king and queen were reunited in the middle of the deck. Larissa asked him to repeat the trick several times, but didn't once yield a smile.

That evening I met my mother at the train station beneath the great tin letters fixed on rails running above the station house's roof. They proclaimed the name of our city in Russian and Yiddish and still do to this day. When a Russian word, running from left to right, meets a Yiddish one, running from right to left, they always draw the eye to the space between them. Now Larissa looked away and searched me out among the figures standing on the platform. She stepped unsteadily across the tracks, her hair escaping from her beret and spilling a gray halo around her. One of the bags slipped from her arms. She stopped, but left it there. Unaccustomed to her desperate expression, I hesitated to help. She didn't tell me about her encounter on the train until years later.

Six

As waving and shouting Jews dangled from the train's windows, Settlement No. 1 ground to a stop on a cold, crystalline afternoon in September 1928. The station was no more than a weather-stained cottage surrounded by a scatter of small wooden buildings and some ambiguously agricultural equipment. Neither the buildings nor the equipment looked new. A wide dirt road trailed past some scrubby, mostly leafless trees and then into a meadow. The view beyond the meadow stretched for tens of kilometers to a low range of pale, gray mountains. The settlers fell silent. Larissa wondered if they were overwhelmed by the fact of their arrival or disappointed by the emptiness of the place. She herself had expected to be disappointed; she was now surprised by the bubble of excitement that rose through her body, squeezed her breasts, rushed blood to her cheeks and ears, and pulsed in her head. She glanced over at Israel. His eyes were as soft as a newborn kitten's.

"It's beautiful," he whispered. "More beautiful than they ever told us it would be."

By the time the first travelers had descended from the train, men and women from the fields and from inside the houses had begun hurrying to the station. A young blond man on a cart, waving a slice of birch—Iosif Reznick, Israel knew him well!—urged his white horse into the deepening pool of arriving settlers. From one of the longer buildings emerged a half dozen uniformed, red-scarfed children. They carried banners. Cries and shouts faintly penetrated the train car's windows.

The adults carried banners as well: "Welcome, Jewish Workers!" "Tsu a Yiddish Land!" and others that Larissa didn't have time to read in the rush to disembark. The passengers lined up to pass the bags from the car and onto the ground next to the tracks. After a month's companionship, Larissa subdued the urge to say farewell to her fellow travelers. She'd be spending the rest of her life with them. Descending onto the earth, her feet tingled, surprised at its solidity.

It was as if the new arrivals had never breathed air before. They stood alongside the train gluttonously filling and emptying their lungs. The tenous, midday sky was enormous and a purplish blue the dark of twilight. Despite the near-freezing temperature, the travelers weren't cold: this electric sensation on their arms and chest and inside their lungs was something better and more life-giving than cold. As the train, with a (congratulatory? derisive?) burst of steam, abandoned them, Larissa sensed that she had been hurtled into deep space.

A dark-haired, grinning-almost-to-tears schoolgirl handed her a bouquet of wild flowers, purple, blue, and orange. The flowers' perfume was of some sweet alien spice. Larissa tried to clear her throat, to offer thanks, but already the girl was presenting a bouquet to another arrival. Around Larissa, freely crying men and women fiercely grappled with each other, tattooing their faces with wet kisses. Something she couldn't see bit her.

Israel had already accepted his bouquet and placed it alongside his bags and was now ignoring the old friends calling his name and streaming past him. He was very still, taking everything in, the entire natural landscape, in the event, it seemed, that he would be forced to leave immediately and would need to recall it the rest of his life. The mountains, the fields, the sky. Did colors like this exist in Europe? Were there *any* colors in the grave-yards and cobbled streets of his ancestors?

Among the last to emerge from the shacks was Leo

Feirman, ambling among the settlers and new arrivals, an unlit cigar in his hand. Like many of the men, he wore a blue workshirt and an oilskin jacket. His face was tanned and he had lost some weight. He nodded hello to a few people and then gazed down at their luggage. He made his way to Israel indirectly, surveying the new settlers. His approach was casual, as if he had seen Israel just the other day.

"Is this everything?" he asked.

"Hello, Leo. Yes, it is. You look terrific."

The cigar twitched like something alive, but Leo smiled and gave one of Israel's bags a little nudge with his foot.

"All personal belongings. Am I right?"

"Mostly books, I suppose. What's the matter?"

Leo smiled in surprise at the question. "Nothing at all. No, it's all right. Have a nice trip?"

"To tell you the truth, Leo, I've already forgotten the trip. Listen, I have some letters from your sister and nephews."

"The only thing is, Israel," Leo drawled, his glance again caressing the travelers' luggage. "The only thing, Israel, is that I have a cable from the Commissariat for Land Issues. It was sent a month ago. According to the cable, you were bringing supplies. More equipment. Plow blades, shovels, seeders, wire. Hammers. Sickles. We need everything. We've already got enough nails for every man, woman, and child, but nothing to drive them in with, and nothing to drive them into. How do you like that? We've been getting cables all summer. The commissariat says there was a 600,000-ruble disbursement made on behalf of Komzet in July. Do you know anything about it?"

Israel shook his head absently, looking now at the structures in the foreground. "These houses. They're *old.*"

"We're renting from the Cossacks. Cash money."

Israel studied the landscape. He counted the buildings and looked toward the horizon for other signs of human settlement. The grounds were littered by a dozen or so gray canvas tents, latrines, and cooking equipment. Finally, he said, "There's no new construction."

"You stupid prick," Leo said gently, almost affectionately. "How can you build a house if you don't have a hammer? Do you know how cold it's going to get in a month?"

A young woman Larissa's age approached her, smiling broadly. She was round and fair-haired and her face was roiled by insect bites.

"You made it!"

Larissa studied the tracing of welts, as if it were a map waiting to reveal important secrets.

"Is everything all right? Larissa, the journey . . ."

"No, I'm fine. It's just a shock." She exhaled a frail chuckle, shaking her head. "You know, I'm sorry, I had forgotten you would be here. As if I were going someplace entirely different, or someplace that was nowhere at all."

"*Gitten yur!* Happy New Year!" When Larissa looked at her blankly, Rachel added, "What luck that you made it in time!"

Rachel handed her something. It was heavier than it looked and unpleasantly wet. Larissa hadn't celebrated the Jewish New Year since she was a small girl.

"It's soaked in honey," Rachel explained. "Cake. For a sweet year. That's the custom." She beamed in apology. "It's the best we can do. We're short on eggs."

The settlers had begun loading the luggage onto Iosif's cart, joking about the bags' weight. One of the suitcases burst open, revealing bourgeois dresses and lingerie and occasioning much laughter that lingered in the open spaces. The settlers straggled across the way. Larissa watched them but stayed where she was, tenaciously, as if she were afraid that the ground would slip away from her. Israel had bent and wrapped his hands around the grips of his suitcases, but now he let go and straightened his back. He smiled. Rachel waited. Larissa was keenly conscious of their presence, and also of love washing over her like a warm bath. She could close her eyes and immerse her face in it. She knew also that the moment she moved, perhaps thirty seconds from now, history would begin moving again too. Her gaze led her beyond Israel, past the settlement, a small pond, a stand of bare trees, a sliver of river, sere meadows, and then all the way to the shadowy borderlands rimmed by mountains.

Orbit

Орбита

To the daring intellect of Soviet man
That first penetrated space.

—Monument dedication, Central Army Park, Moscow

First, they sat for a minute. That was one of our customs of departure. They each took a seat: Yuri, Ivanovsky, Karpov, Kamanin, and the Chief Designer. There wasn't a seat for Titov, who hunkered alongside Kamanin and stared into the floorboards. Not a word was spoken. Outside the cottage a bus raced its engine. His helmet on his lap, Yuri grinned at the Chief Designer.

The Chief Designer strained to return the smile. He dropped his gaze to the clipboard and studied his checklist and the timeline, trying to recall if there was anything they had forgotten. It was bad to return for something after you had left; if you did return, you'd have to look in a mirror and stick out your tongue. Yuri's ventilator hummed.

"All right," the Chief Designer said. His sigh verged on a groan. He slapped and rubbed his thighs and rose heavily to his feet. The men followed him out.

Cheers and rhythmic clapping: Yuri hadn't expected this pool of strangers at the bottom of the steps. A pretty schoolgirl in bows and a taffeta frock rushed up, curtsied, handed him a bouquet of pink lilies, and then rushed back to hide behind her mother's skirt. Yuri's toothy smile warmed the mother's wan, moonlike face. The mother smiled shyly, casting her eyes at her feet. There were perhaps no more than thirty onlookers—approved military personnel and their families—but it seemed like half the world. Later we would throng Red Square. Yuri strode to the bus. The Chief Designer mounted the steps ahead of him and took the ventilator, which was the size and weight of a small suitcase, as Yuri climbed aboard. The crowd cheered again and he gave the thumbs-up sign.

The bus took off and passed the infirmary, across the way from the cottage. Its curtains were parted, but he couldn't see through the morning glare upon the windows. No matter. He didn't wonder when or if he would see the infirmary again.

Nearly everyone at the base knew of the launch. Scores of us lined the road, waving flags and hoisting banners that, because of military regulations, were circumspect in their exhortations: "Manufacturing Unit Wishes You the Best!" "Good Luck on Your Journey, Comrade!" and, simply, "Go!" A detachment of red-scarved Pioneer-scouts waited by the gate to the launch compound, some so stricken by his approach they could do nothing but stare. At the window in the passing bus, Yuri jerked a thumb and offered a smile whose recollection would illuminate the darkest nights of their lives. He blew kisses to the girls.

Wreathed in venting gases, the R-7 rocket and its support assembly were the only objects on the horizon. As the bus drew near, Klaxons sounded.

The bus stopped a few dozen meters from the elevator
that would carry him to the Vostok capsule cabin. At the
elevator waited Leonov and Popovich, as well as more
than a dozen technicians and workers, most of whom he
recognized. Some carried flowers and flags, others clip-
boards and hand tools. Yuri descended from the bus,
holding his helmet in one hand and the ventilator in the
other. The air smelled of kerosene.

"Wait a minute," he said to the Chief Designer.

Yuri walked along the side of the bus to the back
wheels, noting the gentle contours of the tarmac. He
carefully placed the ventilator and his helmet on a nearly
microscopic rise. Turning to the side of the bus, Yuri un-
zipped his flight suit. The Chief Designer, Ivanovsky, and
Karpov, and behind them the technicians, watched attentively as he unfolded his prick from the suit. This
wasn't on the timeline. Yuri placed his hands on his hips.
The stream's arc intersected with one of the bus's tires,
blackening a wedge of it. The urine burned. He gave his
prick a last squeeze and a shake, and the burning sensation returned and intensified. As steam rose off the tire's
mud-caked treads, Yuri wondered whether he was taking
into space a dose of the clap.

It was not anxiety that had kept him awake the night before, nor on any other night. The medics had taped the
sensors to his body and then there had been a dinner in
the cottage, with a big meat *pirog,* followed by a last
round of toasts. The Chief Designer tried to speak a few
words but was overcome by emotion and in the end simply embraced him. Afterwards, Yuri lay in his cot, unable

to sleep, confidence surging through him, something in his blood.

Yuri's confidence existed as a discrete phenomenon, virtually capable of being sized and weighed. His superb physical condition and quick wits had been proven by the most rigorous battery of tests ever undergone by free men. He had been whirled, dropped, scorched, frozen, blasted by sound, left on his own in the dark and the quiet, examined by psychiatrists, and interrogated by commissars. Blind and deaf in the sensory deprivation tank—which in fact had been rife with sour organic odors—Yuri had drifted weightless in a realm of thought. It was then that he had first articulated to himself his awareness of his strength, his imperturbability and his dominating desire to be first.

The Chief Designer hadn't known what he was looking for in the candidate-cosmonauts, his *sokoliki,* his little falcons. The rigors of space flight were mostly hypothetical, yet as the selection process continued and new tests were formulated and new considerations taken into account, the Chief Designer became convinced that he was approaching the definition of the space traveler's essential nature: physically fit, yes; cool-headed, of course; superior lung capacity, yes; height, no more than 167 centimeters, given the dimensions of the capsule; claustrophobic, no—paradoxically in the void of space claustrophobia would be fatal; agile, yes; and confident, yes, absolutely, and it was not only the presence of this confidence that was vital, but its source. It could not derive from loving parents, kind teachers, or achievements on the fields of sport or battle; it had to be something integral to the man, fused with his being.

For months the Chief Designer had postponed his decision. Each candidate was further probed, physically shaken and emotionally manipulated, so that the extraneous bits of his character were flaked off, leaving his naked self. He ran through fields of snow. He jumped from planes. He confessed his secrets. Yuri, Titov, Leonov, Popovich, and Grigoriev felt themselves being remade. They sensed, long before their actual selection, their own elevation as men of the future, spacemen.

The entire enterprise had been nearly destroyed by failure and tragedy. An R-16 ICBM had blown up on its launch pad the previous October, killing Marshal Nedelin, the head of the strategic rocket forces, and 164 other officers, scientists, and technicians. The launch pad had been wrecked. Khrushchev had been furious.

The space program had survived only through the heroism of the Chief Designer, and behind him a corps of workers and technicians, and behind them the entire workers' state, all of us. Look at what we were about to accomplish: sixteen years after the end of a cataclysmic war, forty-four years after deposing a regime steeped in reaction and ignorance, our nation was about to send a man into space. This was not because we were smarter than anyone else; rather, we had organized ourselves to draw the best from each other, from each according to his ability. Yuri's flight would make the definitive argument for socialism. By breaking the chains of gravity, man was about to embark on a new stage of his evolution, a step made possible only by the transformation of society. Within a day, the whole world would know it.

Yuri could not bear to lie in bed awake, not that night.

He pulled on his trousers, shirt, boots, and flight jacket and then stepped from his room, past Titov's, and out onto the porch, gently shutting the door behind him. At the railing he peered into the oceanic dark. The only sounds belonged to the Kazakh wind. A scatter of stars effervesced behind a haze—high-altitude clouds, nothing serious. At ground level, electric lights burned at the edges and corners of a few nearby structures, almost all of them constructed in the past two years.

The air was cold, and he zipped his jacket. Absentmindedly—and this was perhaps his only absent-minded habit—he searched his jacket pockets before recalling that he had finished his cigarettes while Dr. Marshak was writing her final medical report. His hands lightly grasped the railing. The launch pad was in Sector K, too distant to be seen, but the lights around it shimmered on the eastern horizon like the aurora borealis or the first drops of milk in a cup of coffee.

The thought of his last cigarette redirected his attention toward the infirmary, about 200 meters across the scrub. Its white clapboard showed gray and ghostly in the dark. At one of its corners a red light winked. He gazed at the electric bulb and his sense of anticipation became tumescent. Tomorrow: space. Across the darkened American sky, he'd be a light himself. He had always known he would be the first, it was a matter of wanting it badly enough. Already he felt consumed by expectation, pride and, and . . .

A smile crossed his face. Desire. He winked back at the electric bulb.

Descending from the porch, he found the ground hardened from the cold. A few frozen twigs snapped, but otherwise his passage across the empty field was without weight or sound. He was not afraid, he never was.

Deliberately overshooting the infirmary's entrance, he set an elliptical trajectory around the building, past the surgery. Most of the windows were draped or shuttered, but through them drifted soft romantic music from a radio or a phonograph. A radio, he decided, detecting the echoing signature of skip-distance reception.

Beneath his returning arc, behind one of these windows, lay the infirmary's single resident patient, Grigoriev. A victim of the R-16 blast, with burns over 90 percent of his body, he was too ill to move and too ill to recover. Grigoriev had been a candidate-cosmonaut, among the most promising in the nimbus of candidates below Yuri. Yuri respectfully tipped his head as he passed the window of what he believed to be the patient's room.

He came to a large undraped window at the end of a hallway. Its polished wood floor reflected a yellow streak of light. He paused there a moment before moving on to the next window. Its blinds didn't reach all the way to the bottom of the frame. The room was unlit save for the indirect glow reflected from the hallway, like earthshine softening the lunar night. Something stirred in the room and left it. He glimpsed a nurse's white uniform, but couldn't determine to which nurse it belonged. Several were on duty at any given time. He had seen only the girl's back.

Gradually he apprehended a storeroom: cardboard boxes, a shelf of beakers and tubing, and a wall lined by folded linen. With eyes that a famous song would some-day say were as keen as a hunting dog's, he noticed that the side of the window sat unevenly against the frame, not fully in its embrace.

Grinning, he pushed against it and swung the win-dow open on its hinges. He heard footsteps and pulled away. Someone came into the storeroom. Standing among the sparse weeds outside the infirmary, his back to the clapboard, Yuri couldn't guess what she was doing, only that her hands were too full to turn on the light. He gazed across an unplowed field and felt a rising, accelerating excitement. He heard the nurse step away again, humming along to the radio music: "What Moves My Heart So." He turned just as her ankle disappeared around the door. By its slender, sinewy musculature, the ankle declared itself to be Tania's. In a single, effortless motion, as if he were already weightless, Yuri lifted him-self up and through the window.

Tania returned a minute later, contemplation sharp-ening the features of her petite, triangular face. From deep within the storeroom's shadows, where Yuri lurked like an undersea creature, her olive complexion seemed even more oriental, her eyelids even flatter. And every-thing about her face was in perfect proportion, almost isoscelean. Yuri never failed to be astounded by the to-tally anonymous beauties harbored in these remote Soviet provinces.

With a languor redolent of the Tatar centuries, she

placed some folded towels on a pile of linen and reached for something on a shelf above her head. For an extended moment the line of her body, from the balls of her feet through the flex of her ankles and the sweep of her legs, buttocks, and back, was a perfect curve, a single quadratic running through the dark. Yuri waited until she returned to earth before he stepped from the shadows.

The nurse gasped and clutched a spool of bandages to her chest. Another spool dropped soundlessly to the floor. The discomposure of her expression was like the shattering of crystal, which in the spectacle of its disintegration revealed new aspects of its intrinsic beauty.

"Lieutenant!"

He raised a finger to his lips, approached, and then laid the finger against hers.

She recoiled as if struck.

"We must be quiet," he whispered.

"What are you doing here?" she demanded. Her almond-shaped eyes were as dark as the sun was bright. "What do you want?"

"Tania, Taniatchka, relax. I've just come for a little visit. Shhhh."

"How did you get in here?"

"Shhhh," he said, placing his finger again on his lips and then, very gently, on hers. This time she didn't pull away. Heat radiated from the translucent labial flesh. He hadn't been wrong: her single, shyly appraising glance the other day and a slightly lingering touch this evening when she applied the telemetry strip had told him all that he had needed to know.

"Listen, I'm leaving Baikonur tomorrow. In the most extraordinary way. Shhh. Don't speak, Tania. Let's not speak at all."

He removed his finger from her lips and then returned it, pressing more firmly. She kissed it, almost reflexively, but not quite reflexively.

"But what are you doing here?"

He put his arms around her small body, slightly lifting her. The embrace was gentle, the power of his arms merely implied.

"I've come to say good-bye."

A giggle escaped. "Here?"

He ran his hands up her sides. Her body shivered beneath them. It was just a meter or so to the soft wall of linen. With sure, insistent pressure, he danced her back. Her eyes misted and her resistance slowly deliquesced, until the moment her bare calves scraped against the towels. Then she froze and slid from his grasp.

She whispered, "Are you crazy?"

"The doctors say no. I've been tested."

"We can't do this."

"Why not?"

"In the storeroom? Yuri, I can't. For God's sake, you can't!"

"I can."

"Marshak's here!" she hissed.

Yuri was taken aback, at least momentarily.

"This late?"

"All night. It's because of the launch. She's in her office."

Tania moved away, but his hands reached out and touched her wrist. His hands didn't close, it wasn't a grab, but she couldn't bear to move away. And, besides, his foot was against the door.

"Well," Yuri said. "Then you surely can't go. Look what I've risked coming here."

In the stiffening of her facial expression and the clearing of her eyes, he witnessed the physiological consequences of her blood running cold. Yuri himself was not unnerved by the contemplation of the risk, even though it was a little like talking about a plane crash before a flight. For the hundredth time he recalled the moment a few hours earlier when, hunched over the electrical leads, Tania had worked on his chest and the top of her uniform had opened and fallen away, an act of delicious sabotage. Her brassiere had been loose and ill fitting, nearly spilling her breasts, each as round as a planet.

His arms now encircled her again. He pressed his body hard against hers and felt her yield.

A buzzer went off. Although submerged in their kiss, Yuri recognized the low, rasping moan at once: the booster rocket's first stage release indicator. He picked his head up and again heard the signal, down the hall. This buzzer and the one for his rocket had clearly been supplied by the same military contractor in Chelyabinsk.

"I have to go," Tania said breathlessly.

"Where?"

"That's Grigoriev, he wants something. I'm on duty."

"Come back, I'll wait."

"Yuri. I can't."

"You can," he said calmly. "I'll be here."

She made a hopeless little grimace and fled out the door.

A shimmer of domestic perfume remained. He assumed the perfume was domestic—where would she get foreign perfume?—and resolved to send her a bottle of French perfume from Moscow, after his flight, if he remembered.

He rested against the towels and revisited the feeling of her body in his arms and the taste of her lips and tongue. Then he entertained the conceit that the storeroom was the Vostok capsule itself, poised to plunge into the tender blue of the sky. He paced the room, which was illuminated only by the stray outside light, and imagined himself floating weightless to the ceiling, imagined himself pressed against the linen as he accelerated away from the earth, and finally, again, imagined himself pressed against Tania.

Marshak was still in the infirmary. Yuri knew that he should return to the cottage before his absence there or his presence here was discovered, but it didn't seem right, not after getting this far. It would have done violence to his nature.

Sergei Pavlovich Korolev had been arrested early in the morning of June 27, 1938. Precisely one month later, fulfilling a prosecutorial norm, he confessed to "subversion in a new field of technology" and was sentenced to ten years of hard labor. In the unbroken sub-zero temperatures of a Kolyma gold mine, he worked without adequate clothing, food, or shelter. Most of his teeth fell out and a

fractured jaw, incurred during his interrogation, failed
to mend properly.

Five months after his arrival in Kolyma, he was summoned back to Moscow for a rehearing of his case, but
no transportation was provided. A truck driver took him
the 150 kilometers to Magadan, demanding his sweater
as fare. In Magadan, Korolev learned that the port was already frozen and that he had missed the last boat of the
season. Living in rough, makeshift shelters, he worked as
a laborer and shoe repairer to keep himself alive through
the remainder of the winter. He finally managed to sail
to Vladivostok, terminus of the Trans-Siberian Railroad,
but on the journey from there back to Moscow he became disoriented and was no longer able to stem the
blood flowing from his mouth. He had scurvy. With deep
bruises pooling beneath the soft surfaces of his swollen
body, like the lava seas that had once congealed beneath
the skin of the moon, he was taken off the train at
Khabarovsk.

Outside the station he lay for hours on a cold stone
bench, spitting teeth and blood. At some point in the
early morning, two militiamen checked his documenta-
tion, assuring themselves that he had a travel warrant into
the netherworld, and they left him alone. Korolev closed
his eyes but didn't sleep. And then after a long while he
became aware that his carrion body was being sniffed. It
was not an entirely unpleasant sensation: there was a kind
of warmth attached to the scrutiny. Through his muddle-
ment he discerned that these were not staccato canine
inspirations, as he might have expected, derelict in this
remote province, but something much more considered.

When Korolev opened his eyes, the deeply creviced face of an old man in a ratty fur cap occupied his field of view. The man's Asiatic features were surmounted by a large, bulbous Russian nose, from which grew many thick, dirty hairs. But the whites of his eyes were absolutely clear, like two mechanical instruments that Korolev might have worked on in another life. For a long time the old man gazed into his face, in judgment, thought Korolev, who had been denied a trial in Moscow. And then the old man roughly lifted him by the arms and pulled him from the bench to a thin, leafless tree rising off a berm alongside the train station.

The old man deposited him there, his back against the birch, his face opposite the sun that had just crested over the morning haze into an empty sky.

Korolev did not know for how long he was abandoned, but it was long enough for him to become intensely aware of the heat of the sun that fell upon his closed eyelids and face and dried the blood that had soaked into his beard. The sun was a star, less than two hundred million kilometers away, almost close enough to touch. The solar radiation suffused through his tissue. After a winter in which he had witnessed a human death nearly every day, in which his own death had seemed to hover before him just beyond the fog of his breath, the solar heat was a promise redeemed. And it was now, with his eyes still shut, that an idea began to incubate. The idea was nothing grand, nothing ostensibly scientific. It had something to do with an awareness of his determination that was encased within his soft, battered self like a shard of granite.

When he opened his eyes again, a butterfly was dancing in front of them, orange and violet, in a spastic, unballistic flight. It was a gash of color against the anticolor landscape: the black-spotted scraps of melting snow, the concrete buildings weeping dull brown rust at their joints, stones and pieces of rotten timber strewn among prehistoric construction debris, a freight car whose sides had been eaten away by decades of neglect, a smashed toy balsa airplane abandoned in the mud, the mud bubbling gray and oily, the weeds poking out of the mud in rashes, the trash littered around a bin at the edge of a wall. But the butterfly flew above it all, improbably alive. Korolev stared until it dwindled out of sight. He was, in the end, a romantic fellow; we are a romantic people.

And then for the first time in days he truly slept, the kind of sleep we pursue and capture in our dry, straw-mattressed beds, amid the babylike gurgles of steam heat. No dreams visited him as he reclined with his back to the tree.

He awoke with a start hours later, the sun still hard in his face, but now there was a man's finger in his ruined mouth. It was a thick finger, strong and coarse. The old man was stooping before him, a brown earthen pot clutched to his ragged coat. He removed his finger, dipped it in the pot and pushed it back into Korolev's mouth.

As he ran his finger along Korolev's gums, Korolev realized that he no longer possessed teeth. But the firm press against his bleeding, open gums didn't hurt.

"This is *kolba*," the man said, with a high, almost girlish voice. "You will live."

Korolev submitted to the old man's ministrations,

too weak to repel them. The taste of the ointment was similar to garlic's, which was not unwelcome after a week in which he had tasted nothing but blood. Korolev closed his eyes again to shade them from the glare of the sun. A warm washcloth gently massaged his face and beard. He kept his eyes shut a moment longer. When he opened them, the man was gone.

The bleeding had stopped and Korolev now felt well enough to stand. He staggered off and later that day found a doss in a small barrackslike dormitory at the edge of the city. He stayed there for a week, near the stove, resting and making notes on scraps of paper. In that single week, he recalled and improved six designs that he had worked on before his arrest. While other souls in transit bustled around him, Korolev considered the technical problems inherent in flight above the earth's atmosphere, particularly involving the ascent trajectory and in-flight guidance. He became convinced that human flight beyond the exosphere was possible, even inevitable, even obligatory. He jotted notes on the lift requirements for an expedition to the surface of the moon. Alongside a rough diagram of the launch vehicle, he wrote the word *go!*

Then he realized that these sketches were either currently state secrets or would be in the future. If they were found on his person, he would be further incriminated. He burned them in the stove when no one was looking; then he dreaded that someone had been looking, or would somehow recover the embers. He spit over his shoulder, the first time he had done so since childhood. There was surprising, unshameful comfort to be found in this act, at least momentarily. The evil that worked on our lives, producing the world's actual, quotidian brutality, was something magical; to spit or to cross oneself was to pretend to a magic of one's own.

Korolev resumed his journey across the continent. When he finally reached Moscow, his case was reopened and his sentence was reduced, to eight years. Just as he was about to be returned to the Far East, the engineer Andrei Tupolev intervened and had him transferred to the *sharashka* on Ulitsa Radio, the prison-laboratory in which Tupolev and other aviation engineers were incarcerated on political charges no less vague than his.

He spent the war in the Tupolev *sharashka,* the Special Design Bureau of the 4th Special Department of the NKVD, which was eventually moved to Omsk and the Caucasus as the Nazis advanced across Soviet territory. First assigned to the wing design of the Tu-2 light bomber, Korolev then worked on the liquid-fueled rocket boosters for the Petlyakov-2 dive bomber, the auxiliary rocket engines for the Lavochkin-5 fighter plane, the D-1 short-range ballistic rocket, and the D-2 winged guided missile. His mouth was fitted for dentures, but his heart remained weak, his complexion pallid. After the war, although not yet officially rehabilitated, he was allowed to establish a plant in the small town of Podlipki outside Moscow. It was there that, identified in the Soviet press only as the Chief Designer, Korolev developed the R-7. It was the world's first intercontinental ballistic missile.

Yuri had been tested for patience; there had been a battery of clever, sneaky, potentially humiliating tests that he had passed easily and for which he had dissembled his contempt. But he had also been tested for his alacrity and decisiveness. He decided now that Tania had been gone long enough, he would fetch her back.

Opening the door, he peered through the sliver of light and oriented himself within the infirmary. A long well-scrubbed hall stretched before him, its lights dimly, greenishly fluorescent. The shorter hall was to his right. He recalled his passage around the outside of the building. Marshak's office would be on the other side of the infirmary, virtually diagonal to the storeroom. If so, then Grigoriev's room was on this side, down the long hall.

Yuri followed his deduction, padding lightly. The first room was dark, uninhabited, as was the second. A cold radiance emanated from the next-to-last room. He furtively glanced in.

Tania wasn't there. Grigoriev lay in the hospital bed as he had for the past six months, nearly his entire body and head bandaged. The switch to the buzzer was gripped by his right hand, which was unbandaged and immaculate. It was a muscular hand with neatly trimmed nails. It existed in disjointed, mocking opposition to the body. Yuri wondered if Grigoriev always held the switch. And then he frowned. Why hadn't Tania returned to the storeroom? Yuri stepped through the doorway.

First, he felt tremendous elation. Grigoriev was lying there, not him. It could have been him, but he had been in the air that day, training in a Mig-19. Second was the sweet, pungent odor of disinfectant. Never had Yuri perceived such a perfectly disinfecting scent. His body was cleansed just inhaling it. Although the odor was nothing

like Gzhatsk, it evoked his hometown and the quiet,
shrubbery-lined lane that passed behind the house and
meandered to school. He recalled the apple and cherry
trees and the bushes thick with gooseberries and cur-
rants. The odor of the disinfectant was the chemical dis-
tillation of Russia, lush and confident, marching ahead
to the future.

Yuri wondered whether Grigoriev was aware of his
presence and whether he should speak. The patient
gripped the buzzer switch with the vitality of someone
not only awake, but finely attuned to his surroundings.

"Hey," Yuri said. He paused. He felt moved to speak.
"It's me. Just thought I'd drop by."

There was no stirring in the bed, no acknowledgment.

"Yes, tomorrow's liftoff. Didn't they tell you? No?"
Yuri chuckled. "Perhaps you no longer have clearance."

He dropped onto a wooden chair by the bed and slid
it closer. He spoke in a low voice.

"I don't want you to think I'm anxious about the flight.
That's not why I'm not sleeping. The R-7's good, so is the
spaceship, they've been tested. I'm perfectly confident.
Honestly, I'm just wandering around tonight, looking
for a little action. You know Tania, the one who was just
here? Exquisite, really. It's too bad you can't see the
nurses. They've picked them well. I'm sorry for you, pal.
But what can I do? I've got to live my life, you've got to
live yours. Look, I'll give it to her good. Just like you
would have, if you had the chance. So figure I'm doing it
on your behalf. Really, I am." Yuri laughed. "I'm going to
make love to her for the whole cosmonaut corps, for all
mankind!"

Yuri stood, vaguely dissatisfied with his speech. To-morrow he would be obliged to make another one, to the launch crew assembled at the base of the rocket. He'd need to ask the Chief Designer to write it. He wandered over to the window and looked through the blinds. The sky had cleared and Virgo, the Virgin, was visible in the south.

The buzzer sounded, Yuri started. He turned and glowered at the patient, in dismay at Grigoriev's betrayal. They had been through much together: the tests, the training, a survival course in the Urals. Now Grigoriev had slightly raised the switch in his direction, as if he were firing at Yuri with it.

But the gun's retort was not a single, insistent razz. Grigoriev was squeezing the switch to produce a series of short and long pulses. Yuri recognized the letters of the telegraphic alphabet: *Go.* Grigoriev was telling him to leave? Because his visit was unwelcome? Or was the im-perative a warning?

Some kind of quick, surreptitious commotion made itself evident in the corridor, a womanish commotion. There were whispers. A door slammed, alarmingly. Yuri's expression didn't change. It wouldn't be held too much against him if he had left the pilots' cottage to say a few last words to Grigoriev—the visit might even be incorpo-rated in his legend—but he preferred not to get caught at all. And he still had to find Tania.

Grigoriev repeated the sequence. *Go!* Now Yuri took it as an encouragement.

"See you later," he said.

As he exited Grigoriev's hospital room, footsteps approached around the corner. They didn't belong to Tania. They were too heavy. The shoes' heels tapped hard against the wood, their dot-dot-dash spelling Marshak. Yuri scurried in the opposite direction, back down the corridor.

He reentered the storeroom, closed the door, and discerned at once that the blinds had been drawn, immersing the room in a dark more viscid than before. Alert as a wild animal, he paused and considered the significance of the closed blinds. Either Tania had closed them or someone else had. He kept his body very still, sniffing, listening hard, and waiting for his pupils to dilate.

Perfume. Not Tania's. He waited for his night vision to soak up the stray quanta still loose in the room and careening against the linen and the glassware. In the corner where he had hidden earlier, someone else now concealed himself, huddling against a pillar of towels. No, herself. Indeed, two or three women pressed against each other in the corner, given away by the whites of their eyes. Zinia? Maybe also the tall, long-haired nurse he liked. Was her name Ludmilla? The third shade he didn't recognize at all, except to exclude her from the possibility of being Tania.

He did not look directly at the nurses, pretending not to see them. He was unsure of the situation, but guessed that it required a display of limitation. Most of the psychological tests had been like that. Although it was easy to calculate the correct answers to the questions and perform the desired behavior, you had to show that the answers and behavior weren't calculated. The Chief Designer had been looking for a degree of openheartedness and sincerity that would indisputably distinguish the New Man. Yuri had reasoned that his own openheartedness and sincerity would be incriminated by a too-evident manifestation of self-knowledge.

"Tania?" he whispered.

A giggle was brutally repressed.

He whispered her name again. After a long pause one of the girls, Ludmilla, came near. She moved tentatively, reaching out to the room's fixtures for guidance. She couldn't see in the dark. He rotated his body in apposition to hers.

"Yes," she replied in a toneless whisper, pressing against him.

He whispered Tania's name again and kissed Ludmilla, who was nearly a head taller than Tania. Another titter rattled around the corner of the storeroom as Yuri prolonged the kiss, grinding against her. The charade wouldn't last much longer. His hands gently but swiftly probed as much as they could, acquiring a full tactile picture of her legs, breasts, and buttocks.

Ludmilla hadn't expected all this, it was a bit too much, and she was almost pulling away, but not quite. Her mouth tasted minty, as if it had just dissolved a sweet. She was a long and angular girl, not as soft a ride as the others perhaps, but very much all right.

Someone passed behind them, on the way to the light switch. Yuri's right hand squeezed hard between Ludmilla's legs and she gasped just as the room was flooded with light and hilarity. The two other nurses, chief nurse Zinia and the one whose name he didn't know, were laughing, laughing, laughing and trying to smother their laughter in piles of tears-and-mascara-stained linen.

"Shhh," Ludmilla said. She laughed too, a kind of dry, weighted heave that Yuri recognized as forced. Her face had gone blotchy. "Marshak will hear us."

Yuri smirked and feigned embarrassment. He had quickly disengaged himself from the nurse and acted as if he were still blinded by light and surprise. But he didn't want to amuse them so much that their laughter would escape the storeroom.

"The false bride," he conceded. This was one of our customs, to present the bridegroom with an obvious impostor before the ceremony. Yuri knew it well. Only four years earlier, on the day of his marriage to Valya, he had entered a room where her twelve-year-old sister had waited in a white veil, much to the witnesses' amusement. When he removed the veil, the poor girl had suddenly spouted tears. The pretense had been too exciting and had brushed too close to her secret: she loved him too.

Now he said, "What have you done with Tania?"

The nurses responded with every possible expression of stifled amusement. They snorted, snickered, covered their faces, held their sides, and fell against each other. Yuri studied their involuntary contortions; in the future he would become a connoisseur of such lovely, revealing disfigurement.

Only Ludmilla held herself back. She was a country girl perhaps no more than eighteen years of age, with a head of thick, copper red curls and a wide, round face that had still not lost its flush.

"What are you, a Hun?" Zinia said, faking contempt. "Are you going to carry away our most beautiful girl on horseback? Are we civilized people? Are we Russians? There are a few niceties and proprieties to observe."

"Zinia, please. I have to get back to the cottage."

"Go then. We won't stop you."

Tania's demurral, Grigoriev's buzzer, Zinia's prank: these were all signs that he should return to the cottage now. It was not like Yuri to resist portents and omens. But it was one thing to crawl into a window, another thing entirely to crawl out of it, especially in front of these girls. And Ludmilla's embrace had only quickened his appetite.

"Where is she?"

Zinia grimaced. "We have a few questions for you."

"For God's sake, Marshak's going to find me! They'll fly Titov!"

Zinia took a notebook from her pocket. Ludmilla and the other girl sniggered. They gazed upon him with feverish eyes.

"What is the significance of this date? 18 September 1939."

These prenuptial questions were another custom, one of our traditions. How we loved our customs, how we drew a skein of folk belief, tradition and superstition around the most prosaic events of our lives. We would never give them up.

"Tania's day of birth?"

"That was too easy. What does this number represent? One hundred fifty-six."

"Her height," Yuri replied. "In centimeters."

"Forty-eight?"

"Um, her weight, in kilos."

"Two thousand and sixty-four."

"Zinia, I don't know. Just tell me where she is!"

Zinia had a laugh as frothy as steamed milk. "Look how he's dying for it! Girls, have you ever seen anything so pathetic? It's the distance from Baikonur to the village of Kozino, in versts."

Yuri smiled at this. We had stopped using versts before the Revolution.

"What's Kozino?" Yuri asked.

"The place where Tania was born, lieutenant! One should know, after such a long courtship . . . You must pay *vykup.*" Literally: ransom money. It was the custom to pay a token sum for every incorrectly answered question.

"I'm not carrying a single kopeck."

"Then what kind of lover are you?"

"Honestly, girls. Where I'm going, there's not a thing to buy."

"Just like Tyuratum." That was the name of the old Kazakh town outside the cosmodrome. "Has space been collectivized too? Well, go away then."

Yuri briefly flushed at Zinia's political brazenness. "But I have something. A kiss for each of you."

Zinia snorted. "A kiss! He thinks his kiss is better than money." She grabbed at his trousers. "It's going to take more than a kiss."

He pulled away. "It's all I can give."

Zinia said, "All right then. Me first. You call that a kiss? And how do you kiss your mother?"

Yuri grinned. "Wait a minute, I have some questions

for you, some numbers to identify. Eight kilometers per second. Three hundred twenty-seven kilometers. One hour forty-eight minutes."

Now it was Zinia's turn to color. Her expression became serious. The smiles on the faces of the other nurses also faded, though not the shine in their eyes. Zinia said, "Lieutenant, I can only guess at what they mean. I'm sorry, we're not cleared for this technical information."

He nodded soberly. "Better not guess then. Here's one last number, another date: April 12, 1961. I believe you won't forget it."

Zinia said softly, "There's a girl in Room 3 who's hoping to circle April 11 on her calendar."

"Is Marshak in her office?"

"She should be. She said she would take a nap."

Yuri kissed Zinia again, once on each cheek, and tenderly embraced her. Then he kissed Ludmilla and the other nurse. These were chaste, serious kisses; not romantic, almost religious. A new sense of the following day descended upon them, as if the shuttered storeroom had been lit by the dawn. Yuri turned away and opened the door. In the hallway he stopped to listen. The infirmary was still, as soundless as space promised to be. Room 3 was down the hall, away from Grigoriev's.

Yuri had seen the Chief Designer's plans for a spacecraft of the future, a vessel whose great domed living and research quarters would be separated from its nuclear power supply by a long cylindrical axis. The infirmary now offered itself as a model for something similar, a primitive space station, dim, silent, and remote. His soft-soled shoes were drawn to the floor of the hallway not by gravity, but by the infirmary's centrifugal spin through the void. And why not? A man of the future, he would take the girls into the future with him.

Hurtling in the direction of the day after, he turned the corner and nearly collided with another swiftly moving object, in a white lab coat, moving toward the day before. It was Marshak. Yuri hadn't heard her approach.

Several moments passed, her heels clattering, before Marshak fully recovered from the near impact. She was a tall woman well into middle age, with sallow skin offset by brassy red-brown hair. Her plastic, yellow-tinted eyeglasses were perched halfway down the bridge of her nose. She scowled as she identified him in the murk.

Yuri's testicles retracted. He set to work concocting a reason for his presence in the infirmary: the need to stretch his legs, a minor headache . . . He had been in worse scrapes before. This would take some doing, but Marshak would want to believe him.

"Poor Grigoriev . . ." he began.

"Lieutenant," she snapped. "Hurry. Where have you been? Come, come."

She spun on her heels and scurried back down the hallway. For a moment, Yuri wondered whether she had really seen him or was somehow sleepwalking. He decided against pretending to be a dream. He followed her past the door to Room 3, which was closed, but Yuri sensed life—throbbing and abundant—beyond it.

They entered Marshak's office, a small, wallpapered room with a metal desk, a medicine cabinet, a white plaster bust of Lenin worn almost to featurelessness, and, in a shadowed corner, an examination table. A short, stocky man lay on the table with his shirt off and his eyes wide open.

Yuri cried, "Sergei Pavlovich!"

The face of the Chief Designer, as much of a military secret as his name, was paler than Yuri had ever seen it. It was a handsome, frail face, easily betrayed by suffering. A smile now fluttered weakly across it.

"Yuri," he whispered.

In alarm, Yuri looked away, at Marshak.

She shook her head. "It's just angina. I've given him a sedative, but he has to calm himself. He's brought it on through excessive worry." The Chief Designer tried to make a self-deprecating chuckle, but it came out as a faint moan. "Lieutenant, he asked for you, that's why I called the cottage. When you couldn't be found, he became panicked. I thought he would have another attack. And I don't know where my useless staff has gone to . . ."

"Don't worry," Yuri said to the Chief Designer. "Please."

"He's had some kind of premonition. He caught himself whistling indoors. A bird tapped on his window. He passed a woman carrying an empty bucket. He stumbled with his left foot. He discovered that he was wearing one of his socks inside out. Now he wants to call off the flight."

Yuri bit his lip and reached for the Chief Designer's shoulder. The skin was clammy and gave off a sweet, nicotine smell. He smoked several packs a day, the most popular brand. It was named after the White Sea Canal, which had been dug by political prisoners.

"No, you can't call off the flight."

"I've been given too much responsibility," the Chief Designer rasped. "I can't accept it, not with my health. It's not just your life, Khrushchev says the future of the Soviet Union depends on it, socialism, world peace . . . Khrushchev's a madman. He's obsessed by Kennedy. He doesn't care about space or rockets or science, only about Kennedy. He says we have to fuck Kennedy . . . He calls me nearly every day, sometimes twice a day . . . sometimes only to tell me that we have to fuck Kennedy . . . He expects daily, even hourly progress reports, he considers every stuck valve an act of sabotage. He makes threats, terrible threats. But there's too much to do, we're going too fast. We still don't know why the R-16 blew up or what are the effects of zero gravity upon human physiology. How about cosmic radiation? Or micro-meteorites? Will the retro-rockets fire? We need more tests. We have to send up more dogs."

"I won't let a dog fly my spaceship."

"Who do we think we are?" the Chief Designer asked, closing his eyes. "Is man really destined to leave the earth? Now? How can that be? Have we evolved that far? We've barely descended from the apes. We still fight wars and behave unspeakably toward each other. Are we going to take our failings into the heavens with us? What good will that do? We're not ready for it. Our children won't be ready either, I'm afraid. Perhaps their children . . . A generation that hasn't known war . . ."

"Please, comrade, calm yourself." Marshak took his wrist and timed his pulse.

Yuri pulled a stool over to the table and kneeled on it, bringing his face close to the Chief Designer's. The Chief

Designer's eyes were wet and unfocused, their pupils indistinct. Yuri gripped the Chief Designer's other hand as hard as was possible without hurting him.

"Look at me, Sergei Pavlovich. We *are* ready. You've told me so. You've proven it to me."

Yuri then spoke for the next quarter of an hour, in a voice as measured as the feed of a fuel line. He recalled everything that the Chief Designer had told him. The need to explore the unknown was intrinsic to human nature. Space flight was the next logical development in human history, as inevitable as anything set down into print by Marx or Lenin. Titov would fly next, then the others, followed by multicrew spacecraft, space rendezvous and docking maneuvers, and eventually a permanent orbiting station, a stepping-stone to the moon and the planets. Kosmograd-1 was already on the design table, orbiting the earth sixteen times a day. Hundreds of cosmonauts would live and work there; women, too. Children would be born in space and soon a way of life would be established there upon completely scientific principles. Perhaps it was only in space that a true communist society could exist, floating free of terrestrial compromise, its economy as finely regulated as its air and water supplies.

Great vessels would ply the spacelanes between the earth and the moon. Man would settle Mars, colonize the moons around Jupiter, explore and exploit Saturn's satellite Titan. And then the stars would beckon. Man would encounter extraterrestrial civilizations raised by creatures of outlandish biology and aspect, yet their societies would also be subject to the laws of history. Perhaps the extraterrestrials had already reached the final stage of their development. Indeed, because the human race was still comparatively young, living in a universe many times older than itself, it was only logical to assume the technological and social superiority of the extraterrestrials. They would have already abolished economic exploitation, class, national chauvinism, superstition, neurosis, and perversion. There would be much for mankind to learn. But by then mankind would have evolved so far as to be almost unrecognizable to the people of the mid-twentieth century.

"And, Sergei Pavlovich, we shall take the first step, together, tomorrow morning."

The Chief Designer didn't respond. He closed his eyes again.

Marshak kept her eyes trained on her watch. Finally, she said, "That's better. The sedative's taking effect. He must sleep, that's most important."

Yuri nodded. Marshak studied him for a moment. Her expression was soft and distracted.

"You should sleep, too. You have less than six hours. Have you seen the timeline?"

"All right," he said. "Good night then."

As he turned to go, Marshak rushed at him. For a moment, Yuri believed that the doctor was about to strike him, that she was the CIA assassin of whom the KGB had warned. Her body, solid and unyielding, slammed against his before he could defend himself. In his gut he received a presentiment of weightlessness. Then she buried her head in his chest through his open flight jacket. She held him for a long time, her body quaking.

"Thank God," Marshak said at last, lifting her tear-streaked face to him. "Thank God it's you he chose. Go to her now. She's in the next room."

In the next room the drapes were parted and half of Tania's body was silvered by the moon, like an airplane fuselage on a runway. She stood by the window in an open white robe. In the sharp relief of the moonlight, the illuminated curves and spheres of her figure were disconnected by vast occulted regions, positives and negatives, pros and cons, truths and lies. Her lips, the visible portions seeming to hover in space, trembled and then he himself was seized in a passion of anticipation. He took the remainder of the steps toward her. Tentatively, she reached for his hands, gently clasped them, and even more gently carried them to between her breasts. Her body was warm. Let's *go,* she whispered.

In the future, every male cosmonaut would urinate on the side of the bus that brought him to the launch pad: Titov, Leonov, Komarov, Romanenko, Tsibliyev . . . It would become one of our customs. Yuri zipped up and joined the Chief Designer. Some of the Chief Designer's color had returned. He was still anxious but appeared to be relieved and even surprised that the morning had come. He again gazed at the checklist, studying it as if it contained the secrets of the inner workings of the universe.

They walked to the elevator. At the foot of the open elevator shaft, about twenty flight technicians greeted Yuri with sustained applause. It echoed like the sound of buckshot on the flats around the launch complex. Yuri

shook their hands and accepted more bouquets. He
cleared his throat and then spoke in a quiet, passionate
voice, drawing the workers to him. He thanked them,
told them they were embarking together on a great adventure. "Right now, all my life seems to be one wonderful instant," he said, looking at the notes the Chief
Designer had composed on the bus. "Everything I have
ever done, everything I have ever experienced, was for the
sake of this minute."

The elevator began the first stage of his ascent into
space. Although the cabin rose no more quickly than an
ordinary Moscow lift, he soon felt himself enter the rar-
efied, light-soaked regions of the sky. Beyond the passing
red girders that supported the launch gantry, the cleared
countryside spread out like a huge plate. It was hard to
believe that there was even more to the world than this.
At the top of the shaft, in the clean room adjacent to the
open hatch of the Vostok capsule, more technicians
awaited him, their faces luminous. He deposited his
bouquets in a line of vases that had been left there for
him. After some preliminary tests on his suit, he was
helped into the spacecraft. Leads were hooked into the
radio and telemetry jacks. This was followed by repeated
radio checks with the Chief Designer, code-named Dawn.
Yuri was code-named Cedar. The Chief Designer was the
last person he saw as the hatch was shut. Music was piped
in to relax him, the song he had heard the night before,
"What Moves My Heart So." All was quiet as the Chief
Designer, now watching the rocket through a periscope
inside the launch control bunker, announced by radio
their passage through the checklist. He asked Yuri again

how he was feeling and how well did he hear him. Yuri said he was feeling fine, he heard him fine. The start key was put in position. The blow valves were opened and then the fuel valves. The cables to the Vostok dropped away. Yuri said he was ready. He reported hearing the valves working. At precisely seven minutes past the hour, the Chief Designer gave the order for ignition. "Let's *go!*" Yuri cried. That too, would be repeated by each of the men and women who were to follow, another of our customs of departure.

Budyonnovsk

Буденновск

Telephone

A woman in a small provincial town sits at a table in a sweltering kitchen, a bruise rising under her right eye. The woman is silent, the muscles in her face slack. Her hands are clasped on the table, which is bare save for a beige-and-brown telephone. She stares into the table. In another room children are watching a video paced by a strident, tumultuous sound track. The heat of the day smells like blood.

A man sits across from the woman. Sweat trickles along the side of his face. His shirt is drenched and he is keenly aware of its odor. When he lifts his arm, his skin pulls at the table, leaving a pale, glistening shadow. He repeatedly opens and closes his fist, amazed at this simple motor activity; then he conceives that this unpremeditated gesture may somehow be taken for remorse. He stops. Blood pounds in his temples, flickering his vision. And in fact he is touched by the first cold caress of remorse.

The telephone between them bleats twice. They pretend not to hear it. The man suspects some sort of trick. His remorse evaporates. The electrical impulse that induces the noise has been almost certainly generated by his wife's mother. Every peal raises the temperature in the kitchen another degree. Neither the man nor the woman makes a move, as if their argument is about who will answer the telephone. Anger clenches the man's heart. The structure of time now seems constructed entirely from the knells of the telephone, and in the moments between them the world halts its rotation. With a quick, urgent gesture, the man grabs the receiver and brings it to his face.

"Yeah."

There's a brief silence at the other end of the line—no, it isn't his mother-in-law, the silence and subsequent throat-clearing is masculine.

"This is Prime Minister Viktor Chernomyrdin."

"You've dialed the wrong number," the man says. "You want to speak to Basayev. The Chechens have crossed the border and shot up the town. They're holding hundreds of hostages in the hospital. They're demanding safe passage back to Chechnya. The hospital is five thirty-seven fifty-four; we're five thirty-seven forty-five. People are always making this mistake. We get calls in the middle of the night—drug overdoses, heart attacks, traffic accidents. It's a nuisance, sir."

"No, Vasily Yegorevich, I haven't made a mistake. I want to speak with you."

The man doesn't answer. He wishes for a cigarette and suddenly recalls another grievance: there are no goddamned cigarettes in the apartment.

"First, we must be calm," Chernomyrdin says. His voice is gruff but sonorous, resonating reasonableness and dependability.

"I am calm."

"Let's resolve these matters peacefully, without re-sorting to violent measures."

"Fine."

"So, that's agreed. Now, Vasily Yegorevich, I propose that we begin by discussing the situation in its entirety..."

The *situation*. Vasya is overwhelmed by the enormity taken in by this single word. It's like a massive cloud that has floated into the kitchen through the open window. No, it's like a balloon expanding within the walls of the apartment, crushing against him, displacing the air. He pounds his fists against its sides. Choked with anger and frustration, he usually flees to the dusty, frozen, or muddy street alongside the market—no, not today, today bodies lie in the crimsoned gravel—where he passes the tables and kiosks, circles back, lingers, loiters, finds a friend or an acquaintance and, eventually, yes, a bottle comes un-screwed. And then back in the flat, in the permanently damp bed, there's a moment in nearly every passage through the night in which the alcohol he's consumed during the day has exited his system but the natural sleep-inducing chemicals in his blood have not yet suffi-ciently accumulated—and he wakes in the dark, desper-ate to reason, fight, or imagine his way out of this trap, this box, this grave, this *situation*.

Cigarettes

Start with the cigarettes. Vasya buys them, Ira smokes them, perhaps two packs in a single day, less the three or four she sullenly parts with at his demand. At times she's enshrouded in smoke, completely protected from the outside world, barely able to see it. She takes no pleasure in the cigarettes, smoking as mindlessly as she cooks, cleans, and talks. Two packs of Bond cost nearly as much as a liter of White Eagle. But she has somehow computed that a bottle is equal to a certain percentage of his weekly earnings and thus a measurable theft of food from their children's mouths. Despite the softness of her logic— *whatever* the drink costs would be a percentage of his weekly earnings, and why isn't the pack of cigarettes a percentage? and the children aren't hungry anyway, just filthy—he knows that she's right or close enough to right to trivialize his objections, which he cannot in any case articulate. And he usually buys her Russian-made Kazbeks, never Bond. But then, she herself has no weekly earnings from her so-called job in the paper factory, which has been closed for months.

Laziness

Ira says that he's lazy, and it's true and it isn't. Yes, Vasya perceives that he's not making enough of an effort. But this is something in his character, against which he actively, furiously labors. He strains against his laziness like Gulliver straining against the ropes of the Lilliputians. But Ira never acknowledges this effort; she cannot appreciate that laziness is like a chronic illness, a climatic condition, a tidal wave. And at no time of the day does he feel more submerged than when, his head throbbing and his lungs bursting, he sees through sleep's greenish murk the shimmer of morning light several stories above his head. Pedaling his arms and kicking wildly, he never reaches it.

Perhaps it isn't the morning light to which he strives, but something infinitely better. He wakes to find himself beached on the shore of their ill-lit apartment, enveloped in the vapors of cigarettes and fried fish, the cries of quarreling children and the melodrama of the day's first video.

He closes his eyes, shutting out his vision of the hours ahead. At this moment he yearns to make any sacrifice, suffer any hardship, and undertake any kind of self-abasement that would change his life. And then he waits, with dissolving faith, for the inspiration that will show him how.

Missing

If they had all their teeth, their grins would be predatory, but Yura, Borya, and two fellows Vasya doesn't know are missing between them an entire mouth. As Vasya approaches, wary, his own smile flutters like the light of a cheap candle. Borya asks him to guess what's gone. Vasya surveys the park, its crumbling concrete paths nearly obscured by the overgrown grass and shrubbery, its de-slatted benches, its sightless overhead lights. Well, Vasya says, the bottle's here at least, give it over. Borya steps away, hauling it out of Vasya's reach and revealing behind the men a squat gray pedestal. Embedded in the pedestal's granite are two shards of metal in which Vasya perceives the vestiges of two sculpted boots. He stares at these, reminded of a cripple begging in the market this morning, a soldier who lost both feet to a land mine somewhere.

Lermontov's been swiped, sold for scrap, Yura

announces, as proud as if he's done it himself. The men laugh, but Vasya softly says, no, Lermontov's over there, and shrugs toward a still-intact stone figure across the way. They admire the statue for several moments and turn back to the boots. Borya passes Vasya the bottle, its sides slick. Vasya pauses before he drinks. He says, this was Pechorin, remember? You know, from Lermontov's book. The men nod and offer murmurs of congratulation for his literary knowledge. Vasya smiles at the compliments, but the recalled trivia has given him a proprietary interest in the statue and now a tremor of regret at its loss.

G-7

Coffins, say the bills of lading, but scores of Chechen fighters are concealed within the trucks. Arriving in Budyonnovsk, 140 kilometers across the border into Russia, they seize the local administration building in a blaze of gunfire and raise the Chechen flag. They set fire to houses and cars, spray bullets at passersby, and pull civilians out of buses and nearby offices and shops. Several hundred hostages are drenched in gasoline. Then they are marched several kilometers to the town hospital, while the Chechens continue their running gun battle with the security forces, who fire at terrorists and hostages with faint discrimination. Vasya watches it all on television; at one point, the sound of gunfire outside becomes so intrusive that he is forced to close the windows. President Yeltsin leaves Moscow to attend a G-7 meeting in Halifax.

For several days, the Chechens stand off the surrounding police and army units; and then the Interior

Ministry's Alpha Task Force storms the hospital. In the
four-hour assault, dozens of hostages and patients lose
their lives as Alpha fires grenades and rockets into wards
marked with white sheets. Alpha snipers pick off women
and children. When a cease-fire is called, Chechen com-
mander Shamil Basayev frees hundreds of hostages, who
beg the security forces not to storm the hospital again.
Inside the hospital, hostages volunteer to take up arms
against the army and police. The fighters give blood for
transfusions. After a second assault is repulsed with
more loss of civilian life, friends and relatives of the
hostages encircle the hospital to act as a buffer. The attention of the nation rests on the White House in
Moscow, where Prime Minister Viktor Chernomyrdin
has taken charge. He is prepared to negotiate by telephone, on live TV.

Sleepwalker

Pictureless, the television cheers, its static the night's
only sound. Vasya, who has awakened from a moment's
doze jammed with a series of complicated, terrifying
dreams, lifts his feet from the bed and finds the floor.
The fibers of the coarse Ossetian rug, a wedding present,
burn his soles. For more than a minute, he wonders
whether he cares enough to investigate Ira's absence. He
finally stands and pads by the TV set, following the reach
of its gray radiance into the hallway.

At the end of the corridor, in a kitchen suffused by
the television's electromagnetic remains, Ira stands by
the sink, sponging herself. She maneuvers the foaming
sponge in long, errant strokes, washing him out of her,

showing no more determination than when she cleans the breakfast dishes. There is a soft pop as the sponge seals and releases the crevice between her legs.

Vasya is shamed by their bodies, distended, welted, warted, and pimply. Neither of them is yet thirty years of age, but look . . . Outside his cousin's banya, she stands in the snow with her legs apart, the remnants of a perfectly aimed snowball caught in the space between her breasts. She laughs full-throatedly: at her wonder for being here, at the way the cold has tautened her skin, and also at his embarrassed, appraising stare . . . She opens the door to their hotel room in Sochi and behind Vasya, his knuckles poised at the place where the door has been, pass two bearded, middle-aged men in suits. She jumps back as if burned, her tiny hands frantically searching for her sweet spots. As Vasya turns, the two men bow curtly and go on their way . . . On a summer afternoon as hot as today's, but in another decade, her sleeping body stretches across the sheets like a continent.

Mondays

The market is closed every Monday. On this Monday, Vasya brings a folding table to Pushkina, the street that runs outside the market, and neatly stacks piles of dry goods upon it. At adjacent tables, his competitors sell identical goods at identical prices for the same 5 percent commission, which they receive from the same businessman, who comes around to collect their receipts at the end of the day. Before the arrival of the first customers, the sunbeams accumulate on Vasya's face; he stands there as a proprietor, his legs apart, his shoulders straight, and his hands clasped below his waist, rocking a little, unbalanced by anticipation. And then the customers come, picking through the Korean T-shirts, the Bangladeshi baseball caps, and the Indonesian jeans with a listlessness that suggests they have given up finding loose Krugerrands scattered among them. White Eagle and Red Lion ward off the heat and cold. Friends stop by, people he has known his entire life. They take a swallow and congratulate him for his participation in the market economy. This is the best day of the week, even if it profits him barely.

The plant's main building shimmers in the gray distance, flocked by outbuildings so irregularly constructed and located, their purposes so abstruse, that they can never be totaled; men snort and spit in the dressing room under the pale blue eyes of a golden-braided, white-frocked Katya emblazoned on the panelled wall; each man claims his work place, adjusting his chair and placing his favorite tools within easy reach; the machines clatter and sigh; complaint forges bonds of friendship; the cafeteria's white-smocked *babas,* passing bowls of stew over the counter, make rude, self-mockingly flirtatious jokes; the brusque foreman tosses off any suggestion or criticism, but is willing to put his own shoulder to the wheel; newly minted rubles slide under the cashier's grate and crackle like dry firewood in his hands: Vasya's old enough to know what a real job is, but not old enough to have ever had one. By the time he had left the army, perestroika was in full swing and the chemical factory had stopped hiring, and now only fitfully pays its workers. He can no longer search for a job, it's worse than futile, for his inquiries exasperate the acquaintances who may someday be in a position to give him one. When Vasya asks about getting a table in the market, his boss slams his fist against the side of his van, telling him that he's lucky to work Mondays. The number of tables allowed in the market is strictly controlled.

Vsevolod Vsevolodovich

In Ira's face, especially in the narrow, tawny triangle scored by her eyes and the bridge of her nose, he can nearly make out her late father's. The truth is that Vsevolod Vsevolodovich cut a more handsome figure, the flecks of Tartar blood lending his features elements of gallantry that in his daughter have transmuted to insipidity and coarseness. His dignified bearing was something European. An accountant at the chemical factory for more than thirty years, he conducted himself like a government minister, circumspect and ostentatiously discrete. Even as a pensioner, as the contents of his good black business suit diminished, he strolled through the neighborhood coldly surveying its clotheslines and livestock. Liquor never moistened his lips, not even at Vasya and Ira's wedding banquet, not even for the first toast.

Transaction

There is White Eagle and Red Lion. Also Birch Fire, Troika, Star of the North, Tundra Gold, Rasputin, Russian Roulette, and, if someone else is buying, Ivan the Terrible. The bottles are poised like ICBMs beneath the

kiosks' rusting, corrugated metal roofs while, somewhere else, ICBMs are poised like bottles beneath the
rusting roofs of missile silos. His hands parenthetically
at his temples, Vasya peers through the dense glass that,
even when clean and unscratched, refracts the objects
several degrees from the plane of the material world.
Single exemplars of foreign goods line the shelves, Czech
chocolate cherries alongside a box of French tampons,
German condoms in taunting juxtaposition with a jar of
Polish pickles.

Someone nearly invisible, usually a girl, works within
each kiosk, whose goods are identical to those of its
neighbors but are arranged in a slightly different permu-
tation. The spectral presence who possesses the second
kiosk from the corner especially excites Vasya's imagination. What is she doing in there behind the money hole,
before he raps on the vitrine to summon her attention?
He stoops low to announce his choice and within the
kiosk's gloom there is a rippling glimmer of lipstick, a
glint of eye-light, and, perhaps, even more briefly beheld,
an expanse of skin well below her neck. His posture is un-
supportable for more than a small fraction of a minute
and the medium between them is too thick for conversation; he straightens and points to the consumer object of
desire. He places his money in the trap in front of the
hole. A creamy-skinned hand, long and bejeweled, slides
open the little glass gate, emerges from the hole, and slith-
ers around the bills. Its nails are lacquered vermilion to
remind him that they can draw blood. The hand with-
draws as silently and languorously as it has come. Now it
passes among the shelves, lightly caressing the packets

and bottles, until it rests on his choice. It pauses there for a moment. And then the hand reemerges, embracing the object. He would like to stroke that hand but once, as if by accident, as he accepts his purchase.

Kitchen

The kitchen is laid out like a long box (a cigarette pack, a shoe box, a *coffin*), its ceiling low and sooty, its fixtures grease-streaked. Crinkled strips of paint peel from the walls. The cupboard totters over the buckling wooden floor. Wash soaks in the basin's scummy gray water.

The heat of the day has released the kitchen's odors and sensitized the nerves along the lining of Vasya's nostrils. Sour milk pools at the back of his tongue. A cloying sweetness rises from the washtub. The paint's lemony tang stings his eyes.

Vasya recently acquired a toaster oven. Two weeks later he had to sell it. He insists now that they took a very small loss on the appliance, but the counter space it occupied has been left unfilled as a standing rebuke.

The Abortions

The second was a botch, less than a year ago, its bloody and tissue-stained details kept from him. But before the telephone receiver even reached his ear, his mother-in-law had flooded the kitchen with frenzied accounts of her daughter's ill treatment in the hands of rude nurses, complaints about hygiene, demands for money for bribes, calls for fresh sheets and nightgowns, and implied and explicit accusations of his own complicity. Vasya hadn't seen Ira during her entire month in the hospital. Men were kept out of the women's ward for sanitary reasons. It was also for sanitary reasons that he hadn't been allowed to send candy or flowers, though afterwards Ira accused him of not having the money for them, which was true enough, but was not the determining factor.

The first: early spring, early morning, early life. The top of the snow melted the day before and has refrozen overnight, leaving a translucent glaze. Already the sun is working on the ice. Wisps of steam huff off it, patches puddle. Vasya halts on the dry sidewalk by the schoolyard and takes a step onto the berm. His boot crashes through the frosting and finds the cake beneath it spongy and moist. Little clumplets of snow bunch around his laces. He smiles at them and then hurries along, catching up with the shadow-Vasya who hasn't stopped for the experiment.

He crosses the hospital driveway and passes through the double rubber-sealed doors into a waiting room as dim as a tomb. Thinking he's early, Vasya stops at the doors and waits for his pupils to widen. There's a distinct interval, perhaps seven or eight seconds, between the moment he begins to admire the slight, rounded form of a girl stooped over the counter signing a document of some sort, and the moment in which he identifies that it belongs to Irina. Perhaps he has mistaken her for a schoolgirl, two or three years younger than she actually is. The murk evaporates around the room's places of incandescence and reflection. Her black hair, gleaming as if wet and unencumbered by bows or berets, falls down the sides of her face. Only the tip of her nose is visible, hardly recognizable as a nose.

Straightening for a moment, she turns and sees him. He hasn't promised to be here, nor acknowledged anything at all, yet she doesn't seem surprised, only pleased. The pleasure is as clean and lucid as the ice. He returns the smile, sensing that his own expression exercises nearly every muscle and tissue in his body. While Ira completes the document, the bespectacled matron behind the cashier's counter offers him a glance that is friendly and congratulatory. For what, Vasya doesn't wonder. Then, without saying a word, Ira hands him her suitcase, puts her arm in the crook of his and they step from the building, their strides long.

Nine

The cries, shouts, threats, sighs, and moans, the mayhem and the lovemaking, are translated into Russian and voiced over by a single announcer. The English sound track murmurs on underneath.

The video player runs all day in the darkened bedroom, regardless of whether anyone is watching it. Vasya and Ira enter sleep with the films' reflections flickering on the walls and in their dreams.

They own nine videocassettes, each of which they have watched scores or even hundreds of times, attenuating the recording so that the drama is played now against a staticky, ethereal landscape. But Vasya rarely sees a film from beginning to end. Rather, he glimpses it in fragments, its scenes out of order, the violence seeming to operate without cause and effect, just as it does in real life.

Waiting List

Vsevolod Vsevolodovich's death leaves Ira's mother alone in a tottery, battered two-room house with a monthly pension of about 200,000 rubles. For years the house's roof has leaked, streaking the walls first green, then a kind of grayish blue, then an intimately organic yellow-white, and it seems that the walls' decomposing paint and plaster will pass through all the shades of the rainbow before enough money is collected for a *remont*. Then a raging late-winter storm tears off a chunk of the roof and the ceiling below collapses onto the bed. At the time, Ira's mother is taking refuge at a neighbor's.

Having worked with crude, ready material and even less adequate skill, Vasya knows that his repairs won't survive a summer downpour. Ira's mother moves into her other room, and she once again fidgets in her place on the queue for new housing. Ira's parents had applied for an apartment in one of the already decrepit five-story *khrushchevkas* in the year of Brezhnev's death.

Vasya is sent to the chemical factory to plead with the chief to use his influence to help her jump her place on the list. It's a matter of justice, he's been instructed to say. He brings with him an envelope jammed with documents, including Vesevolod's Party card, his twenty-eight—*twenty-eight!*—letters of commendation for dedicated work, and, in a small black case, laid on purple velvet, his war medals. The chief refuses to meet him. In the overbright anteroom, Vasya is made aware of the tenuousness of the material that comprises his slacks and the constraining fit of his sports jacket. He smiles dimly at the chief's bosomy middle-aged secretary.

Incredibly, she doesn't remember his father-in-law, but she attends the particulars of Ira's mother's plight with sympathy. Suddenly, in a rush of emotion, Vasya begins telling her about matters that have nothing to do with the waiting list. He can't check himself. He's still talking twenty minutes later, trying to explain the *situation,* when the chief steps from his office on his way to lunch. Vasya hurriedly shuffles to within his field of vision. The chief's a grim young man not much older than Vasya. Frowning, not looking Vasya in the eye, he replies that there is nothing he can do, times have changed, and he goes on his way. Vasya is embarrassed and, without another word to the secretary, he too leaves. He heads down the corridor in the opposite direction as fast as he can move without running.

He returns home, where Ira and her mother stand vigil. A minute later, her face empurpled, Ira's mother is threatening a stroke. Her rage is directed not at the chief, but at Vasya. She doubts he has pleaded her case properly, presented all the documents, especially the twenty-eight letters of commendation, or shown the chief the necessary deference. She suspects that Vasya has not even gone to the factory, that he has spent the afternoon in the park. Indeed, Vasya's breath testifies that he has recently shared a bottle with some acquaintances, but that was on the way home. And she accuses him of not really wishing to help, his supposed reluctance born from resentment of her late husband's rectitude. And it is true that, despite his initial discomfort, Vasya has taken a modest, delicious pleasure in having failed. And though the next storm will blow the miserable witch into Ira and Vasya's apartment for good, this predicament conspires to work in his favor, because she's Ira's mother, another weapon to use against Ira.

His search for weapons suddenly leaves him fatigued. He flexes his fist again.

Ira

"So, that's agreed," Chernomyrdin is saying. "Now, Vasily Yegorevich, I propose that we begin by discussing the situation in its entirety—"

Vasya cuts him off.

"I want a bus."

The prime minister is silent for a moment.

"A bus?"

"And not one of your shitty army buses, either. A good one, with a full tank of gas."

Chernomyrdin's hand covers his mouthpiece, blanketing some quick, urgent interrogatives. Then, with a burst of static, the hand is removed.

"This can be arranged," Chernomyrdin says.

"No tricks," Vasya warns.

"No tricks."

"And I want safe passage."

"Yes, that's agreed. But to where?"

Now it's Vasya's turn to fall silent. This choice is some kind of sophisticated Moscow treachery, invented by the security organs. Without a map, forced to make a decision on the spot, Vasya won't be able to formulate the correct response. And how can he think in this furnace of a kitchen, with his shirt stinking like a corpse's, with bombs exploding and bullets flying in the next room? He curses himself for his inability to plan ahead. Kabardino-Balkaria, Karachayevo-Cherkessia, Zhezkazgan: place-names tumble through his head like chunks of concrete.

His wife has looked away, showing no interest in the conversation. She gazes through the window at the impossibly empty blue sky. Her face turned so that he cannot see the bruise, Vasya is reminded of it.

He blurts: "Portugal."

"That's impossible," Chernomyrdin replies at once. "Portugal is a member of NATO."

Vasya wonders if he is right. The prime minister is known to be poorly advised, especially about foreign affairs. But he sounds very sure of himself.

"Portugal," Vasya repeats. "Or there's no deal."

Chernomyrdin is gone from the phone a long time. Vasya bitterly regrets that he has chosen Portugal, but if he compromises now, Chernomyrdin will think he's weak.

Ira says, "I want a bus too."

Vasya smothers the receiver with his chest and whispers furiously, "Don't interfere, these are sensitive negotiations."

She scowls. Chernomyrdin comes back on the line.

"It's agreed," he says. "But we will issue a statement denying that our agreement involves any political concessions."

"And I need a hostage, for my own safety."

"What, you don't trust me?" Chernomyrdin sounds hurt.

"I'm sorry, Viktor Stepanovich," Vasya says tactfully, "The state and the governmental organs have lost large measures of public confidence. In general, this reflects society's loss of faith in established institutions and traditions."

"All right then. But it has to be voluntary."

"My wife volunteers."

"And the government accepts no liability for your actions, nor for its own. And I must speak to Irina Vsevolodovna, to confirm her willingness."

Vasya slides Chernomyrdin across the table. Ira lifts the receiver with a limp hand, her eyelids heavy.

"Yeah," she says.

Vasya hisses, "It's the prime minister!"

Irina doesn't change her expression. She is either listening to Chernomyrdin or is about to doze off.

She says, "Uh huh." And then: "Yes, I agree. My own responsibility."

She hands the receiver back to her husband.

"Yes sir?"

"Vasily Yegorevich, everything's agreed. The bus will arrive shortly. You have my word and the word of the government of the Russian Federation."

The line goes dead. They remain in their chairs. The heat of the day still smells like blood. Someone cries out in pain in the other room, probably on television. Vasya and Ira don't look at each other. Yet the muscles around Vasya's heart loosen their grip. He becomes aware of possibilities and potentialities. Is it a breeze that briefly tingles his scalp?

Outside their window an engine mutters and tires gently tear at the asphalt. Trying to hide his anticipation, Vasya slowly rises from the table and steps to the window. A pale yellow bus is parked in front of the building. It's an army bus, but relatively clean and undented. Its door opens and two soldiers in camouflage uniforms and ski masks step from it, waving their rifles ahead of them as if they are clearing cobwebs. They sweep the guns up and down the scorched, noiseless street. One of the soldiers makes a hand signal and another half dozen, hoisting rifles and rocket-propelled grenade launchers, exit the bus. A soldier looks up at Vasya, only his eyes visible. Vasya nods in acknowledgment. Two armored personnel carriers pull behind the bus. The soldiers pile in and the vehicles take off.

Ira noiselessly joins Vasya at the window.

He turns. The heat of the sun, intensified by the surrounding flatlands, reflected by the concrete landscape, and trapped in the confines of the kitchen, is nothing compared to the warmth of Ira's smile.

She squeezes his arm and presses against his side. "You're wonderful," she says.

Vasya sinks his face into her hair, aware only of its tickle. After several long moments he pulls away.

"Let's hurry," he whispers hoarsely. "Let's not even pack. We don't have a minute to lose."

Salt

Соль

. . . a failure, common in Russian economic and political debate, to grasp the notion of creating wealth—that transactions are possible that will make everybody better off.

—Robert Cottrell, *New York Review of Books*

In a certain city lived a certain merchant with three sons: the first was Fyodor, the second Vassily, and the third Ivan. The merchant gave his first two sons great ships with which to seek their fortunes. The first son, Fyodor, went off to the forests of the north and brought back lumber that the city's wealthy used to build fine homes and palaces, and they paid him handsomely. The second son, Vassily, went off to the mountains of the south and brought back coal that the city's multitudes used to heat their homes and shops, and they paid him handsomely as well.

The merchant didn't expect much from his third son, Ivan, who was not quite right in the head, so he gave him a flimsy vessel made from rotten beams and planks.

With this ship Ivan sailed to the Thrice-Ten Lands, where he came upon a beautiful white mountain embraced by mist. He touched the mountain and brought his finger to his lips. The mountain was made entirely of salt, good Russian salt. Ivan ordered his men to load his ship with as much as it would carry, and they sailed until they reached a distant kingdom. There he presented himself and a thimble of salt to the king, telling the king that it was good Russian salt, and that he would be pleased to sell him as much of it as he liked.

The king had never heard of salt. He sniffed it suspiciously and declared that it was nothing but white sand. He sent Ivan away. Puzzled, Ivan wandered through the palace until he reached the king's kitchens, where he witnessed the cooks preparing a meal without the use of salt. When their backs were turned, Ivan opened the pots and tasted the food. It was so bland it was nearly inedible. He withdrew the thimble from his cloak and liberally sprinkled the salt into the pots.

Later that evening the king was served his dinner. At the very moment in which he placed the first morsel in his mouth, a fearful tremor rippled across his face. His queen, grand vizier, and counselors at his side became very still, unable to take a breath. He was a much loved king. As if under a sorcerer's compulsion, the king slowly chewed the morsel. At last he swallowed it and contemplated the swallow and the effects upon his person.

"Delicious," he murmured at last, taking pleasure in the way the word's syllables caressed his tongue and the roof and sides of his mouth.

He consumed the remainder of his meal with a passionate intensity that his courtiers had never witnessed before. They shook their heads in wonder. The king summoned his cooks, who told him that they had prepared his food just as they had in the past and could not explain its change in taste. Then an assistant recalled having seen

Ivan loitering around the kitchen earlier that day. Ivan was brought to the king and freely confessed that he had added salt to the king's food. "But salt, what is it?" the king asked.

"Sire," Ivan replied, "salt is a rare substance collected in the tears of the Firebird on the morn of Michaelmas. A small quantity quickens the appetite, invigorates the palate, and excavates from each element of food its true and unalloyed flavor. Unsalted food is merely the shadow cast by real food. As the first grains of salted food touch the tip of the tongue, a man's salivary glands contract in an exquisite spasm. Can you not feel the ache? The released liquor dissolves each morsel and molecule. In this coupling, the goodness inherent in the food is transferred to our bodies. Salt is the essential ingredient to our lifeblood, to our health, and to our good fortune. It comes from a faraway place, by great difficulty. I have an entire ship of it."

The king took one last bite from his dish, closing his eyes to shut out the distractions of the court. When he finished, he said, "Then name your price."

Ivan trembled at his own audacity. "An equal measure of gold, sire."

The king clapped his hands. "Done," he cried.

The transaction was completed before dawn. Throughout the night, as torches burned on the pier, the king's men carried crates of gold ingots and doubloons to Ivan's ship, to be weighed against similar crates filled with salt that were unloaded by Ivan's men. In the garish, oily light of the lamps, Ivan stood alongside the king's

grand vizier, who ensured the preciseness of the exchange. Dawn broke with Ivan's ship low in the water.
The king himself arrived to wish Ivan farewell.

The ship sailed for neither a long time nor a short time
and was then becalmed on the desert sea. Below deck,
sealed within the mossy saltwater damp, Ivan took the
dampness into his lungs in shallow, pained breaths. The
boards cried out as the ocean thudded against the ship's
hull. Rats skittered overhead, swishing their tails. Sightless in his unlit bunk, he asked himself, am I traveling in
a ship, the idea of a ship, or the word for a ship?

Above the deck the righteous sun never moved;
through the endless day it remained directly overhead.
Ivan leaned over the rail. In the haze, no horizon was visible to separate the atmospheric realm from the watery
one. The sea and sky melted into a single pale blue gauze
that only barely hid what was behind it. The ship's hull
strained against the gauze, close to tearing through to
the truth of things.

The gold seemed to swell in the heat, and the holds
were close to bursting. Indeed, one of the cases had broken, letting loose a spill of ducats. For a long time Ivan
squatted by the case and passed the gold from one hand
to another, trying to feel the weight of its inner substance.

He had once looked upon the gold with pride, eager
to show it to his father and brothers, but that pride had
now dimmed to a memory. Upon inspection (he was con-
stantly inspecting it, rummaging through the holds, or-
dering cases brought into the sunlight, tapping a spoon
against the ingots), the gold appeared to have taken on a

strange, overbright luster, even an odor that was something like licorice. Yet it was steadfastly inert, stupid in
its inertness.

Where resided the virtue in gold? It had little practical use, except for fashioning jewelry, which itself had no
intrinsic value but only an arbitrary, assigned value
based on ephemeral fashion. The metal had a symbolic
use, of course, in trade, in which it took on a value for
which men would labor, cheat, debase themselves, and
even make war. But this value was also arbitrary, established by unspoken consensus or through some kind of
mass hallucination.

Gold was minted into money. In trade men confused
money with the items for which it paid, as if the former
could somehow absorb the qualities of the latter, which
could then be transported in their purses. Money was a
khitraya mekhanika, a deceitful mechanism, invented by
foreigners and Jews.

Wickedness roamed the world. Weathervanes perched
atop church crosses, confounding the most profoundly
spiritual with the most ludicrously prosaic. Clocks imprisoned time in symbolic walls of hours and minutes.
Instrumental music mocked the godly harmonics of the
human voice. Representational art depicted Our Savior
with full-blooded lips, heaving breasts and sinewy muscles, a carnal being. By making Jesus human, the artists
denied His divinity; by denying His divinity, they denied
His actuality, making Him yet another symbol with an
assigned value.

Ivan had gone through life believing that a great secret,
composed of a vast number of small secrets, had been

kept from him and that only he, of all the world's men, was the victim of this conspiracy. The secret had to do with what was real and what was not. For example, was the conventional sequence of the cardinal numbers— one, two, three, four, etc.—their natural order, or a humanly contrived one?

He saw that men earned their livelihoods through the manipulation of intangibles, mostly figures in ledgers and words in books. They talked to each other in a kind of code, about indentures, stock prices, and warrants. They performed transactions after which they announced themselves satisfied and walked away from the table with nothing added to their pockets. The conspirators knew that there was a falseness at the bottom of their dealings, but they would not concede it to Ivan.

Ivan thought he knew what the real world was: it was a *desyatina* of land, a *pud* of wheat, an *arshin* of fabric. You could break your teeth on the real world, but now, out on a sea as still as glass, he had come to wonder if the land, the wheat, and the fabric were symbols themselves, a chimerical overlay for another world that was even more real.

Ivan paced along the deck of the ship, where the sailors drank vodka and played chess. The men were using the various gold coins that had scattered from the storerooms not for stakes, but as game pieces. They refused to recognize the gold's assigned worth. For them the coins had been transformed into the ranks of chivalry, another arbitrary designation. Ivan recalled that in his early-morning departure from the city, the king had stood at the edge of the pier and stretched his arm in farewell. As he had done so, a wan smile had become visible, a watermark just beneath the surface of his face.

Ivan now ordered his men to reverse course, back to the king's city. At once the wind picked up and the sails billowed and grew taut.

They soon reached their destination. Ivan docked his ship in a hidden lagoon and entered the city in disguise. But was this the same city from which he had departed? Its air was suffused with a strange, mellow glow. In his absence, the city's streets had been paved, the homes that lined the streets had been enlarged and more elaborately ornamented, and the dress of the city's inhabitants had become refined.

He stopped at an inn and ordered an expensive meal in its gay and bright dining room. The food arrived well salted, perfectly prepared. Ivan sourly noted that the cooks of this kingdom not only used his good Russian salt, but they used it in ways unknown to the cooks of his own land. At every table there were men and women eating and drinking their fill.

Ivan questioned the innkeeper.

"Has your dining hall always been so successful?"

"No sir, it has been so only since we introduced the rare spice salt to our dishes. Despite our high prices, every night we turn away patrons for lack of tables."

"Are you the only innkeeper in the city?"

"No," the innkeeper acknowledged. "The others are also using salt in their food."

"But certainly if you prosper, it must be at their expense."

"No, they too have few empty places in their halls."

"How is that possible? How can there be an increased number of patrons dining out at increased cost? How do they afford their meals?"

The innkeeper shrugged. "When we first introduced salt into our cuisine, it was an immediate success, but we all had to work harder to afford it. The increased competition closed some unprofitable businesses; people were forced to change their way of working and doing business. In doing so we have become more prosperous. I've bought myself a small coach, which I had never before dreamed of possessing. And there at the next table is the coachmaker."

"If you prosper and he prospers, then who suffers?"

The innkeeper smiled ruefully. "Not everyone can afford to eat salt, sir. There is poverty, more individual cases of poverty than we are accustomed to. But it is quite evident that our land, taken in its entirety, is much wealthier than before."

"Has this kingdom made war on another and looted its riches?"

"No, we are at peace."

"But," Ivan asked, "if the wealth has not come from the purses of the poor, nor from the coffers of the vanquished, from where has it come? Perhaps you have cheated some innocent traveler?"

"We have made it ourselves, sir."

"That is not possible," Ivan replied. "Wealth is a fixed thing, declared to be equal to such-and-such amount of gold. One man can win, rob, or earn another's gold, but the sum of the gold held by the two men stays constant. That is simple physics."

Ivan paid his bill and left, sure of his argument and of the fact that he had been grievously swindled.

Ivan went to his men and gave them great quantities of beer and wine. "The king has turned my salt to gold, and I shall return the favor. Drink up, my comrades."

That night while the kingdom slept, Ivan and his men left their ship in its moorings and silently stole through the city, their bladders full. They broke into all the places where salt was stored. They either urinated on the salt or in some other ways befouled it. On Ivan's instructions, only a single thimble of the good Russian salt was saved. It was spirited away under his cloak.

In the morning, an alarm was raised and the pirates found. A terrible battle ensued in which the city was destroyed and Ivan's ship was sunk, plunging his gold into the murky depths of the lagoon. The king's army cornered Ivan and his men on a bluff overlooking the water and beyond that the ruined, smoking streets of the city, whose people had suddenly been impoverished.

As the king and his men advanced, Ivan removed the thimble of salt from his cloak and held it above the lagoon. The king ordered his men to stop.

"Behold," said Ivan, "this is what's left of your salt. By the iron laws of economics, here is the wealth of your kingdom coalesced into a single thimble. This is the sum of your dreams and ambitions, your scheming and manipulations. Take one more step and it will be lost forever."

In exchange for the remaining salt, the king agreed to

spare Ivan's life. But with his ship sunk, Ivan could not return home. Nor could he recover his gold. He wondered whether he had made another bad transaction, rendering his life equal to a thimble of salt.

After neither a short time nor a long time, another traveler arrived in the kingdom. Upon learning of Ivan's predicament, he offered to organize the men and equipment to lift the gold from the lagoon's floor, even though Ivan was now penniless. The stranger asked only for half the gold that would be recovered.

If Ivan had not been held back by his men, he would have killed the stranger. It was, after all, Ivan's gold. Why should a stranger, this vulture, get any piece of it at all? The king tried to persuade Ivan to change his mind, saying that he would get no use from the gold as long as it was trapped under water. "On the contrary," Ivan replied. "It's as safe there as it would be in a vault."

Despite Ivan's rebuff, the traveler did not leave the city, but employed local artisans to draw up plans for the ship's salvage and to construct the necessary equipment. The traveler financed this by selling to speculators shares of his nonexistent share of Ivan's gold, a swindle that infuriated Ivan, especially because it was accomplished so openly. By some evil wizardry, founded on the chance that Ivan would someday change his mind, the city returned to prosperity. Meanwhile, the traveler and his emissaries plied Ivan with gifts and favors, seeking permission to raise his ship.

Ivan's resolve remained firm until the morning he spied the king's beautiful daughter spinning a length of golden thread. He decided to perpetuate a swindle of his

own. He offered his gold to the king, who believed it
could still be recovered, even though it was long out of
sight beneath the lagoon's burgeoning layers of silt,
drifting down into the underworld of memory and longing, a mere concept of a symbol. In exchange Ivan asked
to marry the princess, as well as for a good, fast ship.

The king clapped his hands. "Done," he cried.

That night there was a wedding banquet, attended by
the king's court and nobility. Jugglers, acrobats, and
dancing bears provided merriment. The guests feasted
on savory dishes prepared with the last thimbleful of
good Russian salt. Toast after toast was raised to Ivan's
health and good fortune. At dawn Ivan and his bride set
sail for home.

The ship sailed for neither a long time nor a short time
and was then becalmed on the desert sea. The princess,
wearing a white cotton tunic, sat at the prow of the ship.
Her eyes were as bright as the word incandescent and her
lips were as red as the idea of red. She stared at the endless sea, her profile etched against the sky. Her hair was
the color of gold.

The princess was beautiful, it was said. Ivan had tasted
the salt on her skin at the nape of her neck. But what did
her beauty consist of? A certain vividness to her features,
an unblemished skin, a posture that conformed to banal
notions of aristocratic birth, a particular shine to her
hair? These qualities meant nothing beyond themselves.
A pair of lustrous eyes did not denote passion but was
something strictly physiological, arising from the eyes'
pigmentation and the flow of moisture from their tear

ducts. It had no practical consequence. And perhaps her hair was not really the color of gold; one might just as easily have called it yellow. A woman declared to be beautiful was only a symbol of real beauty, which itself remained imperceptible to human vision.

Her attractive features were as transitory as they were arbitrary. Her supposed beauty was fading at that very moment, as it had been fading since the night of the wedding banquet. Soon she would be drained, transformed into an empty symbol like a coin declared counterfeit. The memory of the banquet's great festiveness instilled in Ivan an equivalent amount of regret and bitterness. He recalled the king's parting smile.

Ivan now ordered his men to reverse course, back to the king's city. At once the wind picked up and the sails billowed and grew taut.

NOVELLA

Peredelkino

Переделкино

One

Just as in our dreams, a fist thumped at the door, and I opened it and there stood a greatcoated lieutenant of the Committee for State Security. He was at least a head taller than me; that head was blond and square-jawed, without a blemish. Frigid, almost transparent blue eyes floated in their sockets.

"Documents."

I handed over my passport as he allowed himself into the flat. He compared my photograph to my face and then examined the stamp that gave me the right to live in the capital, a right that had degenerated into the occupancy of this tottering apartment building on the outskirts. After checking my face again, he opened a leather purselike bag at his side and removed a sheaf of papers.

I became aware that the apartment smelled of fried eggs. In advance of his arrival I had tried to put the place in order, but the sagging bookcases and the pile of unmarked student composition books gave evidence of its chronic dishevelment. These days I taught literature at the Pedagological Institute.

"Sign here," the lieutenant said, pointing a manicured finger at the top sheet of his papers. "Here. Here. Here."

Another officer of lesser rank stepped into the flat. He carried a brown cardboard carton that later proved to be quite heavy, though he himself didn't show any strain. The lieutenant waved at the table in the little room on the other side of the entrance foyer. The officer deposited the carton there and left, not once looking at me.

The lieutenant inspected my signature and then found another half-dozen places for me to sign on the other pages. As I leaned over the credenza in order to write my name, the lieutenant walked deeper into the cramped, overstuffed flat. He stopped at a photograph of me and Varvara, taken in the Crimea, and then at some unanswered personal mail on a chair. He was most interested in the locked, glassed-in bookcase and its shelf of notebooks. He studied their bindings for a minute.

"My personal journals," I confessed.

He examined them a moment longer and then reclaimed his papers. After patiently confirming that my signature was at each required place, he returned the papers to his pouch and, with a barely perceptible nod of acknowledgement, departed as well.

I remained several minutes in the foyer, breathing deeply, trying to shake off the image of the lieutenant's lacquer-clear fingernails. When my composure had returned, I telephoned Anton Basmanian at his office.

"They've arrived," I said, looking at the carton on the table.

"All right, shall we say"—he paused while, I presumed, he looked at his calendar—"December 3? A first draft, reviewing the trilogy as a whole. Twenty pages double-spaced at a minimum."

"That's fine. That's great. I'm looking forward to reading the books."

"Rem," he said sternly, detecting sarcasm where there was none. "Many on the board were opposed to giving you this assignment. I've gone out on a limb, you know. But it's time to get you back into print, to forget the past. This could be the beginning."

"Believe me, Anton, I'm grateful. Don't worry, I'll do a good review."

"Do a responsible review."

I returned the telephone to its hook and went to the table. Inside the carton, encased in gleaming, wine red leather, lay the books *Malaya Zemlya, Rebirth,* and the about-to-be-issued, still-classified conclusion to the trilogy, *Virgin Lands.* Their author was L. I. Brezhnev. I pulled the first volume from the box. As I lifted its warm, supple cover to my face, I could almost smell the cow chewing her cud. The cow groaned with pleasure as I opened the book. In contrast to the extravagance of the binding, the paper within the book was nearly tissue thin and the type laid upon it was small, about eight-point, and ungenerously leaded. I wondered what portion of these books, the subject of my first writing for publication in ten years, I would actually read.

My stomach turning, I realized that to find the right words of praise, to modulate my lauds into plausibly critical language, to prove my tough-mindedness by offering a few trivial caveats that I would immediately renounce, to concede generously that my own novel on a similar theme could not be rightfully compared with Comrade Brezhnev's achievement, to announce, as I undoubtedly would, that Comrade Brezhnev had raised the art of historical fiction to new and commanding heights—in short, to write an article in which every glimmer of doubt or irony had been eradicated—I would need to read every page of the trilogy, perhaps even twice. The desperate shreds of my ambition would demand it.

Despite the significance it carried for my future, I did not immediately fall upon the general secretary's work. Returning to the hallway where the lieutenant had paused in his inspection of my bookcase, I assumed the same detached and suspicious stance that he had. Relics of a life so distant as to seem nearly prehistoric, the journals ran across the top shelf from left to right. The species had evolved from a single cardboard-bound book that I had been given for my seventeenth birthday. Its cheap binding had broken and now the pages were kept within the covers by force of habit and nostalgia. It was succeeded by three or five very faux-leather notebooks, the detritus of my university years, and then a series of teal, pretentiously unpretentious softbound composition books, which had served me early in my professional career. Then came a long line of black-and-red hardbound diaries that I had purchased twelve years before, in 1966, in a neighborhood stationery store in London. Their confident march into posterity was abruptly broken, and the teal composition books, now simply unpretentious, my pretensions shattered, resumed their course.

Placing my tips of my fingers against the glass at the spot where the English journals were arrayed—the glass was warm, the books smoldered—I marveled anew at the naive confidence of my fourth decade and the century's seventh. And then, as if driven by an itch, the fingers were pushed to the left, to the first set of teal composition books, where I knew, somewhere, lay the notes of my critical conversation with Viktor Panteleyev.

I did not need to fish out the key to the bookcase from my desk: I knew what was in the journals. The bindings were sufficiently mnemonic.

Two

It had been a miserable, brooding weekend under concrete skies, out in Peredelkino. Lydia, my first wife, showed little interest in my quandary. "Do whatever you like," she said. Lydia considered the petition a distraction, a waste of time, yet another seduction to which I was hurrying to succumb. As if she possessed only a single photograph of me, hunched over my desk, she believed I should work every minute of the working day. Time was running out, she always said, not portentously, but as a matter of scientific, cosmological fact. As for herself, she foresaw the diminishing future as a place where she would occupy our newly acquired dacha year-round, tend to the garden, make small repairs, jar preserves, do some translation work, and, above all, read. Her only life ambition was to read every good book that had ever been published.

The text of the petition lay on the kitchen table all that long weekend, pushed aside by the salads and the roast, imprinted by rings of bottles, smeared by cigarette ashes and jam. The cat sniffed at it and slinked away. Viktor had always been a lazy writer. "Beseeching the most respected First Secretary of the Union of Soviet Writers," "stressing the undersigned's conformity to Marxist-Leninist principles in service to the state," "begging for the careful reconsideration of the case of Mikhail Aleksandrovich Vishnevsky," and "reviewing for the First Secretary's benefit the salient facts as we understand them," the petition was like one of Viktor's novels, sentimental and over-participled. I could, on the basis of literary squeamishness, refuse to attach my name to it. The weekend passed into overtime, a tense, loose-boweled Monday.

Yet on Tuesday, back in Moscow, I telephoned.

"Let's meet."

"All right," Viktor replied slowly and thoughtfully, to indicate that he understood the implications of my invitation.

"At the union," I said, and then, with a pretense of casualness, I added, "Would you like to come up to my office?"

Given my low rank and the office's consequent humility, I rarely met people there. The sweep of the door nearly obliterated the room's walking space. The aged, lumpy divan's only charm was its reputation for having once been slept on by Isaac Babel. But the office was adequately lit and well stocked with books and liquor. I found the room a pleasant enough place to write and to attend to union business, especially that requiring discretion. It moreover offered a bright portal onto Gertsena, the always churning street named after Aleksandr Herzen. My pursuit of this office had been uncontested. Most of my colleagues preferred the view of the courtyard, with its statue of Leo Tolstoy.

Viktor arrived on Tuesday afternoon, his face set in a rictus of grim deliberation. He too had traversed a difficult weekend. His suit was wrinkled and his tie undone. His stare was glassy. I recalled that his wife had left him and, I swear, I had a premonition. I motioned him toward the divan, but he ignored the invitation to make pleasantries. Stooping awkwardly, he opened his briefcase, removed the original copy of the petition and slid it across the desk.

I saw at once that I had been snookered. No more than a half-dozen signatures filled the left-hand side of the petition below Viktor's. Viktor had said the week before that Misha Vishnevsky had many friends in high places, and not only in the union. Misha, Viktor said, was genuinely liked and politically well connected. In any case, even among those who didn't know him, there was widespread revulsion at the tactics of the security organs and a commitment not to allow the gains of the past few years to be reversed. Yet most of the names on the list were unfamiliar and those that weren't belonged to individuals of exceedingly modest reputation. Not one of my colleagues in the Secretariat was represented.

"It's early in the week," Viktor muttered, by way of explanation.

"Monday's early in the week. Tuesday's already the beginning of the middle of the week."

"No one's been in their office."

"But you've received commitments?"

He nodded his head in assent.

"From who?"

"I'd rather not say, not until they've actually signed. You know how it is."

I did. I made a falsely hearty mental shrug and signed the petition with an extravagant flourish, plunging my name's descenders to the floor of the next space.

When Viktor sighed I realized that he had been holding his breath. "So, Rem," he said. "That's done." He gingerly returned the document to his briefcase.

"We should talk sometime, Viktor."

He nodded his head again, meaning: not here. Too many ghosts stalked the corridors of this building, a neoclassical mansion that had been built in the nineteenth century for a count named Sollogub. The yellow house, trimmed in white and flanked by two symmetrical wings, was said to have later served Tolstoy as a model for his depiction of the Rostov mansion in *War and Peace*. Many of us, unconsciously indulging the conceit that fiction trumped fact, would insist that it was indeed the Rostov mansion.

"Thank you."

Viktor clasped my hand, and I was surprised by its strength and warmth. Then he left. The whole thing had taken less than a minute.

Now I realized that the weight pressing on my soul the entire weekend was not the fear of signing the petition, but the fear that I would not. With the door closed, I seemed about to levitate from my desk. Or, conversely, I was in the tumble of some glorious fall, the wind sweeping my precociously graying, sloppily long hair behind me. All at once I recalled the sensations—so vivid they were nearly physical—that I had experienced when my first poem had been accepted for publication. Then too there had been relief: I would be a writer after all. Then too there had been a wonderment at my trespass: in that case, across the holy fields of Russian literature. And then there had been the prolonged, deliciously drowsy wait for the journal's actual publication and arrival. (None of the pleasures of publication approach the pleasure of anticipating publication.)

Still buoyed by relief, I turned to the mail that had accumulated on my desk in the previous few days. There was some union business—applications for membership and information about a forthcoming musical program dedicated to a visiting Malaysian playwright—as well as a personal letter from a family friend and a large gray envelope that contained, I knew at a glance, a manuscript from some provincial literary aspirant. I received envelopes of this kind not infrequently and considered the thoughtful reading of their contents an obligation incurred by my profession as well as by my office. My own literary career had begun with a similar packet addressed to Boris Sorokin. I cut open the large envelope and shook out onto the desk a spill of onion skin.

The cover letter contained a few comments about my most recent novel that were perceptive in their artfully offhanded approval. I brought the paper to my face, but the only perfume was the ink's. Sometimes ambitious female writers sent their photographs; Marina Burchatkina hadn't, so I assumed that she was plain. I wasn't disappointed. Already the caress of her praise had produced the accustomed tingling along the insides of my thighs, a quickening of my appetite. If she were plain, I could at least be assured that my response to her work would be based on its merit.

Her letter stated that she was a schoolteacher in Kaluga and had contributed a number of items to a vaguely familiar provincial youth magazine. She asked if perhaps, "respected comrade," I would advise her, on the basis of these stories and poems, whether she should continue her literary pursuits.

I returned the manuscript to the envelope, which I slid into a drawer for later reading, but curiosity prevented me from releasing my grip on it. I pulled out the manuscript. Never did I open an envelope from a novice writer without the trembling hope that it contained something wonderful, something that would change my life or the course of Russian literature. I had yet to be rewarded for this expectation, which I sustained for its evidence of my idealism and open-mindedness. Even today, I pick through the most obscure and irregularly published journals looking for a miracle.

A minute swept away that morning's millennial hopes. Marina had sent me three short stories and a sheaf of poetry, forgettable even now after all that's happened. I remember only my response: a headshake and a dull, leaden feeling. Her work was not as poor as other *samotyok* that had "self-flowed" onto my desk. She had a competent command of the language, but it was put to use for nothing original and certainly nothing urgent. Mired deep within the then loosely watched borders of conventional

socialist realism, the stories were predictable and unper-
suasive. Some of the poems simply failed to scan.

Fortunately for Marina, enough of my good mood remained to compose a few words of mild encouragement.
I rolled a sheet of paper into the typewriter. I told her
that I appreciated her comments about my novel and
was touched by her decision to turn to me for advice. I
commended her careful use of language and her obvi-
ously heartfelt sentiments. All true. And then I advised
her as I would have advised the most inarticulate and il-
literate of aspirants and what I advised myself when my
own work faltered: keep writing.

Three

Of course, it was not only ghosts that stalked the halls of
Vorovskovo, 52. There were corporeal informers and professional eavesdroppers or, to put it more benignly, people
whom we would simply prefer not have auditing our conversations. Viktor's nod had reminded me, as I needed to
be reminded from time to time, that the union was an instrument of the state. It was closely monitored by several
organs of the state, including the Committee for State
Security—that is, the KGB—and the Party. Indeed, several
high-ranking members of the Secretariat passing through
the narrow hallways also held rank in the KGB, and others owed their official positions to inclusion on the
Party's or the KGB's *nomenklatura* lists. This infiltration
was ubiquitous throughout Soviet society. As if placed
in a room with two bright lamps, each organization or

government agency cast a pair of shadows; one belonged to the Party and the other to the security forces.

On the Rostov mansion's polished parquet floors, there were many places where the penumbras of these shadows overlapped. Various union secretaries, section secretaries, deputies, and other officials openly served more than one master. Many of them did it with a grace that lent them authority and propriety. Boris Sorokin was a fixture at Party congresses, where he lectured the delegates on the importance of providing the resources to maintain high literary output. Kind, garrulous Viktor Ilyin, the Moscow branch's organizational secretary, was a former lieutenant general in the KGB, with whom he kept close ties. It was presumed that even Darya Sergeyevna, the stout old lady who had been watching our coats since Gorky's time, castigating us for being underdressed and prescribing home remedies when, as a consequence of our defiance, we became ill, kept a tally of our comings and goings, and especially who with.

The shadows overlapped across our desks. The rank and file never forgot that a full literary career outside the union was impossible: nonunion writers without registered employment risked prosecution as "social parasites." All of us knew our responsibilities as Soviet writers. We had private and public selves. Writing was the work of the public self.

The year-long repairs of the café downstairs ended with it unpainted. The café reopened anyway and after the first weekend a number of comic and obscene graffiti

marked the walls. They were brought to the attention of
Konstantin Fedin, the union's first secretary, who furiously swore he would catch and punish the perpetrators.
Before that could happen, some anonymous hero painted
over the evidence with a copse of graceful palm trees.
Afterwards it was allowed that other writers could add to
the landscape "in a tasteful way," and soon the walls were
covered with more palm trees, Gaugin-esque girls in
straw skirts, dragons, flying fish, and gentle, hilarious
caricatures of our most easily caricatured colleagues.
More than one observer commented that we made better
artists than writers, a remark that seemed less amusing
when Valery Schenëv mordantly responded, "Yes, that is
fair, since the members of the artists' union are better
writers." Indeed, the artists' union, much more political
than the writers' union, was currently consuming itself
with petitions and tracts.

I laid a brush to the middle of the wall closest to the
kitchen and when I pulled it away there remained the
image of a naked, round-faced woman, angelic in her demeanor, her torso almost entirely obscured by tomatoes,
green pepper plants, vines, and a tottering stack of
books. At the woman's shoulder, incompetently foreshortened so that it appeared to be resting on it, was balanced a small, uneven wooden house, our dacha. I
suffered a number of comments about being either so
sentimental or so guilty that I would paint my own wife.

I don't make any claims for the painting's artistic
merit, but I liked it anyway, for its lushness, for its appe-
tizing, perfectly round tomatoes, and for my wife. The

painting was indeed sentimental: the one or two square
meters that it occupied was a map of idealization. I'm
told it remains on the café wall to this day.

My wife Lydia was from the country, a small town in
central Russia, and never seemed to forgive the circum-
stances (admission to the philology department of
Moscow State University) that had brought her to
Moscow. She hated the motor traffic, she hated the
noise, and most of all she hated the food, the dearth of
fresh vegetables and fruit even in summer and their
tinned replacements all year round, the factory chickens,
the pale, tasteless cellulose-stuffed bread and the fatty,
rancid meat. She called it food for slaves. She had hardly
less disdain for the union food packages, containing otherwise impossible-to-get delicacies, that I brought home
from Yeliseyev's Gastronom. Shortly after we married
she established a garden on our fifth-floor balcony. The
balcony was almost always in shade and hardly anything
grew there save her resentment. I could watch her from a
window in my study as she crouched at the root of a
sickly vine, tapping the soil, muttering incantations.
Then she would shake her head, give the root a parting
touch, and go back to her book.

Lydia's passion for reading, her wanton surrender to
an author, was the sexiest thing about her. Embracing a
book, she was completely vulnerable to the author's ad-
vances. She would accept any indignity, swallow any lie,
and remain constant in the face of the author's infidelities
and depravities. Regardless of the wattage of the light
above her head, she gave the text the firm grip of her attention. She was always missing her metro station, even

when she read standing, wedged between the other passengers. Sometimes the text was my own. In the hours when I knew she was reading my work, I lived a kind of distracted half-life, as I imagined the play of my words against her retinae.

One evening earlier that summer, like a gladiator approaching the tribune with booty, I had swaggered into our flat and announced that we had been given the right to rent a small union dacha in Peredelkino, the writers' settlement just outside Moscow. I had expected to be tattooed with kisses, but Lydia was too surprised to even congratulate me. As she stood in the kitchen, tears welling in her eyes, I realized that I hadn't fully gauged the weight of despair that she had accumulated living here in the city.

Even though the hour was late and the juices of a roast were bubbling in the oven, she demanded that we inspect the property right away. By *elektrichka* from the Kiev Station the village was a half hour's journey. In that time she hardly spoke, as if fearing to break the spell. The house was located about two kilometers from the train stop, a distance we covered nearly on a run. We arrived during the prolonged twilight, the shadows long and diffuse, the birds childishly atwitter about their late bedtimes.

The dacha was small, but it was a dacha nonetheless, a wooden, two-room house sitting on a small plot of land and encroached by vines and juniper bushes. The overgrowth made it impossible to see our neighbors, even though they were less than twenty meters away on either side of us. An outdoor dinner party unwound somewhere and a woman's laugh was close enough to promise that I might someday know it intimately. Our dacha possessed neither indoor plumbing nor telephone, but it had a stove and was comfortably laid out and clean. From the porch I watched Lydia till some soil with her foot, testing it.

"No chickens," I declared.

She turned and gazed at me as if I were mad, the mad tsar issuing an ukase to his tenth-of-an-hectare kingdom.

"I'm sorry, but it just won't do," I said. "This is a writers' settlement."

She scowled. "You've never had a real egg, that's your problem."

We moved in the following day and at once set to work clearing the refuse, broken bottles, and abandoned building materials that were scattered in the underbrush. After marking out a rectangle at the side of the house, Lydia laid down a thick layer of fresh topsoil that had been procured at great expense from a truck driver who worked in a nearby kolkhoz. It was already too late in the year to plant anything but lettuce, dill, parsley, and sorrel.

I hardly accomplished any literary work the remainder of that month. Moving into the dacha, as modest as it was, occupied the sum of our energies and imaginations. The first morning I woke in the straw-filled dacha bed, I lay for hours looking up through the square of sky unevenly partitioned by the trunk of a birch tree and believed that I loved the birch as much as I loved life itself. This was not the manifestation of anything as simple as a love of nature. The allocation of this dacha was an enormous professional success, as much as the publication of my first book.

On a pleasant summer weekend, when things were good, Lydia and I would stroll hand in hand down the lanes, blowing cigarette smoke over the hedges of the residences of our greatest writers. On wide Serafimovicha, Korney Chukovsky lived in a yellow-and-brown house with a veranda on which he read his verse and Whitman's to the neighborhood children. A few blocks away, Zinaida Nikolayevna, Pasternak's widow, was living out her last days in their round, wooden dacha. From the street, one could see into Pasternak's upstairs study and, through the line of unshuttered windows, the woods behind the house. Zinaida Nikolayevna's immediate neighbors were, on one side, Mayakovsky's former lover Lily Brik and, on the other, Pasternak's friend and persecutor, Konstantin Fedin.

Each dacha was like a book, in that it represented an author. But there were many more variations among Soviet dachas than there were among Soviet books. Some were located on large grounds and were cottages of more than one story, others were rusticated gingerbread shacks, some were constructed on an individual plan, and many more were built according to a standard design—and each variation spoke of the inhabitants' literary success, productivity, social standing, and political reliability.

Most dachas were owned outright, not rented, by writers who claimed achievements greater than my two novels. I would be reminded of this every month when I paid Litfond, the union's social welfare agency, for the vouchers that I would then give to another clerk in the same office—a pointless, time-consuming task that satisfied somebody somewhere that the capitalist practice of

"renting" had been subverted. The vouchers were not in-
expensive, but Lydia took on some lucrative translation
work and I augmented my schedule of well-paid "creative trips" that brought literary programs to provincial
audiences.

Lydia had immediately declared her intention to spend
every remaining week of the summer in Peredelkino, and
that was fine with me. Accompanied by dozens of other
husbands, I took the train out every Friday evening,
bringing my manuscript and two or three books or
"thick" journals for Lydia. The husbands would return
on Monday morning, looking forward to hot showers in
our newly roomy flats and the capital's parties and romantic intrigues.

We had many friends living in the village. That summer we attended parties extending well into the following morning, parties of great mirth and good feeling,
and I felt more a member of the literary fraternity than
I had ever felt before or have since. Even Lydia enjoyed
these revels, displaying a degree of ease that I had not
witnessed since the earliest days of our marriage. As late
summer gave way to mushroom season, the fungal
equinox, she put off her return to the city.

On the Saturday morning after I met with Viktor, I
woke late and found Lydia reading outside on the porch
swing, her bare legs folded beneath her. Transfixed by
type, she didn't look up. I kissed the back of her neck, recalling that we had made love on the swing the night before. She mumbled something. I made some Nescafé and
watched her read. When she turned the page at the end

of the chapter, I said, "By the way, I signed that petition after all."

She looked up, her eyes unfocused.

I made an elaborate flourish in the air. *"J'ai signé cette pétition-là.* You know, Misha Vishnevsky. They've put him in a psychiatric hospital."

"You signed it!" She appeared surprised.

"I told you I might. It was under discussion, remember? You didn't give me advice either way."

"I said that it wasn't going to do any good."

"That's not advice. Some actions are morally correct even if they have no practical consequences."

"You mean, if you'd like to make a grand gesture."

She had put down her book and had raised and turned herself in the swing, unconsciously choosing the position in which I had penetrated her. I smiled at the recollection.

"All right, so let's say it's a grand gesture. That what's happening now, grand gestures in defense of liberalization. You're right, individually it's not going to have any effect, Vishnevsky will never be freed. But look, we're trying to overcome this monumental legacy of Stalinism. We can't oppose the hard-liners head-on, there's too many of them, but we can reach and persuade high-ranking people in the union and the Party. There are some honest and decent men."

"It's only politics, Rem. You sound like a politician."

"If there's a protest this time, the hard-liners will think twice the next."

"That's something Panteleyev told you," she guessed,

correctly. "Why should they think twice, if there are no practical consequences from the first protest or from any of the others?"

I frowned. I hadn't expected this opposition and hadn't prepared any arguments.

"Let me put it another way," I said. "There's a man. As we argue now in the cool autumn air, surrounded by greenery, he's imprisoned in a so-called psychiatric institution, out of contact with his family, lost to the world. In our own country! Viktor has evidence that he's being tortured and pumped full of drugs—not to cure him of any supposed psychosis, but to induce psychosis. This is being done on behalf of our government and on behalf of a Party claiming to advance the interests of the people. Doesn't that anger you?"

"Do you know this man? Why do you care?"

"It's a writer's duty to imagine other people and sympathize with their situation," I insisted, shaking my head. I looked at a pile of books alongside the swing, just as I had painted it on the wall of the café, and then through the open door at the library that had mysteriously arisen in the front room, like an Inca city in the jungle. Where had all these books come from? I had hardly noticed an attenuation in the thick growth of literature that covered the walls of our flat. "In fact, I would think it's a human duty. I don't understand." I waved at the new library. "What's the point of all these books if they have no impact on your life?"

"But they do."

"They *don't!*" I raised my voice. "They're all about the world and the society you disdain. The characters of the best of them are deeply involved in human life, they're men and women challenged by imperative moral questions, by history, and by the defects of their own personalities. Reading them, you should be moved to reexamine your own character, to question your involvement in society, to act."

She snorted. "Spoken like a Bolshevik. That's not why I read. I'm sick to death of literature as medicine, literature as therapy, literature as politics, literature as the beacon of mankind. I couldn't care less what writers say about the so-called world. Why should they know more about it than I do? Does anyone really believe that a writer, by virtue of his profession, is honest or compassionate or even intelligent? Look at the lives of most writers, the best writers, they're scoundrels and hypocrites. Start with Saint Leo. Why should his view on moral issues be instructive? And the proof of this is in the readers. Are they usually kinder than nonreaders? More moral? Are they more successful at life?"

"I'm not talking about moral instruction, Lydia. A good writer, no matter how much a fool he is otherwise, will place his characters in situations in which their actions have moral consequence. Can't you then, as a reader, imagine yourself in such a situation and learn from it?"

"What a writer says about a particular situation is irrelevant. I care only about how he says it. Style is everything, style *is* content. I don't read Gogol because I have an interest in the depressed state of the landed gentry in provincial Russia of the nineteenth century, or Victor Hugo from an interest in Gothic architecture or Nabokov from an interest in pedophiles. It's their language I admire." She paused to collect her thoughts, speaking after a week virtually empty of conversation. "I don't mean that I simply admire their pretty metaphors. It's the words they choose, when they can choose perfectly good other words, the tone, their strategy for telling the story . . . The means by which they create the illusion of event arise from the convolutions of their individual genius. That's style. That's real art."

The reference to Nabokov stung. I had gone to some great lengths a few months earlier, incurring social debts that would take years to pay back, in order to obtain a British copy of *Lolita* for her.

Lydia asked, "Have you read Vishnevsky's work? I have."

"You have?"

"*Burden of Blood. Across the Tundra.* They're mediocre books, more like tracts than novels, lots of cheap effects and jargon. Also, they're wordy, mean-spirited, chauvinistic, perhaps even anti-Semitic."

I shrugged. "So, he's a bad writer. Bad writers deserve human sympathy too," I said, but I wished Lydia had told me about his work the week before. "And they're citizens just as much as good writers, and they deserve to be treated under the law. Viktor says the authorities have violated their own procedures and decrees."

"Viktor Panteleyev, the noted legal scholar."

I sat down heavily on the swing, spilling some of my coffee. Lydia stretched her bare legs on my lap and I ran my fingers over them.

"Anyway," I said. "This is a small thing. You're right,

it's a gesture. There's dozens of petitions flying about
and they're all being ignored."

Four

I never took note of the arrival of Marina Burchatkina's
second package, though if my memory has correctly ordered the sequence of events, the manuscript must have
arrived sometime early the following year. As I inspected
the return address, several moments passed before I disentangled Marina's name from those of other provincial
writers who had contacted me recently, as well as Kaluga
from Kalchuga, Kalino, and Kalashnikovo. These had
been months of tumescent expectation. Like worms after
a spring rain, would-be writers were squirming up out
of the soil, clutching accounts of Stalinist repression,
famine, and war. Some of these works reached print; all
of them, I presume, reached the KGB. Most were poorly
done, but their quantity testified to an enormous and
somewhat premature national effort to reclaim the
country's memory. As for our petition on behalf of Misha
Vishnevsky, there had been no action taken or any response at all. It was as if we had set it afire and sent the
smoke to the gods. I had no further discussions about
the petition, not even with Viktor. Viktor was becoming
a strange man. I had seen him last at a party, in a dim
corner by himself, brooding into a glass of Johnnie
Walker.

It appeared that Marina had occupied the intervening period in a frenzy of literary activity. What was now

deposited on my desk were no mere poems, but entire poem cycles. Plus there was an epic poem (about the siege of Leningrad) and a ballad (about what, I wasn't sure). The contents of this envelope were in no way an improvement over the first, but the cover letter was more peculiar and more original than anything contained in her rhymes. Marina thanked me. She wrote that in the weeks before she received my letter she had become desperate about her future as a writer. My gratifying remarks had given her new inspiration: every night, when she began to write, she taped the letter to the inside of the door to her communal apartment's pantry. She took it down when she was done. She wrote every night, in her nightclothes, at a folding table in the space made when the door was swung open.

I hadn't saved a carbon of my amazing, inspiring letter to Marina. I wondered if I had confused the bland letter I recalled sending with one to another correspondent, but as I examined this possibility I became convinced that I had not. The evidence was her letter itself, specifically her gush. I suspected that my enthusiasm was a crafty fiction, which she had invented to implicate me in her career. Perhaps she thought I wouldn't remember what I had written. And there was a small flirtation here as well: the invitation to imagine her writing at her table.

"Hey, old man, got a minute?"

Anton Basmanian had poked his head through my door, affecting a familiarity we didn't share. An old schoolmate, he was now the editor of a small literary magazine that made a feeble attempt at liberal fashion.

"For you, two minutes." I lay my watch on the table.

"Nice piece of work in *Literaturnaya Gazeta*," he said, referring to an article of mine the week before. He beamed. "Very nice."

I didn't reply at once. Basmanian had violated an unspoken rule of the professional writer: don't compliment another's work, at least not casually. It was all right, of course, to praise work in a written article, or in a symposium, or even in a serious critical conversation with the author. But we took our labors too seriously to have them evaluated like a haircut or a new tie. We all knew that praise could be too easily given and too easily overvalued; it became then just another soft currency.

"Thank you, Anton. How have you been?"

"No, I thank *you*. Very subtle piece of criticism, but it'll be understood in the right places."

It took me a few moments to figure out what he was talking about. The article had been a general appraisal of current Georgian cinema, based on a week's gloriously bacchanalian stay in Tbilisi. Then I recalled that my review had in passing praised the film *My Father's Orchard*, which was loosely based on some stories by Elgudzhi Piranishvili. Piranishvili had written a bruising attack on the critic Mustai Suleimenov in *Novy Mir* just a few months earlier. This had come, allowing for publication delays, immediately after Suleimenov had blistered Fazil Iskander, who was frequently published in Anton's journal. Sides were being taken. I had somehow blundered into a literary intrigue that, given the number of Caucasians involved, would probably send my great-grandchildren into hiding sometime in the next century. I looked for a way to ease out of the conversation.

"Here's some poems," I said, pushing the manuscript across the desk. "Tell me what you think of them."

"Marina Burchatkina. Who is she?"

"Some lady in Kaluga. She writes prose too, stories."

The quality of his smile changed, showing his nearly radioactive white teeth. The smile was both predatory and congratulatory. At the same time, the image of the poet in her nightclothes penetrated my imagination. The flirtation hit home.

"I've never met her," I said at once. "She just sent this to me. If you don't care for it, fine. You can dispose of it."

Five

From that winter (or was it another?) I remember great gusts of wind spraying loose snow up Moscow's icy streets, blowing off hats and freezing the trolley tracks and tram lines. Through the twilight weeks and months of sub-zero temperature, Lydia remained at the dacha, reading under a sixty-watt bulb by the stove, eating macaroni and the vegetables and fruit she had conserved, plus whatever I managed to bring in from the city. Because of the weather and various commitments, some of which were frankly unburdensome, I couldn't make the journey to Peredelkino every weekend, but she didn't seem to mind my absence or in any way suffer her solitude. She made the acquaintance of her neighbors, mostly the straw-whiskered parents of our literary lions, so she wasn't entirely alone. She raised her head from her books from time to time, I surmised, and gazed through the frosted window pane at the babushkas as they trudged in felt boots through the snow, pulling their groceries and firewood on sleds. When I arrived at the dacha, Lydia and I would mostly talk about what we had been reading. She had no interest in gossip from the city, not even when it involved authors whose work she knew intimately. She hardly showed more interest in my occasional and grossly minimized confessions of marital misconduct, except to the extent that it distracted me from my work.

In the afternoons she led me on walks along the village's icy, rutted streets, and then into the woods on skis, though we rarely got very far before she stopped to investigate some tree stump or burrow. She marveled at the signs of life submerged within the brittle, unmoving landscape: moss on the underside of a rock, a rodent's tracks, a deer's scat, a momentary rustling in the underbrush. The burrows were her favorite sites of investigation. She learned to recognize which animal sheltered within each hole and, more interestingly for her, how recently it had emerged to forage. There were two sides to the woods and it was the unseen one, in wary repose, that carried on life from one year to the next. A creek was interrupted by a sloppy, half meter's fall, at the bottom of which was a pool cloudy with tiny iridescent fish. Lydia gazed into the super-cooled water while I stamped my skis for warmth and made grunting sounds in favor of moving on.

It occurred to me that Lydia might have taken a lover here in Peredelkino, an eventuality that I did not welcome but had in any event prepared myself for. Turnabout was fair play and all that, especially after Tbilisi.

On my return trips to Moscow, I tallied the likely candidates among the village's permanent residents, the ones into whose arms she might that very moment be flinging herself after a weekend's forced separation, and concluded with a very short list. In winter the village was populated by few men of an appropriate age or suitable social background.

I resolved to keep an eye on these three or four hypothetical swains, but the more I dwelled upon them, the less likely the liaisons seemed. There were much younger girls available, and Lydia had never been a flirt, and these guys worked too hard anyway, which is why they lived year round in the village. But rather than take comfort in the deduced proof of her constancy, I became increasingly worried for her. My wife's emotional life was contracting. How could she not be lonely? Was literature and nature sustenance enough?

There had been a time, even before I set out as a writer, when I had believed that it was. As a schoolboy, I had daydreamed of Alpine monasteries and tropical islands provided with nothing but great books. This fantasy was the strongest and most maddening when I was in the army, serving out my conscription in the Turkmen desert and surrounded by men of such low intelligence and negligible curiosity that they were barely more than machines for eating and shitting. After using a month's salary to ransom a secondhand edition of *In Search of Lost Time* from the depredations of an Ashkhabad bookshop, I conspired to obtain two weeks of duty in a remote, vacant guardhouse. The job required nothing but my presence. I had already inspected the building: The unpainted room I would inhabit was clean, warm, and well lit. There was a bed and a desk.

By the second day, by the time Marcel had witnessed the duchess in the chapel of Gilbert the Bad, I was defeated, unable to turn another page. The guardhouse's low concrete ceiling hardly allowed me room to breathe, and I was tortured by a single fly orbiting a bare lightbulb on the other side of the room. Nor could I bear another lap around the muddy meadow outside the guardhouse. I was beset with doubts about my character and identity. To my piercing horror, I now believed that I didn't care to read after all. My literary enthusiasm was no more than an affectation, common to "sensitive" adolescents. The brutes in my company were my real friends, my real brothers. The remainder of the two weeks before I was returned to them seemed as vast as the desert itself. I discovered in myself an enormous capacity for sleep and masturbation.

I eventually returned to Proust, of course, not in a quiet season, but rather in a year of loss and upheaval, when I changed flats and jobs in quick succession and when the connections between one day and the next seemed as tenuous as the skin on the surface of a bowl of pudding. Although my daily ration of reading was limited to a few labyrinthine paragraphs at bedtime, consumed in rough living quarters amid unfriendly strangers, the events in Combray and Faubourg St. Germain never lost their narrative continuity. My conquest of the novel set a pattern for my reading throughout my adult life, all of which seemed to have been caught on the fly.

Although I regretted my chaotic reading and writing

habits, I could never be satisfied with the life of the monkish intellectual. I needed the glitter of society and the refreshment of action. Yet at parties, surrounded by noise and dispute, I would be seized by the desire to return home at once, either to my typewriter or to that evening's book. One desire fed another. Consequently my favorite place to read was on the train, where the book trembled in my lap like a living thing and each page consumed another kilometer or two of track.

In similar regard, the union was the perfect place for me. I loved the unliterary busyness of it: the applications and other forms to be processed, the reports to be filed, and the many meetings to attend in chandeliered banquet rooms, all in the service of literature.

I read much and worked hard the first winter Lydia stayed at the dacha. It was also one of the most unsettling and gayest seasons of my life. Every night in Moscow there were sprawling, sloppy parties, often with marijuana, fisticuffs, foreign girls in miniskirts and vinyl boots, deadly serious political and literary arguments (I don't remember any of them), and, over and over without end, *Rubber Soul.* Many of the foreign girls I brought back to my flat couldn't read a word of Russian, but believed afterwards that they had become experts in contemporary Soviet literature.

And then spring arrived early, promising even more political freedom and travel. Friends went off to Paris and New York and came back agog. The gatherings moved out to Peredelkino, where they bloomed into lovely garden parties with even more foreigners. Lydia consented to attend these parties, chatting amiably with the visitors in their own languages and, in the garden, inspecting with an appreciative, critical eye every flower and plant. She appeared to have come out of the winter without ill effect to her humor or warmth.

My memory of all the parties I attended in Peredelkino have merged into a single gathering, which continued for days and was crammed with *scandale*. For the purposes of this recollection, I have located the *über*-party in Sasha Nasedkin's garden and peopled it with everyone I knew at the time, whether they were in Moscow then or not. The compact circle of chairs around the picnic table dreamily accommodates two hundred guests. Vasily Aksyonov tells a joke about Kosygin, Johnson, and de Gaulle in a leaky boat. Gavril Feldshteyn snaps down the hors d'oeuvres as if he hasn't eaten in a week, which is very likely nearly true. Yevgeny Yevtushenko, a dapper *bit-nik* in a black turtleneck, strenuously flirts with two flushed starlets. Apart from the group, over by the lindens, Vadim Surkov speaks with Lydia. Hello? I screw up my eyes. Surkov spent the winter in Peredelkino, just a few doors from Lydia, but I decide that the conversation is too easygoing for them to be sleeping with each other.

Meanwhile, morose and inattentive, Viktor downs one glass of vodka after another. His conjuration at the party is a bit of a stretch, since he hardly ever went out. He had nearly dropped from sight, though occasionally one heard reports of him emerging from a rain-soaked alley or from the most obscure and remote research rooms of the Lenin Library, always alone. When we occasionally crossed paths, his conversation became guarded and his look furtive. I would sense that I had interrupted a conversation that he was having with himself. At the section of the table where I have placed him, cozy between two women poets of advancing years, he has created a small disturbance, a tear in the social fabric, but the precise nature of his mutters remains beneath human hearing, which is lucky for him.

Six

A train was canceled, I missed my connection, and so I spent the better part of a day in an intermediate station, happily reading Beckett in a glassed-in waiting room perfumed by fresh flowers. By the time I reached Mtsensk, it was late in the afternoon. I was supposed to be met there by a representative of the collective farm that had invited me to read at a "literary evening," but no one was on the platform. I buttoned my jacket against the chill—in fact, it was a superb late-summer afternoon, the surrounding wheat fields incandescent—and stepped onto the gravel beside the station house. Parked there was a mud gray military vehicle covered in gray mud. A middle-aged man behind the wheel, his jaw slack and bristled white, stared directly ahead and took no notice of me.

"I'm Krilov."

The man responded with an almost imperceptible shrug. I went to the other side of the vehicle, a small UAZ truck with a torn canvas top. The door squealed as I opened it. A fecal, alcoholic odor spilled out. I could see the vodka bottle, not quite empty, wedged between the driver's seat and his door.

"Are you in any condition to drive?" I said.

He didn't reply. In any case, I myself couldn't drive. I climbed into the truck, taking care not to bump my head. He switched on the ignition and lurched us onto the road.

"How far?" I asked.

At last he spoke, in a sullen rasp. "Fifty-three."

We drove along a pitted road so straight that its end shimmered and dissolved in the distant haze. I rolled open the window, hung my face out into the passing air, and closed my eyes. The warmth of the setting sun was like a caress.

I usually enjoyed these so-called creative trips to the provinces. For one thing, the per diem for expenses negotiated by the union was usually far in excess of the expenses incurred. Less tangibly, visits from the capital were celebrated as important events in the provincial villages and kolkhozes, which often provided the guests with tours, lavish banquets, and introductions to admiring readers. Writers never tire of readers who admire them. I should have made the journey the night before with the other writers who had been invited, including Schenëv and Basmanian, but I had been delayed by union business. Now I would be lucky to arrive by the start of the evening's program.

I seemed to have left my luck in Moscow. A half hour across the featureless farmland, the driver abruptly pulled to the side of the road and shoved open his door, just catching the bottle as it fell. It was an agile gesture, probably well practiced. He followed it by heaving the contents of his guts onto the gravel. I looked away, but after he slammed shut the door, I became aware that he was wiping his mouth with his sleeve. The stink deepened.

He shifted into gear. As he gunned the engine, the truck jerked forward and fell back. Its engine stalled. I looked down at the wheels. They were mired in the soft, oily mud alongside the road. The driver didn't seem surprised. He put the gearshift back into neutral, stepped from the machine, and began shoving it from the rear. His grunts were arrhythmic and short winded. The truck rocked but remained in place.

I could have put my own shoulder to the back of the UAZ while he worked the gears. But he didn't ask for help and I would have refused him if he had. He groaned and the truck rocked again.

As the landscape bounced in the distance, I marveled at my spitefulness, which was only delaying my arrival at the kolkhoz. It burned in me like a flame. This man was the Russian peasant as he had been known for centuries, a creature of ignorance and superstition, servility and obstinacy, drunkenness and brutality. Fifty years of communism had hardly touched him any more than the previous efforts to reform and Europeanize our country. What could I say that might eventually move him to some awareness of his primitiveness and of his opportunity to escape it? What could I *write*? There was no guarantee that he even knew how to read.

After a quarter of an hour he succeeded in extricating us. The UAZ's front wheels rolled onto the pavement. His face was florid as he returned to the truck, but he made no comment. I looked across the borderless fields and imagined that I saw all the Asian continent before me; it held Muscovy with a gun to its head. We approached the kolkhoz just as night fell. The driver's stink had surely permeated my clothes, but I wouldn't have time to change them.

The UAZ entered a large unlit compound in which were located a number of nondescript but well-maintained agricultural buildings, including several stables. Farm equipment stood idle, as if on display. The compound's most prominent feature was the House of Culture, a white neo-neoclassical structure built from a design used in thousands of kolkhozes, villages, and provincial towns throughout the country. A series of concrete pillars carried the pediment. On it was inscribed a quotation illegible in the dark. I stepped from the machine and walked up to the silent building.

Neither door behind the columns would open. I turned and saw that the UAZ, whose engine had roared like a jet's all the way from the station, had left soundlessly and that now the compound was completely deserted, without even a chicken scratching in the gravel. The evening was calm and the first stars were visible over the purpling fields. I keenly felt my solitude and, even as the nightmarish thought that I had somehow come on the wrong night or even to the wrong kolkhoz slowly descended upon me, I enjoyed the quiet of the evening. I closed my eyes for a moment.

"Rem Petrovich!"

One of the doors had swung open without apparent human agency. I felt a blast of yeasty warmth and found myself at the back of a brightly lit auditorium. Hundreds of heads were turned in my direction. From nearly every face radiated a smile of welcome. As if in a trance, I stepped through the portal, past the shadowed, matronly sorceress who had invoked my name and patronymic.

Is there any question why I went on these trips? It was a full house—of readers, those dear, dear, hopeful, faithful readers, their eyes bright, their fingertips hungry for the touch of the page. Kerchiefed and capped heads testified to the universality of the respect with which literature was held in our country. Jackets and taffeta dresses in turn testified to its high honor. I glided down the aisle past rows of fresh-faced young men and cherry-lipped farm girls. Readers, readers all.

At the front of the room, beneath a red banner, a long dais was covered by a white tablecloth on which stood green bottles of mineral water and a vase of pink lilacs. Basmanian and Schenëv were there, along with a writer I didn't recognize. Another unfamiliar writer, a long-legged girl in her early twenties, stood in front of the table, reading at a battered iron lectern that appeared to date from the early, battered years of collectivization.

Lost in her own text, she was the last in the hall to become aware of my arrival. She was declaiming her words with great feeling and concentration, as if testing their sound against the walls of the auditorium. When she finally sensed the audience's distraction, she glanced up from the lectern and, with a suddenness that surprised us both, her pair of dark, ovaline eyes found mine. I momentarily faltered in my advance to the dais.

Then she glanced to her side at Anton, who had

displayed his full set of teeth at the moment he had seen
me. He said something, the soundless shadow of my
name, and then she too showed her teeth—but it was the
instant before she turned to him that continues to vi-
brate outside time. By some trick of the light or of that
sadistic joker, chance, we had caught each other un-
guarded. Now the girl offered me a smile that was both
warm and embarrassed.

I approached the front of the hall. "Forgive me for in-
terrupting you," I whispered. An empty chair waited for
me at the end of the dais. I kept my head down, as if not
to draw any further attention to myself.

The girl resumed reading. Still waking from the
dreamy confusion of my arrival, I gradually settled myself at the table. A tiled mosaic portrait of Lenin on the
left wall gazed upon a team of farm workers at harvest
on the right. The banner above our heads was stirred by
an unaccountable breeze. The girl, big boned like the
kolkhoz girls and in a plain brown dress, was reading
some prose, either a story or a memoir. I wasn't yet ready
to listen for its meaning, but the sound of her voice was
as deep and clear as a cistern, and in it I thought I heard a
familiar cadence.

She finished. It was now my turn. I removed a folder
of typed pages from my suitcase as the fat, nervous
kolkhoz chairman garbled the title of my first novel by
way of introduction. I replaced him at the lectern and
made a few humorous apologies about my late arrival
(while working in the book's correct title). The audience
laughed as easily as breaking a pane of glass, and in the

shards of laughter falling around me I recognized the girl's, glittering and sharp. And then I decided not to read from my recently published second novel, as I had planned: I would read from my third, still in progress. In the flush of creation, I believed it was the best thing I had ever written. Indeed, I believed it was the best thing *any-one* had ever written. Lately I had been carrying a few completed chapters in my briefcase, not so much to show other people, but as a talisman, a reminder of my talent. I now removed the manuscript from the folder.

Once I began my descent down the first page, I forgot the girl and the rest of the audience. I was the work's only reader, attentive and discerning, its perfect reader, and I thrilled to its broadcast over the hall's modest amplification system. The damn thing was brilliant; there were twists of plot and turns of language in it that surprised me as if I were reading it for the first time. When it was over, I looked up and nearly expected to be crushed by admirers.

I wasn't crushed. The audience remained in its seats and applauded, even enthusiastically, but not as enthusiastically, I thought, as it should have. A twinge of disappointment ran along the left side of my face.

It was only a brief sensation, for the program was ended and, after the kolkhoz chairman, clapping emphatically, shouted his thanks to us, the most appreciative fragments of the audience surged to the front of the hall. Several of the kolkhozniks clutched copies of my novels to be signed. Others crowded around my colleagues, including the girl, who seemed unprepared for the attention. I watched her while I attended to my readers. She had long, straight black hair and as she stooped to take in the words of her interlocutors, it fell across the side of her face. She scooped the hair away from her eyes, an annoyed but fetching gesture to be repeated several times within the minute.

As I signed the last book, the girl approached me, led by Anton. She was tall and moved with a slight deficit of grace that accentuated her physicality.

"I told you he'd make it," Anton said triumphantly.

The girl embraced my hands. Hers were warm and fleshy.

Anton said something by way of introduction. I didn't listen, I was weighing her hands and still considering what had been confessed and exchanged between us. She let my hands go. They remained in the air, buoyed by the remnant heat.

"Rem Petrovich," she murmured, her speaking voice softer and rounder than the one she had used to read her work. "Thank you for everything. None of this would have happened without you."

Anton said, "In September we're publishing two stories and eight poems. They're going to make an impact, Rem. Everyone at the journal is looking forward to it."

"Kaluga," I muttered to myself, the light flicking on at last.

Marina Burchatkina continued to gaze at me with a solar warmth. But then she squeezed Anton's arm. This caused a corresponding compression around my chest. To think what I had done, the promises I had made, the lies I had told, the imbroglios in which I had involved myself, the embarrassments I had suffered, and the pain I had visited upon others, only recently, to sleep with girls half as attractive! I had to look away.

There was a banquet later that evening, the second in as many days, accompanied by toasts in praise of ourselves and our literary forebears, and presentations of the local wine and kolkhoz-made cheeses. It was all very nice—the apparently oafish kolkhoz chairman turned out to be a raconteur and a lover of good literature—but all the while I kept my eye on the girl. She seemed preoccupied. So did Basmanian sitting at her left. I suspected that they were playing footsie beneath the linen tablecloth. Later, in my spartan room in the administration building, an acrid, pale yellow cloud lowered upon me.

Later that year, I saw Marina and Anton together several times in the union café, once at a concert, and at any number of parties. At one of the parties, Anton momentarily disentangled himself from his protégée and approached me.

"Rem, she's enchanting. I owe you one."

"Shit," I said. "You owe me a *dozen.*"

That autumn Marina's work was published in Anton's journal and I studied it, trying to discern those qualities that I had overlooked in my first reading. I sought to approach her stories and poetry with neither the negative prejudice of having already read and dismissed them nor

the positive one produced by their appearance in print.
I was keenly aware that publication adds luster to a work;
a manuscript comes to you stark naked.

But true literature always showed. When I was young,
I wondered if my stories seemed jejune and awkward
only because I was reading them in my own notebook, in
my own clumsy, heavy-footed hand. As an experiment, I
had copied "The Captain's Daughter" into my own notebook, hoping to see it diminished. But before I had completed even the first paragraph, I felt Pushkin's power
flowing in a rush through my arm and the clench of my
fingertips. The words blazed onto the faintly ruled paper.
After the first page, although the results of the experiment were conclusive, I could not resist copying the story
to the very end, merely for the pleasure of witnessing the
words of a genius emerge from under the nub of my pen.

Conversely, ten-point Pragmatica on heavy stock did
not transform Marina's work into something of significant literary value. As poor as it was, the work was not a
particularly freakish inclusion in a literary journal. Every
year the journals printed a fair amount of garbage, either
for political or personal considerations, or simply through
errors of judgment. Although theory held that editors
were bound by the decisions of their editorial boards, in
practice they could publish whatever they wished, and
Goskomizdat guaranteed that a certain number of copies
would be printed. (Goskomizdat also set quotas for pulp-
ing.) One could usually guess the reasons behind a poor
writer's success. Anton escorted Marina around town all
that autumn and winter, basking in the heat of her beauty.

I heard that they were sent together on a "literary youth" junket to Tashkent, her first airplane flight, and never emerged from his hotel room, not even for the gala Uzbek national folk program.

I passed the journal to Lydia and asked her to read Marina's stories and poems.

"Garbage," she announced afterwards.

"Thank you," I said, and kissed her hard on the lips, more emphatically than I had intended to.

She raised her eyebrows.

"Are there any other stories that you would like me to tell you are garbage?"

Later that year, I heard that Marina had submitted a novel to the Sovremennik publishing house, which agreed to bring it out in the spring. Was this Anton's doing? I hadn't believed that his influence extended that far. Was she sleeping with someone at Sovremennik? Who? Or was the novel genuinely good? As Lydia contentedly endured her second winter in Peredelkino, I waited for Marina's first novel with deepening anticipation.

I saw her quite often, at parties and literary affairs, and each time she embraced me warmly. We met in a corridor of the Rostov mansion one evening. Her body pressed against mine a second longer than necessary and I was fully immersed in the nimbus of her perfume.

"Kaluga," I murmured as she slowly disengaged herself.

"Have you been there?"

"I haven't had the pleasure."

"I've moved to Moscow, you know."

There was a rising note of triumph in her voice. It was not easy to get a Moscow residence permit.

"Your own flat?"

"I share it with two girls. But I have my own room. I'm not writing in the pantry anymore."

"Mmmmm," I said, pretending to recall her letter only with difficulty. Then I gave up the pretense and ventured, "And not in your pajamas?"

Her face lit at my concession.

"Sometimes I do," she said.

"They'll be famous pajamas someday."

"And you?"

"I wear a shirt and tie when I write. I like to look my best when I meet the Muse. Of course, I'm sure the Muse is pleased with your pajamas."

"They're nothing special. You'll have to judge for yourself."

When she smiled, her mouth opened, almost carnivorously, it seemed to me. I wondered if she wrote with such heat, by herself, at her desk, in her pajamas. I could hardly bear to look into her face. In the glistening of the saliva on her teeth, I found a world-consuming avidity.

"Sure," I said, backing away.

"Yes."

"I'll come to the opening of the Marina Burchatkina House-Museum."

Her smile cooled. She thought I was a coward. I was.

"I promise," I said, turning to go to my office. "Your desk. Your writing implements. Your first editions. Your pajamas. I look forward to it."

Seven

Because of her later celebrity, Marina Burchatkina looms large in this account, giving the impression that she figured large in my otherwise uneventful life. In fact, this was an extraordinarily busy and creative time for me. My third novel was nearing completion and Lydia was among those who had read sections of it and offered warm praise. Although I retained my snug and noisy office, my position in the union Secretariat improved. I won a trip to London as the more advantageous part of a cultural exchange. In Hyde Park one summer afternoon, on a bench near the Peter Pan statue, I lounged with the sun in my face and about ten shillings in my pocket and daydreamed about quietly defecting to Never-Never Land. I couldn't, of course, but the thought effervesced through the remainder of my days and nights there.

Shortly after my return, in the early morning hours reserved for crises and bad news, the telephone rang. As I staggered into the hall and reached for the receiver, I was surprised by the number of alternatives of bad news that were possible. When I heard the high-pitched, quavering voice of Natalya Fyodorovna, Boris Sorokin's wife, I assumed he was dead.

The story she told was complicated, lousy with red herrings and switchbacks. There had been an incident during the night. Sorokin had woken and claimed to be suffocating, and then to be suffering from a thirst of Saharan proportions, and as Natalya Fyodorovna rushed about to satisfy his various demands, he had fallen from his bed. But the ambulance had come right away, that was the most important thing, she insisted, consoled. I gradually came to appreciate that Sorokin was not dead, but rather, creating more complications, critically ill.

In the taxi on the way to the Ochakovskoye Shosse and the landscaped complex in which Central Committee Clinic 2 was located, I hardly thought of Sorokin. I was thinking mostly of my own life, particularly of how this dash to the hospital was one I would never make on behalf of my father. He was already dead, killed during the war by a sniper in the Carpathian foothills. This sour reflection led to a well-trodden memory, the orphanage in Tomsk to which I had been evacuated with my sister in 1942. My mother had worked in a munitions plant, performing too important a job to be evacuated with us. The walls of the orphanage were lime green and always damp to the touch; the curve of my metal meal dish was broken by a dent that evoked the contours of some foreign coast; I was savagely beaten by boys slightly larger than me, until my face was a mass of tears and blood, and I in turn beat those slightly smaller; by the end of the war my sister was somewhere else, apparently unrecoverable even by the massive investigative machinery of the Soviet state. I remained immersed in the din of war and turmoil through my early life, even after I was reunited with my mother. It was not until I sent Sorokin some prose sketches of Moscow, thereby winning an invitation to be interviewed about my prospects for a literary career, that I began my adult, postwar existence.

So, I arrived to think of Sorokin after all. He was a tough old bastard, one of the founders of the Russian Association of Proletarian Writers, the revolutionary precursor to the present-day Union of Soviet Writers. After publishing nearly a dozen books in the 1920s and '30s, he had established his literary reputation in the strife of the following decade. His four-volume collection of war reporting, which had taken him from Stalingrad to Berlin, was still celebrated as a model of literary journalism. Sorokin had sponsored my first publication and had brought me into the Secretariat. He was a gruff and distant man who never displayed pride in my accomplishments, yet his suggestions about the course of my work and my life had always been deeply considered.

The air of his hospital room was sweet with disinfectant. The bright early morning sun fell upon the heavy curtains, leaving the room submerged in an underwater darkness. Membership in the writers' union gave you admittance to any of the union's special polyclinics; rank won you a private room in Central Committee Clinic 2 and the best medical care in the Soviet Union outside, well, Clinic 1. Sorokin lay on his back, gently stirred by the tides and deep currents. I assumed he was sleeping. I turned to go, embarrassed to be catching him unawares.

"She called you?"

Illness had not lowered the deep register of his voice, but it seemed hollowed out, nearly weightless. I didn't immediately find my own voice.

"Just an hour ago. I came down right away."

"I told her to call you. She thinks I'm going to die—"

"No—"

"The doctors do too. But they're a bunch of incompetents, hacks. You know, 2 was a good hospital once, before everything in this country fell apart."

And that was all that was said for several minutes. Sorokin had always been a big man and in the last few years his body had become swollen and bloated, so that now it was barely contained by the hospital bed and its swathe of sheets. His bald head was like a great stone outcropping, a grim, lifeless rock that rose into view to daunt approaching travelers. He had not yet been shaved or bathed. The excess flesh around his chest and neck spilled from the top of his hospital gown, which, draped on his torso, carried the charge of intimate apparel. In all the years that I had known Sorokin, I had never seen him outside his suit, not even in the garden of his dacha, nor even at his granddaughter's first birthday party. He appeared to have fallen asleep, but I remained at his side, trying to ignore the chill in my gut.

"I was in London," I said at last, softly so as not to wake him.

"I know."

"I liked it."

"Of course you did," he said, dismissively. "How's Lydia?"

"Fine. She's at the dacha. She's translating André Malraux."

A grunt rose from deep within Sorokin's body, from as deep as his bowels. "A prick, a real social democratic prick. Who commissioned it?"

"*Novy Mir.*"

"Tvardovsky has his head up his ass," he muttered, naming the journal's editor. "She should get paid on acceptance. Don't count on publication. Malraux, what a prick."

The odor of his contempt lingered. After a while, I said in a hopeful voice, "My novel's going well. I'm almost done with the first draft. When you're ready, I'd like you to read it. It'll be a success, I think."

"Good," he said.

"I've already talked to Yegor Nikitin. He'll be my editor. He's very enthusiastic. He's even showed Mosfilm the outline."

"Make sure they pay. Don't let them dick you."

I laughed nervously. I'd always been hopeless about money, and Sorokin knew it. Thank God I had the union to protect my interests.

"They won't dick me," I promised. "I expect a good contract. I'd like to build a proper dacha."

Sorokin considered this. He knew better than I did how much I could hope to get for the book and the film rights and how much a dacha would cost.

"All right," he said at last. "Get the money. When you're ready, I'll go with you to Litfond. I know a piece of property, a few blocks from our place. It's right at the edge of the forest. It's not planned for development, I've been holding it back. Just let me know when you're ready."

"Boris Stepanovich, thank you . . ." I stammered.

For the next forty awkward minutes, I made pleasantries, told Aksyonov's joke about the leaky boat, and elaborated upon some union gossip and intrigue. As I left, Sorokin's promise continued to reverberate through me. I knew the piece of property to which he referred. A ski trail ran along its edge, there was a fast, clear stream nearby, as well as what Lydia had once identified as a stand of lindens. I paused outside the room for a few

moments, allowing my eyes to adjust to the light. The corridor was wide and airy, hosed and scrubbed down every
several hours. Clinic 2 was in no way physically similar to
the Rostov mansion, yet given the rotating population of
the union's corridor (Medved had died here; so had Yakov
Baum), it was virtually another wing of the Secretariat.
Sorokin had spent his whole adult life in the union, encased within its protective walls. It was foretold that I too
would one day lie in this hospital, perhaps in the same
bed that now held Sorokin's carcass. I was thoroughly a
union man.

Eight

Sorokin was eventually sent home for a long convalescence. Meanwhile, Marina's novel approached like a distantly heard locomotive. And then it arrived and at a
publication party in the writers' union café, I was congratulated for "discovering" her. With an icy glass of
whiskey in my right hand and a mentholated Rothmans
in my left, I accepted the shower of compliments with the
same equanimity as I might have accepted a soft summer
rain. As for Anton, although he attended the party and
received congratulations for being the first to publish the
new author, he was no longer romantically involved with
her. I knew that Marina had taken up with and dropped
Vadim Andreyev, and had then performed the same in-
delicate operation upon Afanasy Malinin, who, leaning
against the bar for support, his face drawn and his hair in
his eyes, now looked much the worse for it.

The novel was well received: "a fresh voice," "the cry

of brave and wise youth," "a vigorous blow against hypocrisy." For a television interview, she wore a prim gray dress that luridly accented her figure. The camera caressed her. Marina spoke directly into it, to a camera-man with a hard-on. A nation of readers was stirred.

Marina had inscribed the copy she presented me with a stanza from the nineteenth-century poet Fyodor Tyutchev:

> Speak not, lie hidden, and conceal
> the way you dream, the things you feel.
> Deep in your spirit let them rise
> akin to stars in crystal skies
> that set before the night is blurred:
> delight in them and speak no word.

It was an odd, literary inscription to an ordinary, unliter-ary, *anti*-literary novel, which I read with growing disbelief. I had read worse, of course, but probably nothing worse that had been so highly praised for no easily visible rea-son. Contrary to acclamation, her literary voice was stale, her cry foolish, and her stances hypocritical. I counted those who must have been involved in the construction of Marina's celebrity: not only Anton, but the chief edi-tor of Sovremennik, the editors of *Literaturnaya Gazeta* and other journals, critics, and television executives. Could they all have participated in this gross sham? How could she be sleeping with so many of them—and not be sleeping with me?

The volume of the praise forced me to reconsider the novel, and to concede that, whatever its (many, fatal)

faults, there was at least perhaps something engagé about
the book, especially Marina's satirical portrayal of a certain secondary character, a petty bureaucrat. It was
Marina's good fortune that her book was published just
as the press began one of its periodic campaigns against
"the bureaucracy," a charade posited on the fiction that
"the bureaucracy," formless and faceless (save for a few
carefully chosen scapegoats), was something indepen-
dent from the Party. It was "the bureaucracy" that presented the greatest challenge to developing socialism;
the Party needed to "redouble its efforts against the bureaucracy." Although Marina's novel was not in any way
political, she developed a reputation as someone who
could be political, a "reformist," even a literary Young
Turk.

Although my own novel was simply one of scores
published that year and was intended for an entirely different audience, I sensed that it trailed in her wake.
Given my status in the union, my first printing was
much higher than Marina's, but the novel wasn't reviewed as prominently. Nor was I feted on television. As
the weeks passed, several reviews appeared in the papers
and literary journals, huffing their disappointment. The
grievances conveyed by these reviews were consistent
enough to be persuasive.

The gist of the complaints was that my novel, set
aboard a Bering Sea icebreaker, was "ill informed" and
"not genuine." Indeed, a literal-minded review in *The
Baltic Shipman,* by an active-duty mechanic, listed all its
errors and solecisms, which evoked his compassion for

my ignorance about marine diesel engines. It was shame-
fully clear to this and other critics that I had never set
foot aboard an icebreaker.

Yet I never hid the fact that I had no experience at sea
and no interest in going to sea. To write *The Northern
Lights,* I had looked in books and talked with sailors in
order to obtain a few details, but in the end many of
these were discarded or even contradicted for the sake of
the story. I was more interested in imagining an all-male
community in close quarters in a ferocious climate, in
bitter conflict and urgent cooperation, than I was in doc-
umenting anything real. I believed that the novel needed
not to be genuine, but only plausible, so that any errors
would not distract the reader from the main thing, the
story.

This method of operation had served me well in my
first two novels, set respectively in a Kazakh kolkhoz and
in a motorized cavalry unit during the closing months of
the Great Patriotic War. When I was an unknown writer,
critics were unaware that I lacked firsthand experience of
my subjects. Now inflicted with the knowledge that I was
a Moscow intellectual, they squawked that they were
gravely disturbed.

The most savage of these attacks was launched by
Sergei Makarov, whose standing had been recently enhanced by a collection of his travel essays. He took apart
my novel like a kebab, and the other idiots followed suit.
Although my novel was nonpolitical, Makarov leveled a
political charge: to write about workers without having
lived among them, or "as far as we can determine"

without caring about their "real historic triumphs" over hardship and backwardness, was a form of "literary colonialism."

The single exception in this campaign was Marina's long review in *Znamya*. Noting and, I suppose unavoidably, amplifying the criticism I had received, she absolved me of it. Marina conceded that my "pacing and characterization is weak," that the plot "holds few surprises," and that *The Northern Lights* was "a men's novel," but she admired "the vivid portrayal of human frailties and human passion aboard R. Krilov's ghostly death-ship." Her strain was apparent in every line. In the end, her condescension made her review the most galling of all that I had received. Everyone knew, of course, that I had been indirectly responsible for getting her work published.

In conversations with friends and in private dialogue with myself, I hotly defended the book, my ire leading me to make some extravagant claims for it, but when I descended to my desk, the arena of my ambitions, self-doubt coursed through me like a fever. Upon setting out to write the novel, I had been unsure whether I would succeed in believably describing the work of the sailors aboard the icebreakers. Certainly I was not sure of every line, nor of every effect I had hoped to achieve. How could I be? Fiction is a gamble. The thought that I had failed intensified. The sales were very poor. No film was made. The plot at the edge of the woods remained as undeveloped as my critics said my novel's was.

I now wondered whether I had ever wanted to write this novel in the first place, whether *The Northern Lights*, as well as the novels I had previously written and the ones I planned to write, merely conformed to conventional expectation about the work of a contemporary writer (why write novels? why not sonnets or haiku?). Although I confessed pride in my published books, I recognized that they existed alongside another body of work. In actuality, fragments and seeds of this work were located within the journals in my locked bookcase; in potentiality, the work existed in a kind of mirror universe glimpsed on the horizon at twilight or in a glass of ice water at the precise moment the ice has melted or in the polished surface of a quickly passing foreign car. This putative, parallel work was by no means anti-Soviet—I believed I didn't have a single anti-Soviet bone in my body; my father had bequeathed me a name drawn from the words *Revolution, Engels,* and *Marx*—but I also recognized that this writing would never be published here. In the existent passages and stanzas imperfectly set down within my notebooks, there was something too wild and too personal, too much without concession, and perhaps it was simply not very good.

At the euphoric First Union Congress in 1934, Leonid Sobolev announced, "The Party and Government have given the writer every freedom, and taken away from him only one thing—the freedom to write badly." Isaac Babel responded in apparent affirmation, noting that the freedom to write badly was "a very important freedom, and to take it away is no small thing. It is a privilege that we were taking full advantage of." The officials on the dais and in the front rows of the auditorium enthusiastically thumped themselves over this declaration. The rank and file were chilled; they knew Babel was being ironic. Unwilling to give up the freedom to write as he wished, even badly, Babel went on to practice "the genre of silence." Five years later he was arrested at his dacha, brought to the Lubyanka, and executed.

It was some consolation that at least Lydia was pleased with *The Northern Lights* and contemptuous of my critics. If anything, she was annoyed that I saw any merit in their arguments at all.

"Yuri Vorontsov, Sergei Makarov—they're hacks. They think fiction is a dramatization of journalism. They don't respect that the story stands outside reality. To criticize a novel for getting details of a setting wrong is like criticizing a dream for not being true-to-life."

I was sitting on the porch, watching Lydia weed (I myself was forbidden to interfere). She did this with great care in order to remove the root structure without disturbing her cherished tomatoes. I had spent most of that summer at the dacha, traveling to the city for a few days each week only to check my mail and perform some routine union business. I was hardly writing, nor reading much. I had avoided the many parties in the neighboring dachas. I was sure my critics would be there and was unsure how to greet them. With a self-deprecating joke? An insulting one? A punch in the face?

I asked Lydia, "And do readers understand these distinctions, when the critics don't? How about all those earnest letters I was sent by the peasants in Kazakhstan?

They said they loved my novel and then petitioned me with complaints about inefficient kolkhoz directors and unreachable quotas, as if I were working out of an office in the Ministry of Agriculture. Readers *want* journalistic literature."

"There are hack readers, just as there are hack writers. How many good readers do you need? Are you standing for election? This lack of confidence unbecomes you, Rem."

I grimaced my disagreement, though I knew she was right.

"My lack of my confidence is my strength," I said. "It makes me more open to criticism. It allows me to learn from my mistakes."

Lydia straightened and dropped the last of the weeds in a box. She wiped her hands on her smock. "Last year, at Sasha Nasedkin's, I heard Pavel Dubrovski say that he should have won the Lenin Prize for his last novel and that Sholokhov himself had complained on his behalf. You're a much better writer than Dubrovski, but you have a tenth of his confidence."

"That's my point, exactly. If I had his level of confidence, I'd be complacent, and therefore a much worse writer than I am now."

In truth, my inconspicuousness that summer was due in small part to my disinclination to see either Vorontsov or Makarov; the large part was my avoidance of Marina. I didn't want to have to thank her for my defense nor to be obliged to say anything kind about her novel. Yet, on my nights in Moscow when, sticky and logy from the heat, I gazed from my apartment balcony out onto the roaring, frantic city of six million, the capital of an empire, I knew that she was there. When I sat down at my desk to write, she was probably working at that moment too, at her desk somewhere else in the city. She was present like the humidity.

Nine

It must have been the intensity of this awareness that forced Marina's precipitation from the urban haze one afternoon, gently onto the steps of an escalator plunging into the depths of the earth beneath the Kremlin. The complex was at the intersection of two public metro lines, plus a third, famously secret line called Metro-2, built by Stalin for his own speedy exit from the capital in the event of war.

I myself was rising from the Prospekt Marx station, past enormous lamp stanchions topped with white glass globes. A red filament incandesced within each globe, a worm crucified on a bolt of electric current. I had just crossed the landing between escalators and had begun the second stage of my ascent when, beyond the lamps at the descending escalator, I recognized Marina. She was gazing down the length of the tunnel, as blind as a burrow-dwelling animal.

I abruptly turned to face the gray wall sliding by. I was amazed by this impulse, but she had passed before I could overcome it. By the time I reached the top of the escalator, I gravely regretted my cowardice. A barricade guarded by a severe-looking matron forced me to walk to the end of the corridor before I could double back. As soon as I was caught in the flow to the lower level, I realized that I would never overtake Marina before her train arrived.

Pressed at my back by the other travelers, stumbling against the heels of those ahead of me, I sought to identify the cause of my swelling urgency. To be sure, Marina was an attractive girl, but at that very moment equally attractive girls darted at the edge of my vision and bumped against me and besides, I was only three weeks into an intensely physical liaison with a lithe, myopic clerk at the Dom Knigi bookstore. I had been on my way to her a minute earlier.

Marina was a mystery. I hardly knew her, save for what she wrote and the record of our infrequent, occasionally charged conversations over the years. Sometimes I couldn't even picture her face. But she represented a potentiality, and that counted; in those years the potential carried more weight than the actual. I could not bear to define that potentiality.

Now I changed my mind about pursuing her and took a prohibited but unblocked turn on the next landing, through a corridor that I believed would lead to another escalator rising to my original destination, the Ploshchad Revolutsii platform. I must have misread a sign, because it was soon apparent that I was not on my way to Ploshchad Revolutsii at all. The dim passageway wound through the complex without end, sprouting new corridors and escalators and gradually entangling my sense of direction. I lost any idea of which point my underground position might correspond to in the city above. An escalator hundreds of meters long raised me to a distant corridor that, after a sharp turn to the right,

ended in an even longer escalator returning down. The
subterranean heat made me feverish.

I was seized by the idea that I had somehow wandered
into Metro-2. It was said that in the 1950s, after Stalin
began living and working full-time at his Near Dacha in
Volynskoye, construction of the line had been abandoned. Rumors of this sort tended to be disinformation.
The military abandoned nothing. Millions of rubles had
been poured into this tunnel, equipping it with the most
advanced military technology. There were other stations
on the line, vast caverns and intricate warrens. The line
had likely remained a military installation, a shadow city
inhabited by apparatchik-phantoms. The commuters
walking shoulder-to-shoulder with me carried torn string
shopping bags and their clothes were ordinary *univermag*
suits and jackets, but I detected a distinctive confidence
in their stride and a wariness in their glare. Whether
army or KGB, they knew the secret underground workings of our society, which manifested themselves only
obliquely in the events that played out in public view in
our newspapers and television reports, on our boulevards and avenues. Or perhaps Metro-2 was the real city,
and the above-ground Moscow was the one in shadow.

The last corridor discharged onto an unfamiliar platform, which, like every other metro station in the capital,
was lavishly decorated around a particular theme.

This station seemed to imply some kind of southern
motif. The station's supporting columns were tiled with
scenes of swarthy peasant-workers at garden banquets
and vineyards set beneath distant mountains. Grapes and
other subtropical fruit were depicted on the pediments

above the platform. They were alternated with garlanded, hammer-and-sickled seals of one of the organs of power, I couldn't recognize which. Someone behind me took me firmly by the arm and I recalled that it was the emblem of the old NKVD. Through the foggish heat that had descended upon me, I heard my name called.

"I was just thinking of you a few minutes ago. I must be a witch," Marina said. "A picture of your face popped into my head and look, here you are."

"Amazing coincidences happen," I replied slowly, recovering from a series of sentiments that passed through me in the space of a few seconds: first, there had been fright, and then an unspeakable elation, and then embarrassment at the fright and elation. "Even in a planned economy."

We were standing close enough to each other to embrace, or to dance. Buffeted by the rush of commuters, their bags and parcels brushing against us, we began to sway, as if we were indeed dancing—a lazy, slow, subtropical rumba.

We appraised each other again and I was revisited by the impulse to which I had first given in: to turn away. I repressed it and at last said, "How's everything?"

Marina groaned. "Complicated. I'm not with Iosif Spirin anymore."

I bobbed my head sympathetically, but with a slightly quizzical expression fixed upon my face, as if I hadn't known that she had been with Spirin at all. It occurred to me to resent that she thought I was keeping track of her love life, though in fact I was.

She pursed her lips and frowned. "Where are we?"

"I'm not sure," I said. "I thought I was going to Ploshchad Revolutsii. I think my stairs are at the other end of the platform."

"I've never been here before."

"They're always opening new stations," I said and forced a laugh.

At that moment, a train roared into the station, displacing stale tunnel air and discharging a swirl of passengers. Unsure of what else to say, and unable to speak over the noise anyway, I waited until the train left. Meanwhile, Marina studied my face as if she intended to write about it. I wondered if she had been pursuing *me*. Had she too been caught in the labyrinth of tunnels, corridors, and escalator chutes? Before the first train could leave, another arrived from the opposite direction. And then another every sixty seconds, according to the digital clocks at each end of the platform. We had stumbled into the tumult of rush hour.

I asked her if she would come with me for a cup of coffee, but the invitation was completely submerged in the noise. I couldn't hear my words nor even feel their consonants upon my lips. The long hall was scoured by sound, a great onrushing, rarefying force as elemental as gravity or light.

"Marina," I said. "I want to take you home."

This was an experiment. She smiled and pointed to her ears and made a gesture of helplessness.

"You can't hear me," I said, searching her face for any kind of acknowledgment.

She smiled at my persistence in trying to speak.

"Good. Marina, you're driving me crazy. I can't stop thinking about you. I don't know why. Maybe it's your success. I resent it. I resent you."

She shook her head to show her incomprehension.

"But I want to make love to you," I said. "I want to fuck you silly. I want to ride your ass from one end of my flat to the other. I want to smear sperm all over your tits, your face, all over your body. I want to put my cock in your mouth."

I was shouting now and I still couldn't hear my voice. Of course, Marina should have been able to lip-read at least some of what I was saying, but even that, I felt in the white heat of the moment, had no consequence. The safest place to practice the genre of silence was in a tunnel of noise.

Marina laughed, to show that she at least comprehended the dispensations allowed us a hundred meters beneath the Kremlin. She would never be sure of what I said and later I could solemnly deny everything, since I couldn't hear it myself. She could deny it too, even what she was sure of. Now she began shouting too. The trains arrived and left. The clocks were reset to zero. Commuters grimaced at the spectacle we were making. We said whatever came into our heads, whatever we wished. My eyes focused on her finely shaped mouth and, thrillingly, I thought I saw it shape itself around words that encompassed lewd acts. This spurred me on, to match my own lewdness with hers—"let's fuck right here on the platform," I cried—spinning out obscene fantasies with increasing abandon, things I never even knew I could imagine. Then three words emerged from her lips, clearly readable. The words were: "democracy and freedom."

With that, the waves of machinery cast forth by the agate print of the metro schedule met at a point of destructive interference. The station emptied of trains. The noise subsided, despite the hundreds of travelers making their way to the platform exits. Marina and I heard each other laugh, nervously now. I was shocked by the words I had spoken, but even more so by what I believed were hers. We fell silent. Now that she could hear me, I wasn't sure what I wished to say. I looked down the hall, the clock had passed the sixty second mark, but there was no sign of a train approaching on either track.

"Marina," I said.

My voice was perfectly audible. Her smile was warm. Our eyes met as they had the night of our reading.

"Marina," I repeated. Then I said, "Thank you for that review in *Znamya*."

She made a small, disappointed laugh and the air deflated from her.

"There's no need to thank me. I write whatever I like."

"Of course," I said, stung by her rebuke. This did not stop me from adding: "And your novel. I liked that too."

Another train finally arrived and we embraced in farewell. In my arms she assumed a substantiality that I had not expected, as if before I had only confronted the idea of Marina, and this was Marina herself. I began to tighten my embrace, but, no longer smiling, she abruptly brushed my cheeks with her lips, pulled away, and went to the opposite end of the platform. I watched her go. As I returned to the staircase that had brought me here, a second train arrived. It was just then, before the train obscured it, that I looked up to read the name of the station emblazoned on the wall on the other side of the tracks: Beryevskaya, after Lavrenty Beria, the Georgian-born secret police chief executed in the weeks following Stalin's death. At least, that's what I thought I read.

I eventually found Ploshchad Revolutsii and hurried home, no longer in the mood to see my book clerk. Something had passed, I believed. I continued to run into Marina, of course, at parties and literary events, but less frequently, and the encounters carried less weight and possibility. Her novel won a few prizes and subsided from the public's short-term memory. It was said that she was working on a second novel, but she showed it to no one. Despite taking occasional detours, and once even diagramming my recollection of the maze of tunnels, I never again succeeded in finding the metro station in which we had met.

Ten

Cowed by the criticism *The Northern Lights* had received, I put off work on my next novel. The skies grayed late in August, shortly after we picked the tomatoes. The crop was beautiful that year. Lydia and I ate them like apples, the juice running down our shirt fronts.

It wasn't until November that Novel 4 began to emerge from the mists, but shortly afterwards I received a note that, in its powerful effect, prevented me from doing any writing the rest of the day and unsettled me for several weeks to come. The union's Foreign Commission, the letter duly informed me, was negotiating with an American publishing house for the rights to Marina's first novel. I put the note down and stared at my desk for a while, infused with the childish hope that nothing would come of the negotiations.

My own discretion notwithstanding, the contents of the confidential memo became common gossip by the end of the day. I am sure that most of my colleagues initially reacted as I did, if for less complicated reasons. Publication abroad, especially in the West, was always a source of envy. Although the union and the government claimed three quarters of the royalties, and the remainder was transmuted into rubles and vouchers good at hard-currency stores, the balance was still a hefty amount of change. The foundation of many a dacha was composed of foreign royalty checks.

Moreover, translation, even if no further than into the obscure, tortured languages of the fraternal socialist countries, was a matter of great prestige. It made you an international writer, elevated you to panels discussing issues of great import, and won you a greater print run for your next book. Marina would be invited on the best domestic "creative trips"—such as the ones to the Baltics—and even garner foreign invitations. I expected that her novel would eventually be transformed into a film, a mysterious process that enhanced the author (even while it attenuated his work) and brought him even more piles of gold (or its voucher equivalents).

Once the negotiations were completed, several large

numbers were bruited about in the café, but I declined
from using my union position to discover the size of
Marina's royalties. Shortly after the book was published
in America, I attended a small party at Bulat Okudzhava's,
with Marina in attendance. Although the party around
Okudzhava's kitchen table was ostensibly in celebration
of his birthday, Marina sat erect in her chair, flushed and
bright eyed, as if the birthday honors belonged to her. She
received our cheers and congratulations with regal grace.

None of us, however, saw the translation itself until
the following year, when it was brought to Moscow by a
middle-aged Canadian tourist unaware that our customs
officials looked unkindly on the import of any books
about Russia or by Russians, alive or dead, living abroad
or at home, anti-Soviet or not, and would have preferred
that visitors to our country not waste any of their valuable time here reading at all. The book was taken from
her, she was questioned by a matronly guard in a rank
customs booth, and then it was returned to her without
explanation (the explanation would have been that it was
not on the list of proscribed titles). The tourist had returned to her tour group dazed and thrilled by her brush
with dictatorship. No Russian succeeded in parting her
from the book after this adventure, so once the book's
arrival became known by a friend of a friend of her
Intourist guide, it earned the woman an invitation to a
party at Sasha Nasedkin's dacha. The book was passed
around and casually examined by writers and editors
who risked hernias trying to feign their indifference.

"The word made flesh," announced Anton

Basmanian, his grin as sour as good Russian rye bread.
He passed the book to me. The Canadian was at his side,
warily observing the transaction.

In my hands, the object seemed to transmit a kind of
fragile radiance. I caressed the silky dust jacket, printed
as boldly as a call to revolution. Our books were rarely
published with dust jackets. On the back cover were
voiced shouts of praise from Norman Mailer, Alberto
Moravia, and Graham Greene. Inside the back cover the
author herself was pictured, her eyes and hair luminous,
her torso sleek in a tight red pullover. Her posture and
scowl were defiant. But despite the shock that was deliv-
ered by the book's wrapper, nothing prepared me for the
appearance of the words on the printed page. The type
was large, the print so sharply defined that I imagined
that it would have been legible even to a non-English
speaker. My first thought was that this wasn't a novel, it
was a *product,* something like a tube of toothpaste.

Our own books were such paltry affairs, pretty much
identical in their physical form, their paper coarse and
their type small, dense, and erratum-infested. Their bindings were easily broken. Although I never considered our
books "bad" for that—the quality of a book did not reside
in its physical presence, did it?—I could not help but be
impressed by Marina's. With a glass of Armenian cognac
in my left hand and the open book in my right, I began
reading the translation, my eyes gliding over the voluptuous Latinate letters like (I imagined) a Cadillac on a
California highway, the heft and texture of the book mas-
saging and soothing my critical faculties. I ascertained at

once that the translation had been performed competently by some émigré who was no worse a writer than Marina. Part of me acquiesced in the seduction performed by the book's material body; the other part, the critic-writer part, coolly informed me, trying not to raise its voice, that my original evaluation was correct, that the novel was shallow in thought and inept in its execution.

Yet I dimly heard the tourist murmur that Marina's book was selling well after having been favorably and even enthusiastically reviewed by the leading American literary publications. Marina had received tens of thousands of dollars for the novel in advance of its publication and would receive even more once the receipts were counted.

This news worked through me like a poison: the *market* liked her work. Each copy sold for nearly seven dollars. This was in a country where readers were offered a vast choice of attractively packaged books, plus a variety of other leisure distractions that we could barely comprehend, yet a sizable number of Americans chose to read Marina's novel and paid for it in hard currency. For all the approval, comforts, and forest-clearing print runs bestowed upon her more-celebrated elders in the union, it was Marina Burchatkina who was a real-world success. If I could have been so wrong in my critical assessment of her talent, how could I be so sure of my own? Stupefied, I handed the book back to the tourist.

"And are you a writer too?" she asked brightly, in English.

I nodded.

"Would I have read anything you've written?"

"No," I said.

Lydia never saw the book, having drifted to a less populous section of the garden, and as we walked the few dusk-softened blocks back to our dacha, she was unmoved by my descriptions of Marina's book and the self-doubts it had engendered.

"She's not a talented writer."

"Well, someone must think so," I said. "The publisher. The readers. Norman Mailer, for God's sake."

We had just reached a turn in the road. Lydia halted there and tilted her head. She was listening to a bird. I prepared to wait it out. I was usually indifferent to bird song, rarely distinguishing the cry of Bird A from that of Bird B. Yet by some trick of the evening, by the thickened light or the taste of the air or the cognac, I found myself not only attending the bird, but in pursuit of its climb up the musical scale. The song was not pretty. Yet in its ungainliness and rawness there was something ancient that resonated from the age when birds sang without men to hear them. The song was distinctly its own; this was Bird Z.

Then it stopped. We resumed our walk.

"Rem, look at the pornography and detective fantasies that sell millions in the West. The market is the *worst* judge of talent. So what if a few thousand Americans buy Burchatkina's book? Compare that with the hundreds of thousands of Russians who will read one of our talented, serious authors in a low-cost edition—and then save that book as a treasure in their family bookcase."

We walked on a bit, silently reflecting upon the great

spill of sex and violence, dishonesty and tawdriness, that spewed from the West's printing presses. I had no illusions that the same material would fail to sell well here, making millionaires of unscrupulous writers. Only the vigilance of the writers' union and Glavlit, the government censorship agency, prevented our literature from being eroded and degraded by commercial exploitation.

Lydia asked, "And how do you know that the market really finds her talented? Talent may not be the only selling point. She's a contemporary Russian writer. She's a young woman. Merely being published in the West gives her a political aura. Americans are buying her out of curiosity."

It wasn't the novel they were selling, it was the author. This was something I had previously not considered, but knew was true. In the West, literature might not be entangled in political considerations, but it could certainly be knotted in nonliterary commercial ones. I knew that if anything was heavily enough advertised it would sell (our newspapers were always writing about the useless trinkets that, thanks to advertising, Americans thought they could not live without). Even the endorsements on the back cover were not necessarily sincere; they had certainly been solicited, as some kind of favor to someone in the publishing house. This went on all the time. Nevertheless, the fact was this: her novel was being published in America and mine wasn't.

"Her picture's on the book jacket," I murmured. "I suppose it doesn't hurt that she's very attractive."

"Is she?"

I searched Lydia's face for an ironic smirk or grimace,

but her question was asked in earnest. I was taken aback. She knew Marina, had attended parties at which Marina had been marked as the most attractive and glamorous guest. I could recall twice when Marina's presence caused a palpable strain in a party's superstructure, at fracture points of longing and envy—or so I thought at the time. Hanging in midair by its typographical hook, Lydia's question now made me wonder if the young author's beauty was not so obvious. There had been no strain at these parties; I had imagined it. Was there some cosmetic defect to which I had been blinded? Usually it was the other way around: a girl's attractiveness would obscure her personal faults, sometimes catastrophically. Now it was disquieting to have it suggested that Marina's beauty was not self-evident, that there was something more than superficial to my desire. Lydia stared, waiting for my answer, and it seemed that she noticed my confusion, but that might have been a misperception as well.

Eleven

The fall passed in a blur of wet streets and mud. Construction debris flowed over onto Gertsena from the new Prospekt Kalinina, which had obliterated the seedy old Arbat neighborhood and put in its place high-rises gleaming with the optimism of the new age. The jackhammers could be heard in my office. As I had expected, publication in the West heightened Marina's celebrity at home, and there was talk of electing her to the presidium of the union's youth section. I had again established winter quarters in our flat, while Lydia burrowed into her dacha solitude. Our ambiguous conversation of the summer, as I recalled it, proved to be a scratch on the pane of our marriage. My memory would skid past the intervening weeks and snag on that walk back to our dacha. I would wonder about my assessment of Marina's work and her beauty. I lay awake in my bed, listening to the sounds of the city I didn't know, a city of certitude. The city in which I dwelled was cast in shadows.

Late one December afternoon I lifted the receiver of my office telephone and heard a familiar growl: "Rem, come here at once."

Sorokin had been in and out of the hospital all year, his pallor deepening to a permanent jaundice, his mass of flesh rising like a loaf of bread and gradually immobilizing him in his office chair. His demeanor was somber and worried and he sometimes seemed distracted. A few weeks earlier I had come to his office with a package, and, to our mutual embarrassment, he hadn't immediately recognized me. Afterwards he muttered something about my hair getting too fucking long, I looked like a goddam, fucking *khipi*.

Now he said, "We have a problem."

"What's that?"

"Viktor Panteleyev." He pronounced each syllable of the man's name slowly, enunciating it carefully, "Is he a friend of yours?"

Sorokin studied me. Afraid of what I might say if I hesitated, I rushed to answer: "Yes."

Sorokin made a sound halfway between a grunt and a belch and then said, "He must have lost his mind."

"Oh my God. What did he do?"

"Nothing yet. Some agitators are planning some kind of protest at Pushkin Square this evening at six. He intends to join them."

"What kind of protest?"

"What do you think? So-called human rights, I suppose." He sneered and added in contempt, "Decembrists." The Decembrists had been a group of army officers whose pro-democracy rebellion in December 1825 was savagely put down by Tsar Nicholas I and bravely exalted by Pushkin.

"Panteleyev's involved?"

"Apparently. He's a fool. His participation poses a threat to the entire writers' union. It puts our loyalty in question. Certain members of the Central Committee already have raised their voices against ideological drift. Too much publication abroad, too many European friends, not enough editorial oversight by Glavlit. I can't say I disagree. Who has the guts to call himself a Marxist-Leninist writer these days?"

"But Panteleyev's acting on his own!"

"No one acts on his own. He's a member of the union. The union gives him the right to publish, to call himself a Soviet writer. It gives him housing and social benefits, annual holidays and health care. He has responsibilities in turn, and one of them is not to bring his fellow writers into disrepute."

"I'm sure he doesn't mean it that way," I said lamely. "Look, I'll call him. I'll ask him not to attend." This didn't sound strong enough. "I'll stop him."

Sorokin examined me for a moment and then closed his heavy, warted eyelids.

"Boris Stepanovich, do you need something? Some juice?"

He didn't open his eyes. "Just take care of it," he said.

No one answered the telephone at Viktor's. I let it ring ten times and then called again. Then I went down to the café, hoping to find him quaffing a drink before going out to wreck his life. He wasn't there of course, it had been years since I had seen him in the café. A few heads turned in my direction. I offered a smile and they quickly looked away. Nearly all the tables had been taken, but the room was unusually quiet. They couldn't speak of what they most wished to speak. Had I been the last to learn of the demonstration?

It was well past five o'clock, already dark. I went for my coat and took a taxi through the wet, pedestrian-choked streets, not directly to Pushkin Square, but down the boulevard a bit, in the hope that I would be able to intercept Viktor on his way. I stood and looked back to the statue, reverse-shadowed by a layer of fresh snow. Pushkin's curl-topped head was bowed in contemplation. One hand rested in his gown, the other held a derby at his side. In the dark, I couldn't read the inscription on the statue's base, but every schoolchild knew it:

> Throughout great Rus' my echoes will extend,
> And all will name me, all tongues in her use. . . .

No protesters gathered. Only passersby walked through the wet, lightly falling snow. A bus huffed by in a cloud of lingering, neon blue exhaust. Two babushkas swayed across the pavement, lugging what appeared to be either a large package of fruit preserves or pickles. There was no such thing as an anti-government demonstration in the Soviet Union, just as they didn't sell *blini* in the Congo.

I continued to stand there, wondering how Viktor had become embroiled in Sorokin's fantasies. The snow collected on me while it collected on Pushkin, but my overcoat, bought in London, kept me dry. The other pedestrians were also well dressed in warm cloth coats and good boots. To what else could Russians reasonably aspire? With a minute or so left before six, a tall woman in a long black coat emerged from the static that fell across the evening's empty screen. She was beautiful. It was Marina.

She carried a shopping bag from which emerged a long piece of *kolbasa*. She didn't see me at first. When she did, from a distance of about ten meters, recognition spilled across her face like ink tipped from a bottle. She halted, but she didn't smile. She blinked in confusion, a gesture probably reflected on my own face. Then she resumed her approach, moving briskly.

"You're on your way home," I called out, not sure that she would stop again.

She brusquely kissed me twice on the cheeks but continued her motion forward.

"I need to be somewhere."

"Home?"

"Where are *you* going?" she asked. Our questions carried equal measures of hopefulness. Tentatively, she said, "The same place?"

"Home? Your home?" I replied, trying to banter. "Is that an invitation?"

"I have an appointment," she said guardedly.

"At 6 P.M.? That's an unusual time for an appointment."

"A friend."

"What friend?" I asked. "Somebody I know? Let's go for a drink." We were already crossing the street. I blurted, "Are you going to Pushkin Square?"

She smiled cautiously.

"Listen," I said. "Don't go. It's dangerous."

Her face clouded over. I tried to block her but she walked around me. I hurried after her and took her arm.

"Listen, Marina, I know what they've planned. If *I* know, don't you think the KGB knows? Everyone knows! You've been set up!"

"Good. We want the KGB to know. It's *against* the KGB! What would the point be if they didn't know?"

"Marina, where do you think you live? One word from Glavlit and you'll never be published again! They'll remove your book from the libraries. They'll remove *you* from the union—then where would you be? Kaluga? Is that what you want? Don't you want to be a writer?"

"Leave me alone!"

Her long strides had taken us to the edge of Pushkin Square—"Who do you think you're going to help!" I cried—and suddenly dozens of people converged upon us. It wasn't a mere chance eddying of the pedestrian flow. For the most part, they looked like intellectuals, poorly dressed and ineptly coifed, and more than enough were Jews. Marina roughly threw off my arm and rushed to the other side of the statue, disappearing behind a line

of four or five women. They were standing in some kind
of formation, pale and almost mortally self-conscious.

And then several things happened in what must have
been the space of a minute, though the space seemed
even more compressed than that, airless and radiant.

A second hand on some unknown watch lurched into
the cleavage of a twelve and the line of women marched
to the base of the statue. From a worn plastic shopping
bag one of them removed a long roll of white cloth on
which something, some slogan, had been painted. This
woman was middle-aged, squat, with heavy eyeglasses
and a long, nearly simian jaw. Tight-lipped, like a high
diver at the edge of the board, she passed one end of the
cloth to the last woman on the line. It took a moment for
them to shake out the banner; even then, even though I
was only a few paces away, I could not read the words. As
if in another language, or printed in invisible ink, they
refused legibility.

Springing from the soil, it seemed, there were then
many men with bulky, grotesquely oversized flash-
cameras. "They're here!" someone shouted, and others
moaned with surprise and fright. The men wore pale
brown raincoats. Each time they squeezed off a picture,
darting and spinning around us, they grimaced. As the
evening landscape turned stark and two-dimensional,
the flashes made a soft popping sound that echoed like
something from a childhood memory.

It was then that I glimpsed Viktor, standing distant
from the melee, a sign of his own hanging from his
neck. He seemed disoriented and uncomprehending,

an actual passerby. I could read his sign: "RESPECT THE CONSTITUTION!"

In these electric moments, I thought of grabbing Viktor and pulling him away, but the thought barely lasted its articulation. I stuffed my face into my coat and turned to run. Then suddenly dozens of more men, most of them in leather jackets, arrived among us, further outnumbering the protesters. They headed for the women carrying the banners, making detours to push and throw punches at other civilians. Someone I never saw thumped me on the back, a terrific, expert blow that knocked the wind from me and brought me to my knees. When I looked up, two black Volgas had arrived, and the women were being roughly shoved into them, held firmly by their necks.

The woman who had unfurled the banner was the last to go. Her shopping bag had burst, scattering onto the pavement some groceries and several pages of typescript. Both the groceries and the typescript were being frantically collected by a man in a leather jacket. The woman was also taken by the neck, but the plainclothesman holding her missed the opening into the back of the car and, quite deliberately I was sure, smashed her face into the doorframe. From where I knelt, I could hear the contest of bone against steel. Steel won. Her eyeglasses flew off her broken face and into the street. They lay there as the car drove off.

More photographs were being taken and more arrests were being made. I didn't search for either Marina or Viktor. Now I succeeded in getting away, my face covered by the back of my arm. Fifty meters up Gorky Street I overtook pedestrians oblivious to what had just happened, oblivious to my terror. I bumped against them, a few hurled curses at me, and I continued running through the darkness. Down the stairs of an underground passageway across Gorky, I slipped on some ice and took a tumble. As I fell onto the steps, one of my hands was pulled the wrong way, delivering a sharp jolt to my wrist. When I resumed my flight, cold air whipped around my naked left knee.

I was thoroughly winded by the time I reached the union. I didn't remove my coat—"Rem Petrovich!" shouted old Darya at the coatcheck—and went straight to my office. I collapsed at my desk and then, with the door closed and the lights off, I wept, spasmodically trying to catch my breath. The tears sluiced down my face and flowed into the mucous pouring from my nose. I tasted the salts of humiliation for the first time since I had left Tomsk.

I don't know how long I wept. Eventually I removed my handkerchief from my jacket and wiped my face. I was still wearing my coat. I sat in the dark for a while, trying to sort out what had happened, what terrible calamity I had narrowly escaped, or perhaps hadn't escaped at all. The photographers had been all over the place; would the KGB accept Sorokin's explanation of my attendance? But now my thoughts departed from the practical and the actual. The moment I had taken flight I comprehended the full measure of the difference between my size and the size of the power that commanded the man who thumped me on my back. It rendered me insignificant, and all the literary pretensions I possessed—as creator, as an individual whose life was bound to his art, as heir to Pushkin, as, ha ha, the unacknowledged legislator of the world—were rendered negligible. How easily I had fallen to my knees . . . And then at some indeterminate time, hours later perhaps, the door to my office opened soundlessly and a shadow passed through it.

The door closed and the office was dark again. A featureless gray form hovered before me, radiating heat. For a long time I remained at my desk, waiting for the form to define itself. Finally I stood, became a form myself, and the two forms swelled toward each other. She too wore her coat. My hands slid beneath it, along the back of a damp, moist blouse. Her body quavered beneath my touch, but not from my touch. It was fear, at least at first. Her hands ran along my sides and pressed me to her. A stray photon drifted into the room and phosphoresced in a tear swelling at the surface of one of her eyes. I made out the smear of her mascara. That was the last thing I observed, because suddenly I was bereft of language, even language with which to think. Not a single word was exchanged between us.

Twelve

A severe flu descended upon me the following week, and I seemed to be ill the remainder of the winter, which I spent mostly under the blankets, tending to myself. Feverish, congested, and exhausted, I lay in bed brooding about the protest and the events that immediately followed it, but in

these days I could barely phrase two consecutive thoughts.
I drank weak tea with honey and dried berries; then tea
from lime blossoms. I drank warm milk with honey, then
with butter, then with Borzhomi water. I placed mustard
plaster on my chest. I hung garlic cloves around my neck
and stuffed two of them up my nose. That winter I hardly
went in to the office. I was waiting for the next shoe to
drop, but the demonstration, although well known
throughout the city by some kind of jungle telegraph—
not a word about it was set into type—didn't lead to further arrests. No action was taken against Marina, nor
against Viktor. No inquiries were made about my own
presence on Pushkin Square that evening.

I saw Marina on a few occasions, but not in a private
setting, and neither of us took the opportunity to speak
with each other. The glow of celebrity had faded from her
face and her eyes had become dull. In these encounters,
no matter the liveliness of the company, her expression
remained pensive. She didn't offer me any significant
look except, once in the café, a kind, mournful smile.
These days she seemed to be carrying something deep
within her, like the intimate knowledge of her own mor-
tality. In retrospect, I had perceived this the night of the
protest. At no time had our embraces and caresses felt
like something that was beginning. It had felt, right to
the final shudder, like something ending. What was ending, I didn't comprehend until later.

The confused nature of the evening's events, and particularly their lack of record or apparent consequence,
invited me to believe that they had never happened. At
night I lay awake, my fever breaking once again, and tried

to recall what I had seen and felt. Repeatedly I found myself in that elongated moment when the women at the
base of Pushkin's statue unfurled their banners. I stood
there, squinting, trying to hold the moment long enough
to read what was on the banners. Letters and words
swirled along the cloth—fragments of political declarations, fragments of declarations of love, lines from poetry and novels, some of them my own—but they never
remained there long enough to be understood. Always,
in the end, the banner would come up empty, a stretch of
white cloth, anti-Soviet merely by its existence, but offering nothing to be read.

I never said anything about the demonstration to
Sorokin and he never brought it up with me. I was grateful for that. Meanwhile, Marina kept herself out of view
and out of gossip. Many times I dialed the first five digits
of her telephone number, merely for the pleasure of
doing so, but with no intention of dialing the sixth.

Springtime came and my head began to clear. I tossed
aside the notes for my novel and began anew. Then came
an unusually sweltering summer, an odd summer, really,
unnervingly quiet and suffused with expectation, which
I mistook for anticipation of the summer Olympics to be
held in early September. The press and television were
consumed by oracular pronouncements on the prospects
of our swimmers, our runners, our acrobats, and especially our weightlifters. Several of my better-placed
friends and colleagues had wrangled assignments to
cover the games or to join the government delegation to
Mexico City. As I gingerly returned to social life, I found

that my friends did not want to speak of literature, but rather of Janis Lusis, our promising javelin thrower.

I managed to get caught up in the pre-games fervor, at least to some extent, despite the absence of a radio at the dacha and our avoidance of the news from one day to the next. This was part of my convalescence, to seal myself in the dacha with Lydia, her gardening implements, and our books. As August wound down and the afternoons became chilly, I looked with some regret toward my return to the city. Lydia began harvesting and canning her tomatoes, cucumbers, carrots, and cherries, while I watched her from over the novel I pretended to read. She wore a light, full-length dress as she leaned over the rows, not bending her knees. A breeze skittered around her ankles and for a moment plastered the dress against the backs of her legs and thighs. I rose from the hammock to walk off my hard-on and strolled over to the hedge.

The street was quiet. A lone babushka, Vadim Surkov's mother-in-law, pulled a wagon up the street, laying in her firewood early. She was an elderly woman, bloated beneath her housedress, a squall of wrinkles around her toothless mouth. We had never spoken, though Surkov's dacha was located two doors down. Now as she spotted me, her eyes danced beneath her cataracts.

She laughed, a kind of mad cackle, and shouted, "The fascists are in for a hot time now. The whole lot of them."

I smiled. "What fascists?"

"You know, sonny, the counterrevolutionaries. The wreckers. The Right Oppositionists."

The phrase made me smile again. I assumed she had

become distracted from the exertion of pulling the cart, or simply from being old, and had imagined herself to be living in another time. It was a remarkable phenomenon, entirely forgivable, and I thought of all that her generation had seen and suffered. I should have offered to help her with the cart. Instead, to draw her out, to keep the dream going for my own instruction, I asked her, "These Right Oppositionists, who might they be?"

"Dubcek," she spat. "And his ilk! They've locked 'em up, all of 'em! The bastards will hang from the lampposts."

Muttering and sniggering, she made her way down the street. I turned to Lydia, who was working so intently that she had not heard the remark. Her face was entirely composed, self-contained, satisfied with the dirt under her fingertips. Without a word I hurried from the garden, down the block in the opposite direction, to Sasha Nasedkin's dacha.

This had been the scene of a particularly raucous party just the week before. We had attended it, but left early: by chance, Lydia and I had looked up at the same time and communicated to each other the urgent desire to read for a half hour before turning in. This murmured agreement—this congruency of desires—surprised us. We giggled at it. The party had continued in our absence and, like every great party in those last days, had ended at least one marriage and did not wind down until the morning sun had lifted itself above the treetops.

Now the house had the air of centuries-long abandonment. No one was in the untended garden, where some chairs had been tipped over and an empty vodka bottle lay in a vine-choked, crumbling fountain. The windows to the house were closed, but the doorway gaped like a vacant tooth.

"Sasha? Hello? Anyone home? It's me, Rem!"

The inside of the dacha smelled of trash and spoiled food. Papers were scattered everywhere, on the kitchen table and on the windowsills. I found something odd at the foot of the warm stove: half a typed manuscript, the *bottom* half, charred around the upper edges. In the next room there was an insistent radio buzzing noise, which I recognized at once as the sound of the BBC being jammed.

"Sasha?"

Between a bottle of Gordon's gin and one of Schweppe's tonic, a juice glass was filled to the top. Sasha stared at it, ignoring me. He was disheveled, in some ratty dressing grown, unshaven and red eyed. The BBC rattled in the radio like a trapped bee.

"It's Dubcek?" I asked. "I just heard."

Sasha gave a little half laugh.

"Rem Krilov, always well connected and well informed . . . Not to worry, ha ha. Our good Czechoslovakian friends . . . fraternal brothers, friendly friends . . . socialist allies. They've invited us to a party. They asked us to bring our tanks . . . I'm such a great literary critic, how come I couldn't read the writing on the wall?"

"When did this happen?"

"Can't you tell by how drunk I am? Two days ago."

I pointed into the next room. "And the manuscript?"

"Nothing really, Rem. Just some housecleaning. Just cleaning house, getting ready for the next decade, ha ha.

But I don't have the balls for cleaning house. I pulled it out of the fire. What can they do to me? I haven't invited them, ha ha."

Before I left I squatted by the stove and picked up the remains of the manuscript. It was a memoir. Balanced on my haunches, able to read no more than ten or eleven lines of each page, I nonetheless recognized that it was a work of enormous accomplishment, honest and unrestrained, like nothing that had ever been published in our literature. Its phrases even now resonate in my head (later I tried to copy the words into my notebook, but could never get them exactly right). I read the manuscript to the very end, taking perhaps more than an hour, never changing my position. Occasionally I heard Sasha stir behind me. He stretched a leg, he picked up his glass, he sighed, he drummed his fingers on the table. The BBC continued to hiss and moan. When I finished the manuscript, I opened the stove door and gently deposited the pages into the dimming fire.

I returned my stiff back and numb left leg to our dacha. Lydia was in the kitchen, preparing a ragout from a recipe in an Italian cookbook. The cookbook was one of several brought to Moscow by a visiting Italian publisher in the correct expectation that he would be showered with lapel pins and would want to give something in return. Lydia had made his acquaintance at a party and, though no lapel pins had been exchanged, the book became one of Lydia's earthly treasures. When I told her the news, she raised her hand to her face and made a little soundless moue of pain. She looked back at the recipe. Stained and swollen, evidence of cosmopolitan tastes and foreign

contacts, the book was now enveloped in the aura of
samizdat.

Anyone who had spent an entire life in the Soviet
Union—indeed, a week would have served, and been far
more convenient—knew at once that the Warsaw Pact invasion of Czechoslovakia would be accompanied by a
crackdown at home. I realized now that we had been expecting this always, even counting on it. The expectation
had fevered our social gatherings, our love affairs, and, especially, our work. Night would follow day; it always did.

Most of the trips to Mexico City were canceled. The
apartments of dissidents were searched, as were those of
nonconformist journalists, lawyers, and trade unionists. A
demonstration in Red Square lead to seven arrests, including the arrest of a woman wielding an empty baby carriage. On the carriage was hung the banner: "To Your
Freedom and Ours!"—Aleksandr Herzen's cry in defense
of Polish rebels a century before. First Secretary Alexander
Dubcek and his colleagues were abducted to Moscow and
forced to recant the heresy of reform communism.

Even in the best of times, our news reports were deliv-
ered by radio and television in a harsh drone nearly devoid
of information. Across the airwaves, the standard words
and phrases churned and boiled like the Baltic in winter.
After heralding the delivery of "urgent aid to the fraternal
Czechoslovak people," "in defense of peace," a harsher
tone was taken, with many references to "traitors" and
"agents of world capital," but the roar itself remained
constant, an almost soothing accompaniment to one's
breakfast or dinner. This is how it had always been. And
then one September morning, in this ocean of radio

noise, the words "Marina Burchatkina" surfaced like an enemy submarine.

I was home, making coffee in my bachelor kitchen and glumly looking ahead to my day's work, which had faltered since my return from Peredelkino. Taking the broadcast of Marina's name as an aural hallucination, I decided that my obsession with her had finally overcome my senses. I could still feel her touch echoing off my skin.

This acknowledgement meant that my life would be different now. I would have to pursue her, win her, and marry her; otherwise I would know no mental ease. I loved her. The hallucination then deepened, deforming reality itself. I heard the following:

". . . outrage at her selfish and criminal anti-Soviet actions. We cannot understand how someone raised under Soviet rule, whose education and professional status were provided by the toil of common laborers, can so unscrupulously libel our way of life. Burchatkina's letter serves only the interests of Western reactionary circles opposed to the efforts of the Soviet Union to foster peaceful coexistence. She who blackens her country and people and tries to turn back history deserves only contempt and indignation."

Thirteen

I forced myself to finish breakfast, not fully understanding what I had just heard (but understanding enough). I dressed and hurried to the metro. The train arrived as I reached the platform and I was carried by the masses into the central car, whose atmosphere was thick with the odors of garlic and sour milk. Pressed against my body, the other passengers showed me their faces of ash and their blind, watery eyes. They were not only my compatriots, they were my readers. Emerging from the Krasnopresnenskaya metro station, I deeply inhaled but failed to taste fresh air. Inside the Rostov mansion reigned a deep, muffled silence. A few colleagues crossed my path, but they didn't look my way. Something had slightly altered the building's dimensions, narrowing the foyer corridor and deepening the tread on the little steps down to the café. Desperate, I went to the publications office and found Anton Basmanian at a desk, studying a sheet of galleys.

He had gained some unbecoming weight in the last few years, especially in his jowls and belly. With his head down, the thinning of his hair was apparent. It was probably just as well that his wife had come up from Yerevan. Meanwhile, he had kept control of his journal by fluttering it to the right side of the innocuous.

"Anton," I said.

He kept his eyes fixed on a line of type.

"Rem."

"Tell me. What did I hear on Radio Beacon?"

"A Bach cantata, perhaps. 'Sleepers Awake.'" Now he put down his pencil and looked up. He strained out a smile. His teeth were as gleamingly white as ever. "She wrote a so-called open letter to the Politburo. She appears to be a bit put out by Czechoslovakia."

"It was published?"

"In *Le Monde, Corriere della Sera*, the *New York Times, Die Zeit*."

The title of each foreign publication struck me like a body blow. I collapsed into a folding chair. I had known that she had done something terrible, but nothing as terrible as this.

My mouth was parched when I spoke next. "Well, she's finished."

Anton chuckled, monstrously. "No, she's just beginning. I haven't told you the best part."

"What?"

"The letter was written in Paris. She has a visiting lectureship at the Sorbonne. On what subject, I don't know. In Kaluga she taught arts and crafts to twelve year olds."

My brain had slowed nearly to a stop; I could barely make out Anton's words. I felt as if I were still in the metro, surrounded by strangers. I closed my eyes and felt a filament of steam from a cup of espresso tickle my nostril hairs.

"She's not coming back." I tried to make it sound like a declarative sentence, but there was a childish, hopeful interrogative rising at the end.

He laughed at the possibility. She had already been stripped of her Soviet citizenship, of course.

Anton said, "I suppose you haven't talked to Sorokin, or been by your office, have you?"

"I've just come in."

"There's a union petition against her. You'll have to sign. And I suppose there'll be a pro forma expulsion. That'll be on the agenda, a real spectacle I'm sure."

I slumped my shoulders.

"And let me give you some advice, Rem, my friend."

I looked at him dejectedly.

He said, "It won't hurt for you to be the one to submit the resolution. People have memories, you know. They know about the role you played in her career."

"I hardly had anything to do with her. Anyway, she's in Paris now. People should forget her."

"You don't understand, the entire union is under a microscope. Not just the leadership: the rank and file too. They're talking about a new censorship regime, closing literary journals, ending foreign travel."

"Because of a single letter in *Le Monde?*"

"It's the whole international situation. They're going back through everything that's been written in the past ten years, looking for divergences from Party views. Suslov's involved! The pressure's incredible. The union has to respond in a positive way."

"Fine, I've got no objection to that."

"Look, Rem, all they're asking for is a little self-criticism. It's nothing."

"For what? For reading her work?"

"For recommending her for publication. You know, write about how your proletarian vigilance had been relaxed, about how you were misled."

"But *you* published her!"

"I'm also writing a letter of self-criticism. I'm pouring a bucket of shit on my head."

"And you had an affair with her! You spent a week with her in Tashkent!"

"That's personal. It had nothing to do with politics," Anton said. The recollection brightened his smile.

Later that day, the text of Radio Beacon's attack on Marina Burchatkina was posted in the glassed-in bulletin board in the lobby outside the café. It was signed and ostensibly written by six Heroes of Socialist Labor, members of the mechanics' union at the Zil Autoworks.

In September 1944, as the Red Army pressed on toward central Europe, an ineptly planned uprising by Slovak partisans was countered by the 357th German Infantry Division and the 108th *Panzar* Division. Rushing to the Slovaks' aid, the Red Army descended from its positions in the Carpathian mountains and met the Germans in and around Krosno. Two days of close fighting ensued. As it advanced into the Dukla Pass, the 38th Red Army's first Guards Calvary received orders to open a narrow corridor, less than 2000 meters wide, between the villages of Lysa Gura and Gloitse. Leaving behind its heavy weaponry and much of its ammunition, the Soviets passed through a zone raked by machine-gun and mortar fire. My father, a young lieutenant who had won decorations at Lvov, took a sniper's bullet in the throat. It was not necessarily a mortal wound, members of his company said later, but without quick medical attention he bled to death on the pass's wooded slopes.

As our government propagandists reminded us, the Soviet people had paid a high price for the liberation of Czechoslovakia. Even among my liberal friends, there were now murmurs that Dubcek had left us no alternative.

Meanwhile, news of Marina Burchatkina had, by way of returning travelers and those who had access to Western media, filtered through to the Rostov mansion.

She had appeared on French TV. From there she went to America. It was said that her publisher offered her a lucrative contract for her next work, a book of political essays. She became romantically linked to a famous Hollywood director.

Every piece of news was treated with ironic contempt by my colleagues, but I kept my silence, trying to identify the precise nature of my loss. I now spent hardly any time at the union, not even in the café. I worked every day at home, when I did any work at all. In the evenings I stayed home too; suddenly, there were no parties, no salons, no encounters with foreign guests. Out at the dacha, I mentioned Marina's spectacular defection to Lydia, but she shrugged it off. For her, the invasion of Czechoslovakia had more serious consequences: the flow of foreign books into Russia, whether authorized or not, was slowed to a desperate trickle.

I had never told her about Pushkin Square. Now I didn't tell her that I had been asked to sign another petition, nor that it had been suggested that I sponsor a resolution. The only piece of writing that I produced that autumn was a lengthy and flamboyantly damning letter of self-criticism, which I tore into little pieces and flushed down the toilet.

A few weeks after my encounter with Anton, I was called into Sorokin's office. He shoved a piece of paper across the desk.

"Read this."

Marina Burchatkina's open letter to the Politburo, published all over the world, had been printed on a numbered document that was labeled the property of the

Committee for State Security. I had not heard of anyone
who had actually seen the letter, among neither travelers
to the West nor the privileged recipients of foreign newspapers. I took a seat and read it, aware that Sorokin was
closely reading my face, on which I had pasted a stern,
worried expression. I immediately recognized that the
letter was no great advance in the literature of political
philosophy; it was an absurd amalgam of special plead-
ing and whiffy analysis, to which were tacked irrelevant
quotations from Gandhi, Tolstoy, the Czech statesman
Jan Masaryk, and Lenin himself, and then John Lennon.
When I reached the end ("Comrade Brezhnev, please give
peace a chance!"), I said, "It's vile."

"I'm relieved to know that you think so. Because
some suspicion has been voiced that you might sympathize with these anti-Soviet sentiments."

"I can't believe—"

"So why isn't your name on the union petition?"

"I wasn't happy with the wording. You know, as a
writer, how you hate to put your name on anything that
you haven't written yourself."

In fact, Sorokin probably didn't hate it at all, he probably took it as a matter of course. He responded to my
well-rehearsed evasion by pressing heavily with his el-
bows against his desk. His face flushed and his arms
trembled as he rose from his seat. By the time he reached
his feet, he was breathing heavily. He moved with an unfamiliar, listing limp across the room to a gray gunmetal
safe implanted in the wall between two bookcases. He
blocked my view of it as he turned the wheel. He removed

something from inside the safe, brought it back to his desk, and laid it carefully before me.

It was Marina's portrait, encased in a thin crimson border: the cover of *Time* magazine. I recognized that I was not meant to touch it. The picture had been done in oils, and my first thought was that it was not a good likeness, that this was not as I had known her. While the artist had succeeded in making her attractive, he appeared to have added years and hard experience to her beauty. As she gazed up from the cover, her face was drawn and slightly battered. The resolute set of her jaw raised a faint crease along the base of her left temple, her moral fiber made visible.

The gross tangibility of this image gave me pause. I had to concede something to the vision of the artist, even if he were merely a workaday magazine illustrator. Action was character. The actual Marina Burchatkina was not the person that, entangled by desire, I thought I had known. I gazed into the printed eyes, unable to turn away. Sorokin spoke over my shoulder, his voice thick.

"That's their new heroine, their Joan of Arc. She pours lies and filth on the name of the Soviet people. They won't rest until the Soviet Union is destroyed."

I studied the picture, trying to commit it to memory. I thought it was the last thing I would ever know about her.

"No, Brezhnev's destroying it himself," I murmured, not bearing to look at Sorokin. "This invasion puts back the political development of our country twenty years. It's a disaster for my generation."

This was the first time I had ever articulated this thought. It was not even something I had known I believed. The force of my belief made me dizzy.

Sorokin belched. It came out in a growl.

"Rem, you're so fucking smart. Tell me then, how did I learn in advance about Pushkin Square?"

I turned to face him. He was leaning on the desk, towering over me.

"I don't know. From one of the security organs, I suppose."

"Damn straight I did. But who in the security organs?"

"How would I know? I don't care. I have no idea how the KGB operates. They must have placed an informer among the demonstrators. I know they have contacts in the union." I waved vaguely with my hand, not wanting to directly accuse him.

Sorokin continued to stare, his eyes brimming with disgust.

"What?" I said.

He didn't reply.

"Bullshit," I said. "I don't believe it."

Now Sorokin's expression turned smug. He enjoyed this, it recalled the literary wars of his youth, against Zamyatin, against Babel, against Akhmatova. The color that had come into his face made him look healthier than he had in years.

"It's impossible," I protested. "She was probably one of the ringleaders."

"Yes, that's right."

"What's right?"

"She was a ringleader, she was an agent provocateur.

She smoked out the so-called dissidents. Too bad you
didn't stop Panteleyev. We wanted to keep the union out
of it."

"How can that be! She just defected! She wrote an
anti-Soviet letter to *Le Monde!*"

"That's what's so despicable. Here is someone, a sup-
posedly loyal citizen of the state who, after years of delicate cooperation, suddenly has a so-called 'crisis of
conscience.' She changes sides, acts the pure innocent,
the defender of liberty against the very system that
helped bring her to prominence in the first place. She
planned this, she knew she was going to defect when she
applied for the trip to Paris. She wasn't coming back. The
KGB searched her flat. It was cleaned out, not a single
manuscript or notebook or address."

My voice was no more that a whispered croak: "When
did she apply?"

He was distracted by his anger and didn't answer at
once, not understanding the import of my question. I repeated it.

"Last winter. Right after Pushkin Square." Glaring, he
said, "Write your own statement." He added sarcastically,
"I want that you should be satisfied with the wording."

He returned the magazine to his safe.

Fourteen

The resolution had been circulated among the executive
members of the Secretariat several days before the meeting, but had been left unsigned. Anton told me that he
offered to sponsor it, but the offer was refused: First

Secretary Fedin demanded a higher-ranking official. Anton said that Sorokin demanded me—"Idiot, she's in California! What do you care? They can't touch her!"—but I wasn't approached again. Indeed, hardly anyone spoke to me that week. Now Anton avoided me as well. I gave off the odor of bodily corruption. At the very last moment an unknown children's poet was flown in from Irkutsk, presumably on the principle that if rank would not serve, then "the people" would. In the poet's address, she expressed the indignation of all the Far East writers of children's literature at Marina Burchatkina's "betrayal of high principles," which aimed to "mislead and pervert incorruptible Soviet youth."

As the evening wore on, the speeches became more hysterical. Marina was called "a prostitute" and "a traitor"; the threat she "and her masters" posed to the Union of Soviets was as great as that of the armies of the Third Reich. I hardly paid attention to the crash and pounding of the rhetorical surf. Instead I took into account the ten hours' time difference and, assisted by several glasses of whiskey administered shortly before the start of the evening's program, I saw Marina waking late at her director's Pacific beach house. She luxuriated for several minutes in the big bed and soft white linen, marveling at the paleness of the light playing against the room's trim, understated furnishings and fixtures. (At the microphone, someone cried, "Marina Burchatkina, did you receive your thirty pieces of silver?") Placed in a sunny mood by her surroundings, she rose from the bed, wearing the director's pajamas, slipped her feet into an ex-wife's slippers, and summoned one of the servants to serve her coffee on the terrace. She brought her expensive fountain pen (a gift from the director) and a tablet of writing paper (I assumed she had purchased that on her own) out to the glass café table and, after sipping the coffee and smiling at some seagull swooping over the water in search of its own breakfast, she began her day's work.

There was an end to the speeches and then the hall was quiet. Sorokin spoke from his place on the dais: "Any more comments?" His gaze passed across the surface of the audience like a spotlight. It avoided me, but I felt its heat just the same. This was my last chance to make amends. Hiding in the third or fourth row, I kept my gaze straight ahead, at a portrait of Gorky on the wall behind the dais, and tried to demonstrate my obliviousness.

After a while a vote was taken. It was unanimous. From exhaustion, even I raised my hand in favor, though the official observers of the vote would have recorded that my arm was not fully extended and by how much. I knew that my friends at the meeting, Anton and the others, who had chosen not to sit with me, would be relieved: a difficult chapter was closed. I sought relief as well, but was instead visited by a strange foreboding.

There was more business at hand, of course, including a report on our accounts, a report about our increased membership, and even a resolution lauding the Czechoslovak writers' union, which had been brutally reconstituted after the invasion, for its "brave defense of national sovereignty."

Then the floor was opened to "questions from the floor," and someone I didn't know approached the microphone, a hefty dark man in a gray pullover. He identified

himself as a poet-miner from Kemerovo. I idly wondered
how many words rhymed with "shovel" and "bitumi-
nous." As I began making a list of rhymes, as I had done
with the aid of my father's dictionary when I was first
seized by the idea of becoming a poet myself, I became
conscious of the furtive looks again glancing off me from
around the hall. The attention was disturbing, but not as
much as the furtiveness. The miner predictably encoun-
tered difficulty reading his own speech, mispronouncing
and replacing many words, but it seemed to be in general
praise of the Soviet medical profession.

A hospital had been built in Kemerovo, providing free
medical care to all workers. The miner-poet went on for
some time about the hospital and about the general ad-
vances in medical care throughout the Soviet Union,
rambling a bit and thus giving evidence that he might
have written at least part of the speech himself. My attention abated again, but part of me continued to follow in
parallel his spiraling oration down some very nasty hole.

It reached the bottom of its descent when he warned
against "gross libel of the Soviet psychiatric profession."
He reminded us that, while psychiatric care in the West
was a luxury of the rich and pampered, Soviet psychiatry
served "working-class men and women with working-class
problems." During the Great Patriotic War, honorable
men of the psychiatric profession had served on the front
lines against the Nazis, risking and often sacrificing their
lives to treat the psychological effects of war on the heroic
defenders of liberty. Was this the reason "shell shock," as it
was called in the West, was virtually unheard of in the Red
Army? Today Soviet psychiatric medicine was poised to

advance to the furthest reaches of human consciousness, promising relief from anxiety, stress, and neurosis, if only it were not impeded by the forces of reaction.

When Viktor Panteleyev's name was read out by the miner, I knew that all was lost. My name and a few others, belonging to men who were far more surprised than I was, shortly followed. The air in the room turned cold; there were gasps of surprise. Sorokin asked if anyone wished to speak on the question. No one did, not even those who had been named. Viktor, of course, had not bothered to attend the meeting. The news of his expulsion from the union would come to him in a registered letter, which he might well neglect to open. When eventually arrested for "social parasitism," he would go without protest. This time the vote was opposed by a few liberal stalwarts with secure reputations, but it passed easily. Men rose from their seats. As if the vote had somehow reversed evolution, not one stood fully erect. They staggered from the hall.

This was expected of me as well, but I found myself paralyzed and my vision dimmed. Sorokin stood at the podium in a shaft of avenging light, the dome of his massive head radiant. He glowered at me, focusing all the attention in the hall. He had silenced the audience, even their incidental coughs and rustling of papers. At last I climbed from my seat, tripped over some legs, crawled out into the aisle, and left.

I struggled up the carpeted, chandeliered stairway to the third floor. As I entered the corridor in the after-hours murk, I could see four large cardboard boxes neatly stacked outside my office. I approached them warily, my legs shaking. My home address was neatly printed on the top box. I opened the door to the office and flicked on the light. The room was perfectly empty, much larger than I had remembered it. The office needed a new paint job, but it would have taken the most rigorous forensics to determine that I had ever inhabited it.

I returned downstairs, claimed my coat (Darya Sergeyevna gave it up reluctantly, scowling), and left the building.

The snow was falling thickly by the time I disembarked at Peredelkino, the only passenger stepping from the dark and frigid train. When I reached the end of the platform I turned and saw that the snow had already covered my tracks. The streets of the village were unlit except by the radiance of the snow itself, which swallowed the sound of my footfalls.

Once the train had pulled from the station, the village offered the illusion of being completely detached from the world. It was self-sufficient: fed, heated, and powered by the imaginations of its inhabitants. I crossed over the frozen brook unwinding along the station and headed up the hill. The air was scented with sweet chimney smoke. Someone was burning cedar, an extravagance. The lovingly maintained fiction was that this village was a republic. Its only currency was language, and its military was composed of readers, partisans who would defend it at any risk to themselves. Its laws were just and mostly grammatical, but no less severe for that. The village was a confident one and defiant in its knowledge that it had chanced upon the most perfect political economy.

As I crossed our gate, I suffered a premonition that I was about to be surprised for the second time that evening. I stopped at the window, expecting to see Lydia in Vadim Surkov's embrace.

But Lydia was alone, sitting in her upholstered chair, fixed in the amber cone of the reading light. A fat book rested on her lap. It was mine, *The Northern Lights*. She was entirely motionless, as if holding her breath. I could not make out the movement of her eyes. After a while she turned the page. She would not have seen me even if she had looked up, because I was standing in the dark behind the glass, in the dark nowhere place from where authors always watch their readers. To disturb her would have been as if to ripple the surface of a clear mountain lake in which the moon and the cosmos were perfectly reflected. I knew that shortly there would be many explanations to be made, however imperfectly, and then confessions and recriminations, protestations of grief and loss, and then at last hard, practical calculation. Before that, I wanted to absorb—place into words I would always be able to summon—an image of her like that, the passionate reader. I watched for a long time, letting the cold seep through my coat and skin. The snowflakes, like a precipitation of type, collected in my hair and upon my eyelashes.

KEN KALFUS was born in New York. From 1994 to 1998 he lived in Moscow with his wife and daughter. He is the author of a previous collection of short stories, *Thirst*. He now lives in Philadelphia.

More fiction from Milkweed Editions

To order books or for more information,
contact Milkweed at (800) 520-6455
or visit our website (www.milkweed.org).

Agassiz
Sandra Birdsell

What We Save for Last
Corinne Demas Bliss

Backbone
Carol Bly

The Tree of Red Stars
Tessa Bridal

The Clay That Breathes
Catherine Browder

Street Games
Rosellen Brown

A Keeper of Sheep
William Carpenter

Seasons of Sun and Rain
Marjorie Dorner

Winter Roads, Summer Fields
Marjorie Dorner

Blue Taxis
Eileen Drew

Kingfishers Catch Fire
Rumer Godden

Trip Sheets
Ellen Hawley

Cracking India
Bapsi Sidhwa

The Crow Eaters
Bapsi Sidhwa

The Country I Come From
Maura Stanton

Traveling Light
Jim Stowell

Aquaboogie
Susan Straight

The Empress of One
Faith Sullivan

The Promised Land
Ruhama Veltfort

Justice
Larry Watson

Montana 1948
Larry Watson

Interior design by Donna Burch
Typeset in Legacy Serif
by Stanton Publication Services Inc.
Printed on acid-free 55# Sebago Antique Cream paper
by Maple-Vail Book Manufacturing